INTO THE WILD

(A *Tigers* TALE)

D.V. WILLIAMS

Published by Claw Mark Publishing

www.dominic-williams.co.uk

Typeset in Palatino Linotype

Photography by Brian J. Davies

ISBN: 978 0 9957715 0 5

For Kathy, Owain and Rhys.
Perhaps someday I hope to repay your patience.

CONTENTS

To Yasmin,
Don't do anything
I wouldn't do!

Dom W.
xx

ACKNOWLEDGEMENTS

In a world already teeming with hopeful writers it is sometimes hard to keep on believing in the face of apparently insurmountable odds, so my heartfelt thanks go out to everyone who has helped turn the dream into a reality. If I fail to mention any of you here, you know who you are. Please forgive me.

In particular, I would like to thank MD for his artistic talents, help and advice with the website, and a host of his other skills and knowledge too numerous to mention; Brian Davies for his wonderful photography; Kate Davies and Sue Meek for their editorial input; and everyone who read the early drafts and provided such invaluable feedback and suggestions, including (in no particular order) Alex Bryant-Evans, Lynsey Rogers, Kate Davies, Simon Blake, Karen Bailes, Liz Crippin, Jo Custy and Sue Meek.

Thanks also to Alex for being the daily sounding board for my ideas. For two years, Rebecca's story has been my principal topic of conversation and you had no means of escape. You deserve a medal, sir.

To the real world and online writers' communities who have been a source of encouragement, information, and advice, I thank you. I would like to include in this a special mention to Julie Archer for answering all my questions so patiently. This has been the steepest learning curve of my entire life, and I include gaining two graduate qualifications and becoming a parent in that.

Lastly, and by no means least: thank you to Kathy my long-suffering wife, and to my family, for living with my obsession on a daily basis. If there is one thing I would like us to take from all of this, it is that nothing worthwhile happens without sacrifice, but living vicariously is not the answer either. If we ourselves do not have the bravery to live more inspired and inspiring lives, then we cannot hope for our children to do the same. We need to think bigger, dream bigger, live bigger. Perhaps this is the sentiment that gave birth to Rebecca's story in the first place.

Dominic

'O tiger's heart wrapped in a woman's hide!'

William Shakespeare

PROLOGUE

What do we see when we look in the mirror? Is it the same thing other people see? I'm not so sure. There's always so much more to each of us than the face we show the world. It's like stripping away layers of wallpaper to reveal the imperfect beauty of the plaster beneath, to find the truth behind the veneer of civilised normality, the animal that lives under the skin.

It's often something people won't admit to themselves, either. Many prefer to remain dazzled by appearances, never daring to look too far beneath the surface of anything, including themselves. Perhaps they are afraid of what they might find.

But not me. I learned to embrace it.

When I look into my own reflection, behind the gentle, blue eyes and softer features I see another pair staring back at me; eyes that blaze golden and intense. Together, she and I have experienced things I could never have imagined in the cosy little bubble of my early childhood, but somewhere along the way I came to a simple conclusion; something I've tried to live by ever since: when you're born with a yearning to fly, there's no point living life as if you're afraid of falling. Rules and conventions exist to be broken, boundaries to be pushed, limits tested. After all, that's how we find out who we really are, how we prove to ourselves that we're truly alive.

Along the way, I have lived and loved so completely that it's no surprise I've been hurt, but pain is a part of living no matter who we are; there's no avoiding it. Without that wellspring of light and darkness on which to draw, I could not hope to touch the lives of others in the way that I do.

I think it's the people we love, for better or for worse, who most shape our outlook on life and in ways we could never imagine at the time. Perhaps it's them I really ought to thank because I haven't always been so bold. I became the way I am. Of course, I had dreams, everyone does, but I never dared to believe I would actually have the chance to live them.

Looking back now, it's hard to say exactly when the balance tipped, but from that point on there was no turning away from the path on which I had already set out. Maybe it was the first time I . . . but I'm getting ahead of myself. I do that sometimes; it's the Aries in me, or so I've been told.

Allow me to explain . . .

CHAPTER ONE

We stumbled up the stairs to my bedroom, laughing, dizzy with excitement and breathless in our anticipation, barely able to keep our hands off each other. I couldn't even remember crossing the courtyard to the house but somehow we must have got there. I gently pushed him ahead of me into the room and still facing him, closed the door behind me.

At least in part, I had my best friend to thank for all of this. If it wasn't for her I don't think I would ever have had the courage to act on my convictions, but I was glad I did, even though it had the potential to stir up so much trouble. I still couldn't quite believe it was happening, and even then I had no idea how pivotal a moment in my life it would be, or how my world would be changed forever by the events that unfolded in its wake.

So how did I get there, and why the potential shit-storm? To explain that, I really will have to go back to how I met the most extraordinary girl in the whole world: Linda.

-0-

It can't have been easy for Mum, raising my younger brother and me on her own. After my parents split up when I was four, we saw my father less and less. The last time I didn't see him was when he failed to turn up for my eighth birthday. I guess it wasn't too much of a loss.

Despite caring for two young children, Mum never lost her passion for acting and singing. She worked a series of day jobs to pay the bills as well as performing whenever she could, and even though we didn't have very much, our little home was always filled with love, laughter and music.

My mum's record collection became the soundtrack to my childhood, and I soaked up every note of it like a sponge. Rob (or Bobby as we used to call him when he was little) not so much; he had other interests. I was always prancing around the house with a hairbrush for a microphone or keeping family and friends pinned to the sofa while I put on a show, often accompanied by Rolo the poodle who seemed to find the whole thing a huge source of excitement. Nanna and Pappy would sit patiently through hours of my little performances without complaint. They were my regular captive audience.

Now I realise how much pride Mum must have swallowed to ask for their help and how bitter a pill the inevitable 'I told you so' from Pappy must have been, but when you're a young child, things like that pass you by. However coloured hindsight might be, it's only when we look back through the tinted lens of experience that everything comes into focus.

As I grew, my love of music naturally progressed to piano and singing lessons. The discipline of vocal training came easily, but to my piano teacher's frustration, I spent more time trying to copy music I'd heard or inventing things of my own rather than practising what she'd put in front of me. I can still see Miss Macpherson's spinsterly finger rapping on the sheet music and hear her reedy Scottish accent.

'Focus, Rebecca! Focus!' was a phrase I heard rather a lot.

My first proper guitar was a Christmas present from all the family. Mum, Nanna and Pappy clubbed together to buy it for me. I had already helped to hand out what I thought was the last of the presents when Mum reached around behind the Christmas tree and produced a beautiful acoustic guitar with a red bow tied around the neck. It was inlaid with mother-of-pearl and abalone down its rosewood fingerboard. The top of the body was a fine-grained wood of a deep honey colour. She held it out to me.

'Thank you, thank you!' I gushed, eyes bright, flinging my arms around everybody in turn.

Sitting down on the sofa with my guitar, I tried to form my fingers into some of the shapes I'd watched guitarists make on the telly when they played chords. It wasn't as easy as they made it look.

'It won't happen overnight. Patience and perseverance will pay off. We'll get you some lessons too.' Pappy's words came from somewhere in the distance, but I was already focussed on the job in hand.

By the time I was thirteen I had abandoned the piano in favour of the guitar and started trying to write my first proper songs. Most of them weren't very good, but I had to start somewhere. I suppose everybody does, even the greats!

I must have been getting on for fourteen when Mum met Jeff. She found some session work, recording backing vocals for an up-and-coming band. Jeff Taylor was producing the project at his studio a bit over half an hour away from where we lived and Mum came home every day with a new spring in her step.

Despite his busy schedule, Jeff called over a lot at weekends and we would all go out together for the day. In the evenings, Mum and Jeff could be found snuggled up on the sofa with a bottle of red wine while I kept Rob company, usually playing on his games console even though it wasn't really my thing. There was a warm glow surrounding Mum that I'd never seen before, not even when my dad had been around. She'd always been beautiful to me, but now she radiated confidence and happiness. Her wavy brown hair had more bounce to it. Her skin seemed almost luminous.

We spent more and more time at Jeff's house although it was to be a year or more before we eventually moved in. Even so, a whole new world had already opened up. Compared to the cramped terraced house we had called home, 'The Gables' felt enormous. The building which began life in the eighteenth century as a row of timber frame and red brick cottages had been extended backwards on the ground floor, modernised and opened out downstairs to make one large home. The whole thing nestled in two acres of land that had once been part of a farm on the outskirts of Westerbridge, Kent.

There was something organic about the way the house had evolved over the years, and it kept much of its period character despite the obvious intervention of an interior designer. But the best thing of all, the thing that made it a wonderland to me, was built in a converted barn to one side of the house: Jeff's recording studio.

I would often sit quietly at the back of the control room while he worked, watching the painstakingly slow process of shaping imagination into sound, listening as layer by layer, instrument by instrument and sometimes note by note, something magical took form and gained a life of its own. Musicians would come and go, each contributing their own piece of the puzzle, and all the while Jeff masterminded proceedings, weaving his magic and coaxing the best from every one of them. He was usually aided in his wizardry by Steve Bowes, his studio engineer and, despite their age difference, his closest friend. Jeff never went off on a job without his right-hand man.

There were plenty of private schools close by and Jeff was quite happy to pay for me and Rob to go to one of them, but Mum insisted we should go to the local comprehensive school.

'I know you can afford it Jeff, but I think it's important they keep their feet on the ground,' I overheard her say while they were talking in the kitchen. 'I don't want either of them thinking opportunities are something you can buy; they're something you make. Besides which, it's a good school anyway.'

I could hear the frustration in his sigh.

'That's fair enough Avril, but it takes more than just merit to open doors. At least let me help.'

'Helping is okay, but they have to find their own path in life. It's about their choices, not ours,' Mum said, remaining resolute. 'Some things are more valuable than money.'

Jeff conceded, holding up his hands in surrender.

'Okay! Birchwood it is!'

He kissed her on the forehead and pulled her close. He must have been a fair bit taller than she was, but what Mum lacked in height compared to Jeff she made up for in other ways. She was every inch a force to be reckoned with.

It was then that Jeff noticed me standing in the doorway.

'Hey, Beccs!' He gestured for me to come over and wrapped his arms around the two of us. 'Looks like you'll be starting at your new school on Monday. You ready?'

'I guess so,' I replied.

I was excited by this whole adventure but still daunted by the prospect of starting over and having to make a new set of friends. I wasn't exactly what you'd call gregarious.

When Monday came around, Mum dropped us off at Birchwood dressed in our pristine new green and grey uniforms. Our new school was fifteen minutes' walk from the house and despite the fact that it was a beautiful spring day with only a smattering of clouds to mar the otherwise clear, blue sky, Mum somehow felt it her duty to drive us there. I quickly kissed her goodbye, and although I wanted to sprint through the entrance to put some distance between me and parental control, I waited for Rob to catch up.

Not cool!

Mum meant well but even so, I vowed to walk as much as possible in future.

At the front desk, the receptionist despatched Rob off

to his form room and looked over her glasses at me.

'You're in form 10J, Mr Travers' class.' She handed me my timetable and pointed down the corridor somewhere into the distance. 'Room twenty-three.'

I made my way down the by now nearly empty hallway and knocked hesitantly on the door. Most of the class were already inside and they stopped what they were doing when I stepped into the room, gawking blankly at me like a field of cows. One face stood out from the crowd: a tall, thin, dark-haired girl with an oval face and glasses who eyed me with a quiet curiosity quite unlike the empty stares coming back at me from the rest of the class.

Mr Travers smiled at me, somehow managing to make me feel more at ease. He was large and round-faced, with a kindly manner and a huge moustache. To me, he looked like a walrus in a tweed jacket.

'Okay everybody, this is Rebecca. She's joining the school today and I'd like you all to make her as welcome as possible.'

He gestured to the dark-haired girl to come over.

'Rebecca, this is Linda Maloney. She hasn't been in the school long herself. It looks like you're going to be in many of the same classes so it would be a good idea if Linda shows you where everything is. Are you okay with that, Linda?'

'Sure,' she replied coolly in a Northern Irish accent which had softened to a gentle lilt, then turned to me. 'Come on over and sit down. We'd better have a look at where you're going before the bell goes.'

We took our seats and the hubbub of the class returned to normal. Maybe she could see how self-conscious I was and took pity on me.

'Never mind this lot,' she added conspiratorially, with an air of self-assurance beyond her years. 'They're harmless enough once you get to know them. I felt a bit out of place on my first day, but you'll soon settle in; I did. You see Liam over there, the one with the ginger hair?'

I looked across the classroom at a burly, red-haired boy who was busy slapping his mate round the head.

'Likes to throw his weight around a bit,' she said. 'Picks his nose all through lessons. A bit of a knob really, but easy to put in his place if you stand up to him. And Sylvie over there.' She gestured towards a girl with ratty hair who was sitting on her own.

'Mm-hmm. I see her.'

'She's got victim tattooed right across her forehead. Needs to learn how to stand up for herself, or she's going to be like that all her life. The point is: they all have their stories to tell; they're all just people. Anyway, let's have a look at this timetable.'

Once the bell had gone, we gathered up our stuff and made towards stairwell A, then up and along the top corridor to where our first lesson was. I was so glad I had Linda to navigate for me, even though I'd been given a map of the school; the whole place was like a rabbit warren.

'You see the two teachers we just walked past?' Her lips barely moved.

I turned around to see a man and a woman in their thirties walking in opposite directions down the corridor.

'Yes.'

Linda checked over her shoulder then lowered her

voice.

'I'd bet money they're having an affair. They're certainly having a relationship they don't want people to know about.'

'How do you know? Has somebody said something?'

She shook her head.

'No. I just watch. Most people will make eye contact when they greet each other in the corridor, at least for a moment. They didn't; they avoided it. They're hiding something.'

'I hardly noticed them at all.'

She didn't look at all surprised.

'Most folks don't. I just like watching people. I find them fascinating.'

'What about me then?' I had to ask.

Linda pursed her lips.

'You definitely fascinate me, in a good way, though,' she added, stopping to look me up and down. 'There's something wild and untameable about you. I can't quite put my finger on it but there's more to you than meets the eye. Maybe you have hidden depths you've yet to explore. Let me know if I get anything wrong.'

She waited for a response, looking pleased with herself. I just stared at her, open-mouthed. Where did all this stuff come from? How did a girl my age end up with such a worldly head on such young shoulders? Unconventional didn't begin to cover it.

'You're not exactly run of the mill yourself,' I said.

'Listen, you have no idea; you haven't met my family yet.' We set off along the corridor again. 'Anyway, here we are, first lesson: Science. Mrs Appleton does go on a bit, but she means well.'

Throughout the day, her sharply observed commentary on both teachers and pupils had me in fits. It nearly got us into trouble once or twice. I liked her ready wit and irreverent sense of humour. She was a curious mix of quirky outsider and social butterfly, floating from person to person and introducing me to more people than I had any hope of remembering names for. When the final bell went at the end of French, she turned to face me.

'Do you want to stop off at my place on your way home? It's on your route.'

'Sure! I'd better phone home and let Mum know what I'm up to. She'll only worry otherwise.'

On our way out of the door, I rummaged in my school bag for my mobile phone. I located it down the side of my pencil case, dialled and put it to my ear to block out the hubbub of the people going past us. By the third ring, Mum picked up.

'Hi, Mum!'

'Hi, sweetheart! How was your day?'

'Good thanks, really good. In fact, I've been invited to stop off at someone's house for a bit if that's alright. Rob's already on his way back. I'll tell you about everything later when I see you.' My eyes flicked up and met Linda's, looking back at me with gentle amusement.

'It's good to know you're making friends already, sweetheart. Be back by six in time for dinner, okay?'

'Okay, Mum. See you later!' I rang off. 'What? What's so funny?'

'Nothing! It's rather sweet in fact. Your Mum's obviously very protective.'

'I suppose she is. Isn't yours?'

Linda looked thoughtful.

'Yes, but it's different with my family. Everything's a bit different with us.'

On the way back, we rounded the corner about five minutes from Jeff's and came to a large, square, smartly kept house which had a grand-looking, roman-style portico over the front door, supported by two fluted pillars. It had an equally large and immaculate front garden, in the centre of which stood a tall stand of pampas grass. It was the sort of suburban pile estate agents might rather pompously call an 'executive style home'.

'This is us! Come on in. My brother Ryan's probably home already and Mum will be there. Don't worry, though, they don't bite.'

We entered the hallway and Linda poked her head around the lounge door. Ryan was still in his school uniform, fishing for the television remote down the side of the sofa. He found it with a look of triumph.

'Hey Ryan, there's someone I'd like you to meet. This is Rebecca. She's just started at our school.'

Ryan stood up to face me and politely held out his hand to shake mine.

How very proper! My internal monologue elbowed me knowingly in the ribs and I blushed.

He was a few years older than Linda and tall like her, with a slightly unruly mop of sandy coloured hair and a disarming smile which somehow took the edge off his formality.

'Hello, Rebecca. How was your first day?'

'Um,' I felt suddenly tongue-tied, 'so much the better for meeting Linda, to be honest. It would have been very different without her.'

'Aye she's a treasure, isn't she?'

Linda poked out her tongue at him. He grinned.

'I'm going to get some lemonade. Do you want some?' she asked him.

'Not for me, thanks. I'm okay.'

'Would you like some?' Linda seemed to be addressing me now, but my eyes were still fixed on Ryan. 'Then I'll show you around. Mum should be upstairs.'

'Thanks, yes,' I said. 'Nice to meet you, Ryan.'

'Likewise, I'm sure.' Still there was that infectious grin I could have watched all day.

When I found Linda again, she had reached the fridge and was filling two glasses. We were heading up the stairs when Linda's mother appeared from the office on the landing, removing her spectacles with a hand that still held a pen clutched between its long, elegant fingers.

'Hello! I overheard you guys downstairs. It isn't very often that Linda brings a friend home.'

'Mum, this is Rebecca. It's her first day at Birchwood; she's new to the area.'

Linda's mum gave me a gently appraising look.

'So what brings you to Westerbridge?'

'We just moved in with my Mum's boyfriend, Jeff. They're getting married later this year.'

'And how do you feel about it all?'

I shrugged my shoulders.

'It's all a bit new, but good, though. Jeff's great. Mum's really happy, and as long as my brother Rob's got his sports nothing seems to faze him.'

She nodded, processing my words. I could see where Linda got her analytical nature from.

'But what about you?' she asked.

'I'm still getting used to everything, to be honest. It's certainly different.'

'Hmm, exciting times! Well, make yourself at home. Sorry to love you and leave you, but I have an article to finish and a deadline to meet. Linda will take good care of you, I'm sure.'

With that, she returned to the office and we took our drinks into Linda's room. Like the rest of the house, it was spotless yet comfortable and relaxed. I'd been in my newly decorated room less than a fortnight and already it looked like it had been hit by an air strike. Linda put some music on to play in the background while we lay flopped forwards on the bed with our feet crossed in the air behind us and talked about life.

'We came over from Ireland five years ago. Mum's a journalist and Dad does something big in a haulage firm; I don't know exactly what, but I don't think it's very interesting. We moved here at the start of the year when he took charge of a different part of the company. Ryan's in the final year of his A-levels. Everybody reckons he'll get top grades despite having to change schools this year.'

Something told me Linda was no less academic. Despite everything she'd said her family didn't seem all that unusual to me.

'So what do you want to do with your future?' I asked.

Linda thought for a moment, brushing her hair back over her shoulders. I was almost envious of her beautiful, straight, dark hair; so dark, in fact, it looked almost black. Back then I might even have called my hair mousy. It was wavy like Mum's, but lighter brown.

'Something involving people; I do people,' she said. 'Anyway, what about you?'

'I want to make music.'

The words bypassed conscious thought and fell out of my mouth before I could stop them. I'd never really considered any other options for my future. Even so, it must have sounded ridiculous. Linda wasn't laughing, though.

'Go on,' she said.

Having opened a door I could no longer shut, I thought I might as well justify myself.

'I just love to sing and perform and sometimes I feel like I'm so full of music that if I don't let it out I'll burst. Now there's Jeff's studio at home I'd like to record my songs if they'll let me.'

'It's not for the fame then?' Her green eyes looked right through me.

'No, but I guess fame sort of comes with it.'

'It kind of goes with the territory I suppose. Didn't I say you had hidden depths, though? God, I love being right!'

We became so engrossed in our conversation about bands that we liked, pop stars and actors that we fancied and about how annoying brothers could be even though we loved them very much, that it was only when I noticed the fading light through the window and reached for my phone to check the time. Ten minutes to six!

'Shit! I'd better get home. Mum said dinner would be at six.'

I grabbed my school bag and we bounded down the stairs just as Brian Maloney was coming in through the front door. One glance told me where Linda and Ryan got their looks from. Facially, they were like carbon copies of their parents except that Brian had dark hair and his wife

Loretta was sandy blonde.

'Hi! Bye! Sorry!' tumbled from my mouth while Linda's dad watched me dashing out of the door with benevolent amusement.

'See you in the morning!' Linda called after me. 'Drop by on your way to school and we'll walk in together.'

'Okay, see you then! Bye, Mr Maloney! Bye, Ryan! Bye, Linda!'

There was a muffled voice from the lounge that blended with the sound from the television. It sounded like it was directed at me.

Turning towards the road again, I sprinted the remainder of the journey home and down the long driveway, gravel crunching beneath my feet as I went. I was finding it hard to suppress the smile that had started in the corners of my mouth and spread rapidly to become a grin.

When I piled, breathless, through the front door at the stroke of six, Mum was in the kitchen serving up. Something smelled good, really good. It made me realise how hungry I was.

'So?' Her tone was questioning rather than accusing.

I dropped my bag on the kitchen stool and beamed at her, pausing to enjoy the words that were about to come out of my mouth.

'I think . . . I think I'm going to like it here.'

CHAPTER TWO

Aside from the sound of my own breathing and the pounding of my heart, the booth was unnaturally quiet. The white, padded walls closed in around me in deafening silence. Through the glass I could see Jeff and Steve sitting at the computer screens in the control room, their lips moving soundlessly as they prepared for the take. While I stared at the lyric sheet in front of me, Jeff's disembodied voice appeared over the headphones, seemingly from midway between my ears.

'Let's try it from the top. Remember, relax and enjoy yourself with it. You know the song. You've already heard it a hundred times and it's only a demo, so just go for it. Okay?'

Awkwardly, I raised my thumb in acknowledgement, partly because my mouth had gone too dry to speak, and positioned myself with the pop shield between me and the microphone just like I'd seen real singers do.

Five minutes before, I had been sitting in the control room as I often did, while Jeff put the finishing touches to the backing tracks of the ballad he had been writing. Then he gestured for me to stand up.

'Your turn!'

'What?'

'I know you're keen to have a go and I've heard you humming this song all over the house, so come on, let's have some fun with it. Your Mum thinks it's about time you had a go too.'

Mum had already recorded what Jeff called a guide vocal, which was what I'd been listening to so far. Now that had disappeared from the playback and I was on my own.

'It's not karaoke,' he said. 'I don't want to hear you singing along. I want to hear you carry it yourself. Don't worry about making everything perfect, it's the feel, the spirit of it I'm looking for. Let's just go once all the way through to start with.'

I wasn't sure I was up to this, but I had to try. This was what I'd wanted after all, wasn't it?

Acoustic guitar and piano led the wistful introduction, while Jeff's outstretched finger remained poised to cue me in for the first verse.

'And . . .' intoned Jeff's voice in my head, the finger gesturing in my direction.

I opened my mouth and began, hesitantly, to sing the opening lines.

There's a yearning
Inside the heart of everyone

After the first few faltering notes where my mouth just didn't seem connected with my brain I realised I couldn't do any worse and just let go.

And I'm searching,
Thinking you might be the one
For all my travels lead me back where I belong

Gaining a little in confidence, I opened up slightly more.

Just go for it. You know the words anyway.

I closed my eyes and sank into the melody. String parts, drums and more guitars joined in at the start of the second verse.

I've been longing
To share this with you
And I'm hoping
You feel like I do
One single moment could stop the turning of the world and
change everything

Now standing on a mountain top in a vast landscape I could look around at the vista below me and shape its textures and colours, dive into its seas and return with shimmering pearls from their hidden depths. Every note appeared three-dimensional and softly coloured, like a living thing in the air in front of me, every word a halo of meaning surrounding the notes.

One single lifetime is never enough
To find the love we seek, it's tough
But every road I take keeps leading back to you
I find my way home

Eventually, when the last chords died away in the headphones I opened my eyes. Steve and Jeff were staring at me. I shied away from the microphone.

I've blown it. They won't ask me again.

After what felt like an age, Jeff leant in towards the talkback microphone on the mixing desk.

'Now you're on a roll, let's go over the first verse again. Keep it contained like you did the first time, but I want to hear some of the same confidence the rest of the song had. Okay?'

I nodded.

The familiar opening bars began again and I stepped back into my landscape, allowing the notes to form themselves in front of me and immersing myself in the music once more. A few notes after the end of the first verse the music stopped abruptly, snapping me out of my reverie.

'Good. I'm going to try something, Beccs. Think you can sing a harmony to the last line of the second verse and the bridge? After that, we can add harmonies to the chorus.'

He sang the notes softly to me. Although he didn't have a powerful voice, in my head I could hear what he wanted. I nodded again.

'Oh, and it's alright to speak between takes,' he said. 'You'll come through loud and clear.'

I nodded yet again. Jeff shook his head in wry amusement and looked back towards the screen in front of him. After we'd overlaid the verse and bridge, Jeff carried straight on to the chorus and once again I found myself on the mountaintop, singing the words while the notes painted themselves in front of me.

Open your heart and I'll be there waiting
Take me in your arms; I don't want to be alone
Tell me I'm yours, and I'll never leave you
I've found my way home

The faces on the other side of the glass shot another glance towards each other at the end of the take. Again, there was a pause.

'One more thing if you're still up for it. I'd like you to have a go at improvising the end section, so there's one chorus after the big key change then go for it. I know it's not how your Mum sang it but I'd like you to give it a go. Just do your own thing with it, okay?'

'Okay.' What did I have to lose?

The music rolled again from the last chorus and I found myself transported once more. I was an eagle, soaring high over rivers and valleys. Long, sustained notes floated me on the air currents before I dived to chase descending waterfalls of droplets on their journey to earth.

Everything reined in for the final chords. Only the strings and the acoustic guitar still lingered in my ears when the sterile booth came back into focus. There was another long silence, an interminable wait while there was much activity on the other side of the glass.

'I think you might like to have a listen to this. Stow the cans and come through.'

I hung up the headphones as requested and, leaving the silent cocoon behind me, crossed the performance area and made my way through the heavy, sealed doors to the control room.

How bad is it? Jeff wasn't giving much away.

'Just listen to this.'

Steve tweaked a couple of controls on the screen and hit the play button. Both of them were looking at me, waiting for my reaction. I listened in silence while the music swirled around me and eventually died away.

'That was never me!'

'It bloody well is! I don't think you have any idea just how much of a natural you are.' Jeff looked at Steve. 'Can we have a quick mix of that so I can play it to Avril?'

'Sure! Give me half an hour so I can tidy up a couple of things and balance the levels a bit, then you can have it.'

'Come on! Time for a well-earned tea break,' said Jeff briskly, turning back to me.

We made our way out of the studio, across the courtyard and in through the end door of the house, inside which was a small vestibule with a stairway which led to the upstairs rooms, including mine. Another door led through the utility room to the heart of the house: the kitchen. Everything seemed to happen there. We didn't use the big lounge much either; mostly we preferred to use the snug for watching TV. It still felt like a country cottage, despite being part of what was now a big, sprawling house on the edge of a suburban town to the south of London.

When we came in, Mum and Linda were sitting in conversation at the breakfast bar while Rolo patrolled the kitchen.

'Hi, Linda! Is it that time already? Have you been waiting long?'

She shook her head.

'Only about ten minutes. I didn't want to disturb you while you were busy in the studio.'

'Tea anyone?' asked Jeff, filling the kettle. A roomful of hands went up.

Linda's face puckered.

'Can I be a real pain and have a coffee, please. Sorry, Mr Taylor, I'm not big on tea.'

'Sure. No problem . . . and it's Jeff, okay?' Jeff retrieved five mugs from the kitchen cupboard and began filling them. He placed them in front of us on the breakfast bar along with the sugar bowl and fetched the milk from the fridge.

'Why don't you two take Linda's stuff upstairs? I'm going to have a chat with Mum,' he said. 'We can have these in the studio. I've got to take Steve's out to him, plus there's something I think you need to hear, Avril.'

Linda grabbed her overnight bag and picking up our mugs, we headed up the back staircase to my room. The sound of explosions and screeching tyres could be heard coming from Rob's room, which was further along the landing on the other side of the bathroom. No doubt he was playing on his games console as usual.

The past few weeks had seen us settle into our new life in Westerbridge. My fifteenth birthday had come and gone, Linda and I were practically joined at the hip and I was even being given the chance to record. Now Linda had come over to stay the night because her parents were having another one of their parties. I couldn't keep track of their hectic social life. Linda often came to stay at weekends because they were either away visiting friends or throwing a 'do' of their own. Ryan stayed with friends a lot, too.

My room was in its usual state but at least the double bed was clear. I usually shared it with Linda when she came to stay; that way we could stay up, watch movies and talk until we fell asleep.

Linda placed her backpack on the rocking chair in the corner of the room and we knelt on the bed with our arms resting on the windowsill, looking out over the back garden to the fields beyond. It was starting to spit with rain.

'Your mum said you were going to do some recording today. Did you?'

'Yes. I had a go at Jeff's latest song. It's a power ballad. Not exactly original, but he says they're never really in fashion, so they never really go out of fashion. Always a good bet for the end credits of films, according to him.'

'How did it go?' She looked unusually excited about it.

'Oh, he called me a natural but I'm not sure I really believe him; I think he's just saying it to keep Mum happy. Families are weird. Despite everything you've said, your family still seem pretty normal to me.'

She snorted.

'Don't be fooled by appearances. We're not your average anything. Anyway, you're alright. You and Rob have folks that are keen to support both of you in whatever you want to do. You've got a proper little nuclear family going on here.'

My head filled with the image of a mushroom cloud spreading over The Gables.

'You make them sound radioactive.'

'No, nuclear as in self-contained: a tight little unit.'

'I suppose we are, although the family's about to get bigger. Anyway, you and Ryan are well supported too.'

'Oh, it's not that; it's just . . . What do you mean bigger?' Linda looked shocked and surprised all of a sudden. 'Oh, my God! Your mum's not pregnant is she?'

'No, nothing like that! We're getting a kitten next week. She's slinky and grey with the most amazing eyes. We're calling her Fluffy. It's Rob's idea of a joke 'cos she isn't fluffy at all.'

'That's a bit like . . .' Her voice tailed away.

'A bit like what?' I asked.

'Oh, nothing!' She was practically biting her tongue. 'Anyway, have you got any pictures? I'd love to see what the kitten looks like.'

'Yes, I have. I took some on my phone when we went to see her.' I picked it up off the bedside table and showed her the handful of shots.

'Oh, she's so cute! How do you think Rolo will react to having competition around?'

'He'll get over it,' I laughed.

Mum knocked and poked her head around the door, beaming.

'I've just been listening to what you recorded today, Rebecca. It sounds amazing. Is it something you want to do more of?'

I nodded.

'If that's alright. I enjoyed it.'

'Sweetheart, we'll support you all the way if that's what you want to do in life. It's the same with Rob and his sports; you don't know what you're capable of until you try. There'll be a lot of hard work if you want to take it seriously, but when it comes to living your life to its fullest there are no trial runs; you just have to embrace it.'

'Thanks, Mum. Was it really that good?'

She looked overcome with a mixture of emotions.

'Darling, you've got a very special gift, and if you feel inspired to use that then Jeff and I are right behind you. You have a world of opportunities at your disposal that were never available to me, so make the most of them, okay?'

'Okay, Mum. Thanks,' I said, trying to keep my voice level.

She disappeared around the door again and I turned to Linda, excited.

'Maybe I wasn't that bad after all.'

'I think you were probably more than okay. Your problem is you're too modest, but at least that's better than being too cocky. Nobody likes a precocious brat; there's a fine line between self-belief and arrogance. Anyway, dig out the DVDs. Let's decide what we're going to watch.'

'What sort of thing do you fancy?' I asked, reaching for the top drawer of the cabinet underneath the telly. Only the downstairs TVs had been hooked up to all the movie channels, so I kept a good selection of films up in my room for when Linda came over.

'Oh, something classic with plenty of action and humour.'

My fingers naturally fell on an old favourite.

'I think I know just the thing.'

We stayed up late, watching movies, eating tortillas and salsa we'd raided from the kitchen cupboards and laughing until our sides ached, but somewhere in the back of my mind I still had the nagging feeling that there was something she wanted to talk about but couldn't or wouldn't: something big. Nevertheless, I put the thought to one side until she was ready to share it with me. She could be so mysterious at times.

The weeks rolled by. Most weekends would find me being put through my paces in the studio with Jeff and Steve during the day. Linda often sat on the sofa in the control room, listening and watching with her usual cool detachment. Some of what we did was Jeff's own songs, some of it other peoples, but the one constant thing was change. Rock, dance, funk, jazz, intimate acoustic songs, soul: he threw everything at me. I drew the line at sea shanties.

'Sea shanties? Really, Jeff? What's the vibe we're going for here, Spongebob Squarepants?'

He was belly laughing.

'I was actually joking about the sea shanties, but there is a serious point to this. If you enjoy something and you want to be good at it, you have to explore every avenue. You need to push the envelope to find out where your limits are, otherwise, how do you know what you're capable of and what's right for you?'

'And what are my limits? Have you found them yet?'

He shook his head.

'Not so far, no! There doesn't seem to be much you can't do when you put your mind to it.'

-0-

School was . . . well, school really. I had made other friends, Sophie Parkinson and Jayne Tripp in particular, but no one like Linda. We both saw everything from the outside in our own different ways, never quite fitting in with the crowd. With each other for company, neither of us had to pretend to be anything other than ourselves.

Most days I would stop off at Linda's on the way home and we did our homework together. Ryan was usually there, sometimes with a few of his mates. 'Mr Popular' was always in demand. Guys liked him. Girls liked him even more.

When he wasn't surrounded by his friendship group we would sit and watch the telly together if Linda was busy. Watching the wrestling became a bit of a regular occurrence. We both knew it was ridiculous and staged but couldn't help getting worked-up over it anyway. Sometimes we'd realise Linda was watching us from the lounge doorway and smiling to herself while we both shouted at the screen. Neither of us had the faintest idea how long she'd been standing there.

The confirmation of his place at the University of Westminster to study for a BA in Business Management arrived that summer. He was hoping to go on to do a Masters Degree and aiming for a job in one of the big shot companies in London. He had it all mapped out, the clever sod! I could imagine him being at home mixing with the hoi polloi at the Henley Regatta or punting a boat down the river Thames. If ever there was someone who seemed destined for success and at ease with the prospect, it was him.

In September, Ryan left to take up his studies. Apart from holidays, he was going to be away for at least the next three years. It seemed like forever. I was going to miss his easy charm and that smile; especially that smile.

By then, I was starting to really get the hang of writing songs and we'd even recorded some of them. Jeff and

Steve both helped out and made suggestions. Steve was particularly helpful, brushing back his shoulder-length blonde hair from his face while he showed me new and exotic chords, patiently maneuvering my stubborn fingers into place. Even the music theory stuff, which might have been dry and dull, was made more enjoyable by his mischievous humour; there was always a sparkle of enthusiasm in his eyes. Although he must have been in his mid-to-late twenties, he seemed younger; his boyish charm remained.

Jeff was just turning forty, but he seemed more his own age. Maybe it was because Jeff had become more like a dad to me. It might also have had something to do with the grey hair that was beginning to creep in around his temples. It made him look distinguished even if he did still try to act a bit trendy sometimes.

Mum and Jeff were married in the autumn. Steve was Jeff's best man, but his wife was away in Spain, visiting family. It wasn't a grand thing anyway, but intimate and relatively low key with all our immediate family around us. They both looked so happy. Mum deserved some contentment after all the time she struggled to bring us up on her own. All three of us took Jeff's surname and I was happy to be able to call myself Rebecca Taylor instead of Rebecca James. After all, what had Robert James ever done for us? Not that much when I thought about it.

It was towards the end of that year when Jeff sat me down in the snug and had 'the chat'. It wasn't the birds and bees chat that every parent dreads and every teenager dreads even more, it was about the music. He was trying to put me at my ease, but I could tell he was uncomfortable himself; he seemed unusually hesitant.

'You might not realise it Beccs, but you're at something of a crossroads and there are decisions to be made. Before you do, though, there are some things you need to think about.'

He took a deep breath and placed his hands around mine.

'You have a talent for music; it's a raw, natural, wonderful gift, but it takes more than talent to make your way in the music world. There's no such thing as guaranteed success, no matter how talented, hard-working or well-connected you are, but if that's the career path you want to follow then your mum and I will support you all the way, and I can help to open doors for you. You need to know what you're getting into before you make that decision, though. There's no getting away from how big a commitment this is. It will influence the whole course of your life.'

Suddenly my arms and legs were made of lead, rooting me to the spot. I'd never seen the usually laid back Jeff look this serious before.

'No one with your fierce, individual creativity is going to be content to spend their life dancing to someone else's tune. So if you are looking towards a solo career in popular music, and it seems to me that that's where you're heading, then you only have until the end of your teens to begin to break into that market. The music industry isn't interested in new artists unless they have youth on their side. Once you get past twenty your chances of achieving success decrease dramatically every year, so it means committing one hundred percent from this point on if it's what you really want. Not only that, but you will have to learn to be strong and determined in ways you never imagined to survive what the music industry does to people like you: people who have the soul of a true artist, who really love what they do, because it chews them up and spits them out and throws them away when it thinks it has made all the money it can make out of them. I've seen it happen time and time again.'

There was bitterness in his voice and his intensity was unsettling. He wasn't done yet, though.

'It's hard to make a living doing something you love without eventually sacrificing the very thing that made you want to do it in the first place. You put your heart and soul into everything you do. You give yourself so completely to the music I must admit I worry about what that life will do to you. The music business and its pressures have even been the ruin of many, even its biggest names. Elvis Presley, Michael Jackson, Jimi Hendrix, even Whitney Houston: it's a very long list.'

'Weren't a lot of those cases drug related?' I asked him.

He nodded.

'Yeah, but drug abuse, prescription or otherwise, is a symptom of the disease; it's not the cause. The point is, no matter how successful you are it can still mess you up. Pretty soon, if you decide to take the plunge and if your career takes off, there will be all manner of people and things to contend with, all in addition to the stuff I know you love: the writing, performing and recording. I will shield you from as much of that pressure as possible for as long as I can, but it's not an easy life and it's potentially a lonely one. We live in a world driven by commercial concerns, not artistic ones. You'll be surrounded by people for much of the time and yet alone because everybody, the public included, will want a piece of you and yet none of them will know and understand the real you. None of them will be able to follow to where you go in your head when you create or walk a mile in your shoes.'

I froze. How did he know where I went in my head? I'd never told him that. I'd never told anybody that, not even Linda. Maybe we were more alike than I'd realised. I think Jeff could see the effect all this was having on me. He was calming down now, but he still looked upset.

'I think of you as my daughter: the daughter I would never be able to have if I hadn't met your mum and I just want the best for you, but what that is can only be your decision. You have to make that choice for yourself because it will mean growing up fast whether you like it or not. I just need you to know what you're getting yourself into and what the dangers and pitfalls are.'

I flung my arms around him, resting my head on his shoulder.

'It's alright, Dad. I know what I'm getting into and with your help, I'll be strong. I'm not going to be a victim in all of this but music is it for me. There's never been anything else.'

He pulled back and held me at arm's length to look at me.

'You called me Dad,' he said, regaining his senses.

'Of course I did. You're the only real dad I've ever known.'

He began to brighten and put his arms around me.

'Just think carefully about what I said, will you? I'm

always here if you need to talk.'

'Thank-you.' I said, before making my way thoughtfully up to my room.

I was pleased he'd opened up about his fears for me, but what else was I going to do with my life? What else could I do? I wasn't academic, not like Linda. If I wasn't going to make music I'd spend my whole life trying to be something other than me.

I lay down on my bed and stared at the ceiling, turning everything over in my mind until it eventually stilled, the turmoil replaced by calm resolve. If I was really serious about it, I would have to devote my life to the music from this point on. There could be no half measures, no second best. From now on I was going to find myself increasingly thrust into an adult world and I had to be ready for that.

All of a sudden it seemed my childhood was over.

CHAPTER THREE

I was sitting on the edge of my bed, trying out ideas for another song. The chords were great and I liked the vocal melody, but I just couldn't get the lyrics right. It was supposed to be about relationships but what did I know about those? How could I lend some reality to the words when that kind of love was something I had no experience of? To be honest, for as far into the future as I could imagine what chance did I have? I'd somehow bypassed the years of carefree teenage exploration and been catapulted straight into a world of adult expectations. The real pressure wasn't on yet, but it soon would be. Like Jeff had said, though, at least it had been my choice, my decision.

It had been a hotter summer than usual. Sultry, late summer sunshine streamed in through the window of my room filling it with a golden glow, but I was feeling none of its warmth. I needed a change of scenery, a chance to clear my head.

With a sigh, I put down the pencil and paper and placed my guitar carefully back on its stand next to the bed. I always kept it to hand these days, along with a pad of manuscript paper so I could jot down ideas as they came to me, which was often first thing in the morning. I would wake up with music whirring around in my brain which I had to write down quickly before it evaporated into the ether, only to be lost forever.

My GCSE exams had come and gone since Jeff pulled me aside for our little chat. To be fair, Jeff opening up to me like that had brought us closer, but it was becoming clear just how much I would have to sacrifice to make music my life. While other people at school had social lives and boyfriends and some even had part-time jobs, I was squirrelled away in my bedroom, writing songs and working towards a future in music that might never happen. If fate wasn't on my side it could go nowhere, no matter how hard I worked, and I would miss out on so many of the experiences people take for granted when growing up while pouring all my energy into chasing an illusion.

It did feel like all the effort was paying off, though. I'd come so far, but I still wanted to know so much more, and the whole process of recording fascinated me. Even when Jeff wasn't there I would interrogate Steve while he worked. With patience and good humour, he explained about microphone types and placement, isolation, acoustics, sequencing, effects and processing, multi-track recording techniques and the differences between analogue and digital signals as well as expanding my music theory.

It wasn't just the technical stuff either. He was a really good musician too and had an encyclopaedic knowledge of music history. Like me, he was an enthusiast. He didn't have to spend so much time helping me; it wasn't his job to do that but nevertheless, he did, and I liked being around him too. What shone through everything was the fact that he was doing what he loved and loved what he did. Like the Spanish Inquisition, I wanted to know everything. I would sit on the swivel chair by the mixing desk, swinging my legs as I listened and watching Steve's hazel eyes dancing while he answered all of my questions with his usual generosity.

When I came down from my room after my aborted songwriting attempt, Mum was in the kitchen putting the shopping away. Fluffy surveyed everything with haughty suspicion from her favourite vantage point at the end of the worktop while Rolo stretched and got out of his basket to greet me. I patted him on the head, reached into a bag and began helping out by stacking some tins in the cupboard.

'Are you still planning on going over to Linda's?' Mum asked.

'Yeah, I'll probably go over earlier than originally planned. I need a break; writer's block has struck again.'

'It'll do you good to get out for some fresh air. You spend so much time shut away in your bedroom with your music. When you're not doing that you're either doing homework or in the studio. Are you staying over there tonight?'

'I don't know yet, but I'll phone and let you know later. Don't worry about dinner, though; we might go out for something to eat.'

'Have you got enough money?' she asked.

'Yes, Jeff gave me my allowance yesterday. Where is he today anyway? Has he gone into London again?'

'He's playing golf with a contact and taking your latest demos along to play to someone quite high up. I can't even remember which record company it is this time. It probably won't be long before you'll have to start going with him. I think there are a few labels interested now but they will all want to meet you and eventually, they'll be looking for some showcase gigs too. They'll want to see the performance side of things before they commit to anything.'

I said nothing, just nodded. It was one thing recording in the studio; I felt at home there now. Standing up in front of strangers was going to be something else. I'd performed in school, of course, in concerts and things like that, but it was nothing like taking my singing out into the wider world. Although I knew I could do it, it still felt daunting.

'When are you going out, Mum?' I asked.

'Bobby's got a training session at two so we'll be leaving in about fifteen minutes.'

'Rob, Mum!'

'Sorry?'

'He wants to be called Rob now, remember? He says it's more grown up and manly.'

The last word came out with a little more sarcasm than I intended. Mum chose to ignore it.

'I forget how fast the two of you are growing up sometimes. Anyway, grab yourself some lunch before you go over. Make the most of what's left of the summer holidays. You'll soon be back to school for the sixth form and you've got a big year ahead of you . . . on all fronts.'

'Oh, don't I know it!' I said with an air of resignation.

I'd done okay in my GCSEs, so at least I had some half-decent qualifications behind me. Although I was going on to take Music, Performing Arts and English

Literature in the sixth form, I had no idea whether I would get to finish the courses or not. It depended on whether anything else took off.

I made myself a sandwich and cleared up again before heading over to the Maloney's. Linda's dad was cutting the front lawn when I arrived. The engine of the mower ground to a halt when he saw me heading up the drive.

'Hi, Rebecca! Linda's in the house if it's her you're after.'

'Hi there, Mr Maloney! How come you're at home on a Friday?'

'Oh, I took some time off to get on top of a few jobs. We've got visitors coming this weekend. Anyway, go on in.'

What, again? More visitors?

'Thanks, Mr Maloney. I'll see you later.'

He gave me a genial wave and returned to the task at hand.

Ryan appeared from the kitchen when I passed through the hallway, handing me a cold drink of sparkling elderflower cordial. He looked as dreamy as ever in a pair of camel coloured, slack shorts and a white, open-necked shirt. I looked forward to his visits during the holidays.

'You look different.' He cocked his head to one side. 'I think it must be the summer dress because jeans and a t-shirt is normally more your style. I didn't realise you had legs.'

I took a sip of my drink and punched him playfully on the arm with my free hand before heading up. At the top of the stairs, Loretta waved a hand in greeting when I passed the office, still engrossed in whatever was on the computer screen in front of her.

'Hello, Mrs M.'

'Hello, Rebecca. Linda's in her room.'

I opened the door and Linda looked up from her book.

'Hey! What are you reading this time?' I asked, sitting down on the edge of the bed.

She held it up so I could see the cover.

'The Story of O? What's that?' I asked.

She reddened. That didn't happen very often.

'It's um . . . it's a classic of its genre, although it was banned for many years. It's hard to believe it was written in the 1950s. Back then the average person, in Britain at least, would only admit to doing it on a Saturday night in the missionary position with the lights off. It blew people's minds.'

She handed it to me and I read the blurb on the back cover. It was my turn to blush.

'I suppose that's about as close as you get to reading romantic books,' I said. 'It all sounds a bit twisted.'

'I suppose, but it's also rather beautiful in its own dark way.'

'A bit like you then.'

Her green eyes burned with some complex mixture of emotions I couldn't quite fathom. She looked so different now that she wore contact lenses most of the time instead of glasses. Gone too was the gawky, skinny girl I had first met. What had begun to replace her was a young woman with the same slender elegance as her mother. I handed the book back to Linda, who placed a bookmark in between the pages she had been reading, put it back beside her bed and turned to face me with a resolved look.

'Listen,' she paused and took a deep breath, 'there's something I've been meaning to tell you about for a long time. The problem is we have to keep very quiet about it. It could cause all sorts of problems if word got about. Ryan and I had to swear not to talk about it but I need to share it with you, otherwise I'm going to go crazy. I don't like keeping things from you, but to be honest I didn't know where to start.'

She had my complete attention.

'You know my parents have a rather full social life?'

I nodded. Linda was watching me closely, awaiting my reaction to whatever she was about to tell me. The air in the room had turned to treacle; so thick you could have cut it with a knife.

'. . . They're swingers.'

'You mean like . . . ?'

'I mean they enjoy having sex with other people, yes. It's all strictly couples with them. They're very happy being the way they are, and they love each other very much. Everything's by agreement. Nobody goes behind anybody's back about any of it but they don't have an exclusive relationship.'

She sat back, waiting for me to say something. At first I was lost for words, but eventually my speech returned.

'How long have you known about it?' I asked.

'Since I was twelve. I've been dying to get it off my chest and I'm so glad I finally have, but it's hard to know what to say and to whom. I didn't want to scare you off and I had to swear not to talk about it to people. You're not mad at me are you?'

'Why would I be mad? Just . . . no more secrets, okay? I'm not going to tell anybody.'

She flung her arms around me in what was, for her at least, an unusually open display of affection.

'Thank you. I promise there will be no more secrets.'

She looked relieved. All the tension seemed to drop away from her.

'Do you get it now with the pampas grass?' she asked, grinning.

My brow furrowed. I didn't get it.

'It used to be a bit of a cliché among swingers to have pampas grass growing outside the house as a signal. It was already there when we moved here, but we kept it for a laugh. It was Mum's idea of ironic humour, a private joke. As far as I know, nobody does that anymore. It's just as much of a myth as the lucky dip with the car keys to see who gets who. That's just so 1970s.'

'How does all this sit with your family being Catholic?'

'Lapsed Catholics,' she corrected, 'very lapsed! Can you imagine us being practising Catholics? We'd never be out of the confession box. I'm most definitely not, for all sorts of reasons, and as for Catholic guilt: don't get me started. Why the fuck should anyone be made to feel guilty for simply being what they are and obeying their nature?'

She spat the words out with a vehemence which took me by surprise. I was beginning to regret asking and changed the direction of the conversation to calm things down.

'So, what about you and boys?' I asked, lying down on the bed next to her.

'I've got my eye on a couple of possibilities,' she made it sound like she was interviewing them for a job, 'nothing definite at the moment. I'm not really interested in heavy relationships; I just want to keep it fun. What about you?'

I sighed heavily.

'Relationships aren't really on the cards for me either: not because I don't want to, but because with the whole music thing I couldn't commit myself. Besides, I've had the odd snog and a grope with a couple of the boys in our year, as you know, but they're just boys. I want someone with a bit more about them, a bit more . . . maturity.'

She regarded me for a moment. I could almost hear the cogs grinding in her head.

'Who says you have to have a committed relationship to get what you want. No princess really expects to find her prince first off anyway! Besides, kissing frogs can be fun.' Her eyes narrowed. 'Something tells me you've got your eyes on someone older. Have you?'

I blushed.

'Certainly not!' I replied in a huff.

She sat up and changed tack, still obviously keen for more information although I had no idea why she would be so interested in me; I knew she'd been seeing boys from school on and off for months.

'Don't you wonder what it would be like, sex I mean: how it feels?'

'Yes, of course.'

'Do you think you're ready?'

'Oh, God yeah! There's just nobody to do it with. I must admit I am spending rather a long time in the bath lately.'

Shit! Me and my big mouth again!

'Tell me more.' All of a sudden Linda's eyes were

bright.

There was no point stopping now; the cat was out of the bag.

'Well, it's the warmth of the water and the bubbles and it feels so sensual and I . . . I just get all wrapped up in the moment.'

Linda's cheeks were unusually flushed and her eyes had a hard glint in them.

'Fingers?' she asked.

'Mm-hmm!'

'Do you orgasm?'

I puffed out my cheeks and exhaled, raising my eyebrows.

'Oh yes!'

'That's my girl!' She grinned.

'Anyway, what about you?'

Linda winked at me.

'Given my taste in bedtime reading, what do you think?'

'I guess you've got a point there. Silly me for asking!'

Confessions over, we fell about in fits of giggles, two teenagers just laughing about life. It felt good.

CHAPTER FOUR

It was towards the end of the year when school was well underway again and I was working closely with Steve on perfecting my songs that I overheard Mum and Jeff talking about how Steve had separated from his wife, Valentina. He stopped shaving and let his beard grow for a while, and I could see the pain in his eyes whenever his thoughts got the better of him, but for the most part, he hid it well. I felt for him, although I didn't know what the cause of their problems was. Jeff was away more and more, but Steve was always on hand to help despite his troubles, and there were times when I just wanted to hug him.

Actually, I wanted to do more than that: I wanted to kiss him; I wanted to . . . do other things. Every time we were around each other my mind ran riot but I had no idea what to do with all the thoughts and feelings that went through my head. He was Jeff's friend and colleague. Why would he have any interest in a silly teenage girl with a crush?

Yes, that's what it is: a crush. Stop being so stupid!

By January I noticed a change; he seemed to be more himself again. The beard had gone and his youthful bounce was returning. I'd share in his excitement at every musical corner we turned, every breakthrough we made, but I was starting to find it hard to concentrate when we were in the studio together.

Once, when I leant across to see what was happening on the screen in front of us, he turned to talk to me and my hair brushed his face. I pulled back as if I'd just had an electric shock, suddenly feeling self-conscious and mumbling my apologies. Another time our eyes locked and I turned away from him, red with embarrassment at the thoughts running through my head. I could smell the clean scent of his hair, his skin. It was driving me crazy.

I'd never really noticed how lithe he was until then, how lightly he moved. Damn, he was starting to look good in a pair of close-fitting jeans! Containing my frustration was getting harder and harder. The only cure, albeit temporary, seemed to involve a lot of long, hot baths.

I confessed all to Linda while I was over at her house after school one day.

'I'm starting to get all fingers and thumbs around him. I feel like I'm making such an idiot of myself but I can't help it.' I stared into my lap and fiddled with my hands. 'Every time we're alone in the studio I want to touch him but whenever we get near each other I fall to pieces and I don't know what I can do to change that. He's been such a good friend and teacher and I don't want to mess that up.'

'Didn't I tell you? I knew you had your sights on an older guy.'

'It's not like that. I never asked for this,' I protested.

'Not relevant, not important! The question is: do you

want him?'

I rested my head in my hands then lifted my face towards her.

'Yes. Yes, I do.'

Linda leant forwards and took my hands in hers.

'Then you need to tell him. Don't put on an act. Don't try to seduce him. Just be honest with him. Tell him how you feel. Tell him what you want.'

'But he's ten years older than me and he's Jeff's best friend!' I wailed.

She waved her hands in the air.

'That's just numbers and politics. You need to tell him,' she repeated. 'Do you know how he feels about you?'

'Well not really, no.'

'Then talk to him,' she handed me a tissue to mop up my tears, 'before you drown us all.'

Linda turned and disappeared out of the room, returning moments later with a small box which she placed in my hands.

'Where the hell did you get these?' I asked.

'Ryan's room! He keeps a stash in his bedside drawer. Since he's away at university he won't want these ones in a hurry. Look, I'm not saying you'll need them this week, next week or next month but there will come a time, and probably not too far away when you will. You'll be glad they were there, but for Pete's sake, talk to him!'

'Alright! Alright! I get the message,' I said, putting the condoms away in my coat pocket. I decided to change the subject. 'Anyway, how is Ryan?'

'He's doing alright for himself. He's a popular lad, too. I don't think he gets cold at night very often if you know what I mean.'

I did know what she meant, and was that a pang of jealousy I felt in the pit of my stomach? I resolved to talk to Steve soon. This was going to be awkward but I knew Linda was right. It had to be done if only to clear the air, so I could get over the rejection and move on.

The next two weeks were torture. All the opportunities that had been there while Jeff was elsewhere and Mum had taken Rob to some football match or training session vanished. Everything seemed back to normal, all except for me. I wasn't even sure if I'd just been imagining the chemistry between Steve and myself or not. He was his usual self while Jeff fussed about song arrangements and harmony parts. On the other hand, I was living in a dreamlike state, going through the motions in a vain attempt at normality. I even tidied my room just to keep my mind occupied. Everything now had its proper place and my stuff had all been put away in drawers or hung up on hangers in the wardrobe. My clothes were even arranged in groups so I didn't have to hunt for everything.

By the third weekend, though, everybody was due to be away on the Saturday, except me and Steve. By now, my head was filled with scenes which alternated between a horror show in which I made a complete fool of myself in front of my stepdad's best friend or was swept off into the sunset by a valentinoesque romantic hero and all points between. The one thing that steered my ship between the rocks of these wild extremes was Linda's voice inside my head.

Don't put on an act. Just be honest with him. Tell him how you feel.

I knew Steve was coming over mid-morning, so I showered after breakfast, put on minimal make-up and dressed very simply in a denim skirt, white blouse and flat pumps. He can take me as I am or leave me, I thought. I just needed to lay this ghost to rest.

I heard his VW Golf pull up in the driveway in front of the house. I knew it was his by the sound of the engine. From my room, I could hear his feet on the gravel as he crossed the courtyard and went in through the studio door. I headed downstairs to the kitchen and made us two mugs of tea just like I had a hundred times before.

When I entered the studio, Steve was sitting on the swivel chair in front of the mixing desk, firing up the Mac that operated most of the software. He was dressed in his customary blue jeans along with a shirt which had fine, vertical navy and white stripes, tailored in slightly at the waist and a pair of casual brown leather shoes worn without socks. He looked so laid back, so at ease, so . . . damned hot.

'Morning!' I breezed, handing him one of the steaming mugs which he stood up to accept.

'Morning!' he replied. To my ears at least, his voice was like butter. 'So, what's on the menu for today?'

My insides were turning to mush but my brain resisted.

'*Focus, Rebecca! Focus!*' intoned a voice with a Scottish accent somewhere in the back of my head.

'I've got something different I need to run past you.' I was trying hard not to let my voice betray my nerves.

'Okay, shoot! I'm all ears.'

'Listen, it's a bit more . . . a bit more personal than usual.'

Suddenly he looked rather less comfortable, but he persisted.

'Okay.' He could clearly sense my awkwardness and gestured towards the sofa. 'Sit down and talk to me,' he said calmly.

I sat at one end, he sat at the other, and we placed our teas on the table in front of us.

'I don't really know where to start.'

At least I was being honest! I took a deep breath and exhaled steadily.

'I need to know what this thing is between us.' The words came blurted out in a rush.

He swallowed.

'Ah, the elephant in the room!' He smiled awkwardly, trying to make light of it. 'Yes. Me too!'

'So I'm not imagining it then?'

Steve shook his head.

'No.' At least it seemed we were both in the same disorientated boat. 'Tell me what you think this is,' he said.

'I'm attracted to you.' I couldn't think how else to explain myself. 'I have been for some time, and I know you probably think I'm just some girl with a crush and no sense but I can't help feeling the way I do. I fancy you and I just can't help it,' I gushed.

He put his hand over his mouth and closed his eyes for a moment then opened them again, searching me for information.

'Why are you interested in me? There must be guys your own age who are falling over themselves for you.'

It was my turn to shake my head.

'They're just boys. They couldn't possibly understand

where I'm coming from right now, but you know me. You understand me.'

'I also know you're the stepdaughter of one of my closest friends who also happens to be my employer, and I don't want to let him or you down. You are going to go incredible places with your life and I won't be responsible for jeopardising that by entering into a relationship that can't possibly go anywhere.'

'I'm not talking about forever. I want to learn from you. I want to experience things and I can't think of anyone I'd rather share that with, than with you.'

He looked shell shocked. I was offering him a free pass to an all-you-can-eat buffet. I don't think I was much less surprised myself.

'Look,' I said, gathering all my wits, 'I know that for a long time into the future serious relationships aren't going to happen for me, but that doesn't change the fact that I've got the same need to explore all the sides of who I am. I can't help wanting you and I hope you feel the same way. There are no strings. I can hardly afford long-term ties myself, can I? Whatever I can have of you is better than none, but if you don't want me then I understand and I promise I'll never mention it again.'

He mustered himself, trying to find the right words.

'I'm not going to pretend to you that it hasn't crossed my mind; I'm only human. You've blossomed into a very beautiful young woman as well as being smart and talented, but don't you see how complicated things could get? Jeff's very protective of you. God only knows you know your own mind better than many women far older, but I'm sorry, I just can't go there; I've been promising myself I wouldn't.'

Steve got up. His hands were shaking. I stood up too. He put his hands on my arms, gently pinning them to my sides and kissed me tenderly on the forehead.

'I'm sorry. I ought to go.' He turned to leave and reached for the door handle.

My heart sank. I'd blown it.

Rebecca fucks it up again! At least I knew where I stood but I'd made such a mess of everything. I had to try and retrieve what I could.

'Don't go, Steve. Look, I was out of line and . . . and I shouldn't have put you on the spot. You're so kind and helpful to me and I owe you so much. I don't want this to affect anything. If you go now it will be much harder for both of us to get past this and it will be my fault. Please, let's just get on with what we're supposed to be here for. I want you to forget we ever had this conversation. Deal?'

He exhaled slowly, let go of the door handle and turned to face me. It felt like a long time before he spoke.

'Deal!' Suddenly it was business as usual. 'So what have we got today?'

'There are a couple of new songs I've been working on. I can't get the lyrics right for one of them even though I've been trying on and off for months so that will have to wait, but the other one has some potential I think.'

'Fire away then. Let's see what we can do with it.'

My guitar was still up in my room so I picked up one of the acoustic guitars from the rack in the performance area, slung it around my neck and produced a plectrum from the back pocket of my skirt.

Steve grinned.

'Ah, you're a proper musician now if you're carrying plectrums everywhere you go.'

I smiled shyly at him, relieved that everything seemed to be getting back to normal, sat down and began to strum the opening chords.

'You'll have to forgive the rather stilted vocals. It really needs two voices because the vocal lines overlap, but anyway, here goes.'

Then it struck me what I was about to sing, but it was too late; I'd already started so I had to see this through. There was a rising tide of discomfort that began in the pit of my stomach and moved upward till it prickled in my scalp. I opened my mouth, wondering if the song's simple honesty would be too much. It hadn't really dawned on me till now how much this song laid my soul bare . . .

I can't, I can't help the way that I feel
You know, I hope this feeling is real
Not quite a woman, yet more than a girl
Suspended in motion to wait on the world

In my head, other instruments were already joining in: bass and soft, relaxed drums, resonating gently with the guitar.

How long must I stay here floating in space?
Waiting for contact, the touch of your face
This radio silence is killing me slowly
 But I wait . . . oh
Drifting . . . oh, drifting

I closed my eyes while I sang. At least that way I didn't have to face him. In my head, ascending strings joined the swell of the music. I tried to focus on those over the coursing of the blood around my body and the heat spreading to my cheeks. I wasn't succeeding.

Whatever happened to me?
The age of innocence is gone
Whatever it is I'm feeling
It can't be wrong

I could feel myself choking on the words. My voice was breaking up. The notes would barely come out of my mouth but I had to try.

You know I don't . . .

I faltered and ground to a halt, unbidden tears welling in my eyes while gentle hands took the guitar from me and helped me to my feet. Steve cupped my face in his hands and tilted my head back, giving me no choice but to look at him as he wiped the tears from my cheeks with his thumbs.

He rested his forehead against mine, with his eyes closed and our lips almost touching, hands on either side of my head. I could hardly breathe. Steve opened his eyes and our lips met, simply, passionately. When he slowly pulled away, his lower lip dragged languidly against mine. I could still taste him.

He suddenly snapped to.

'I'm . . . I'm really sorry. It won't happen again.'

Steve turned, picked up his jacket and walked out of the door which closed behind him, leaving me still reeling, unable to move my feet. I longed to feel his lips against mine again but he was gone. I was stunned, unable to decide whether to whoop with joy that I'd just had my first ever proper kiss or burst into tears because there wasn't going to be another. I touched my fingers to my lips, willing them to be his mouth once more, still in shock. The only sound was the faint hum of the computer; otherwise, the control room was silent.

I was still standing frozen to the spot where he left me, staring towards the door when it burst open again. Steve stood framed by the light in the doorway for a moment, looking towards me, then quickly crossed the room and drew me into his arms with his hands in my hair. I could hear the rise and fall of his laboured breathing, feel the heat of his skin, smell the faint remnants of his after-shave.

'I don't know what it is you do to me, but I couldn't leave it like that. I just couldn't do it.'

'Then don't,' I said.

'You do know what you're saying to me, don't you?'

'Yes.' I was resolved. 'Yes, I want you.' The words arrived in a kind of breathy gasp, a voice barely my own.

His lips closed urgently on mine and I responded with a force I never knew I possessed. My hands were tearing at the buttons on his shirt in my sudden need to reach his skin. My heart was threatening to leap out of my chest.

He pressed my hands together between his and pulled back to look at me with a new and savage heat burning behind his eyes, something glorious and unsettling, dangerous and undeniable that melted me inside. He was shaking slightly, wide-eyed with adrenaline, though whether from nerves or excitement I couldn't exactly tell.

'Fuck it!' he said. 'Who wants to play by the rules anyway?'

CHAPTER FIVE

Steve and I found ourselves stumbling across the courtyard and up to my bedroom, so absorbed in each other and the moment that we couldn't even remember how we got there. Lips pressed tight and eyes locked, we barely paid any attention to where we were going. I closed the door behind me and stood, looking at him, still unsure what would happen next. My heart was thumping and I tingled with excitement.

'What am I going to do with you, Miss Taylor?' His words dripped with suggestion.

I stepped out of my pumps and kicked them across the floor.

'Everything, I hope, Mr Bowes.'

He looked at me in amazement at my boldness. I had no idea where my confidence had come from, but I liked it.

'That's a pretty long list,' he said.

'Well then, we'd better make a start, hadn't we?'

Steve looked nervous all of a sudden, his expression becoming more serious.

'Are you absolutely sure this is what you want? It's not too late to change your mind.'

'Shh!' I soothed as if calming an infant and touched his lips with my forefinger. 'I think I made my feelings perfectly clear.'

'Yes.' Steve's eyes still hadn't left me. 'Yes, you did.'

He wanted me too; I could tell by the hunger in the way he looked at me. It scared and excited me at the same time.

I took hold of the front of his shirt with both hands and drew him towards me. He kissed me hard, our tongues exploring each other's mouths. Making out with boys my own age had never been like this, even if I did have to draw myself up to my full height to do it. I'd never thought about how much taller than me Steve was. Even though he wasn't big-built, up close and personal he wasn't small either.

Feeling my way with nervous fingers, I began undoing the remaining buttons on his shirt. The rest of them must have been on the floor of the studio control room. I would have to pick those up later, but not right now; I had more urgent things to attend to. Before I even realised what I was doing, I had peeled Steve out of his shirt, thrown it into the corner of the room and was running my fingers through the smattering of hair on his chest. Steve didn't bother undoing all the buttons on my blouse; he simply lifted my arms and slipped it off over my head before tossing it into the corner to join his shirt.

His lips hovered close to mine while he stroked me through the material of my plain, white bra, and I let out a short, involuntary gasp at the shock of his touch, followed by a much longer sigh when his fingers located the clasp, freeing my breasts. He trapped my stiffening nipples between practised fingers and rolled them beneath his thumbs. Nothing could have prepared me for how I felt; it was all so new and startling to me, but so wonderful too.

'Are you alright there?' he asked.

I nodded dumbly. I didn't want him to stop.

Cupping and kneading my breasts in his outstretched palms, he lowered his head to nuzzle my neck just below my earlobe. The effect was electric; I would never have expected that part of me to be so sensitive. It was like being introduced to the body I lived in for the first time.

Every muscle in my lower body clenched in response to Steve's hot breath fanning against my skin. His lips brushed my throat and worked their way down and across my breast until his mouth closed over my nipple. He swirled his tongue around it, sending tingling waves of sensation rippling through my whole body, then pulled back to blow gently on my wet skin, the cool rush of air stiffening my nipple still further. Turning his attention to the other side, he did the same again. It was driving me to distraction, the trickle of moisture inside beginning to feel more like a flood.

Without warning, Steve stepped back and holding my hands firmly, moved them down to my sides. Undoing my skirt, he let it fall to the floor in a heap around my feet and stepped back, admiring the view. I stood, dressed in nothing but my white cotton knickers, my breath heaving as this beautiful, carnal man took in every inch of me. I could tell by the bulge in his jeans that he liked what he saw.

'Definitely all woman!' he announced, kneeling in front of me.

Steve brushed his lips against the flat of my stomach,

inhaling my skin while I ran my fingers through his mane of blonde hair, then holding my hips firmly he dusted me with kisses down to the line at the top of my underwear and hooked his fingers into the waistband. He looked up at me as if waiting for permission.

I nodded.

'Please,' I added, just to make sure. I wanted him. Despite my obvious nerves, I wanted him so much it hurt.

Inside I was already raging, but Steve was clearly not a man to be rushed. Slowly peeling my panties down over my hips he caressed the rounded swell of my buttocks before finally sliding the last defence of my innocence down over my thighs. I parted my legs slightly to ease the flimsy garment's passage to the floor and stepped away from the crumpled heap of clothing at my feet.

Taking my hands he steered me towards the rocking chair and sat me down on the cushion then knelt between my legs, raining gentle kisses up my thighs and brushing his fingers through the soft thatch of my pubic hair.

'You . . . are . . . Venus,' he insisted, his words a punctuation between the touches of his lips. 'I don't think you know how beautiful you really are.'

I had an idea what was coming next, but I was unprepared for the feeling of total abandon when Steve's hands gently parted my thighs still further and his mouth closed around the folds of my pussy, sucking my lips between his, his tongue probing the space between and sliding upwards to find the sensitive bud at the apex. I gave in to the sensations, melting into the chair and running my fingers through his hair while his tongue continued, gently seeking out my most sensitive places then darting against me before he hungrily devoured me again. It seemed that all the moisture in my body had abandoned my mouth and headed southwards, but somehow I managed to speak.

'Oh my God, Steve! Where did you learn to do that?'

He looked up at me, eyes sparkling with mischief and lifted my legs up, holding them apart. Hooking them over the arms of the chair he pressed the flats of his hands to my inner thighs and moved them apart slightly, exposing me still further to that wonderful, wickedly probing tongue.

'Fucking hell!' I squealed, eyes wide, throwing my head back, barely able to breathe as he kept up his exquisite torture.

In a moment of madness, I grabbed the back of his head, grinding his face into me. I would have apologised but he seemed to be enjoying my abandonment; I could feel him grinning.

'I want you, Steve! I want you inside me!'

He stopped dead.

'Shit! I haven't got anything on me. I'm not used to having to think about that.'

'Don't worry,' I assured him. 'Bedside cabinet, top drawer!'

Once again, Steve looked surprised.

'How come you're so prepared?' He sounded both relieved and amused.

'A girl's got to think of these things, and besides, it pays to have friends with older brothers.' I was feeling very pleased with myself at that moment.

When Steve kissed me again I could still taste myself on his lips. If anything, it turned me on even more. He stood up, guiding my hands gently towards the waistband of his jeans. For a moment our eyes met, then transferring my focus to what was in front of me I undid the buttons of his jeans and slid them down over his thighs, taking his underwear with them. His erection sprang free from its confines and I could finally admire him close up.

I wrapped my fingers around him and I liked what I felt; hard and velvety all in one. He seemed to be thrilling to the touch of my cool, hesitant fingers almost as much as it thrilled me to touch him. His mouth hung half-open, breath catching in his throat as I stroked him gently, running my fingertips smoothly across the swollen head. Gripping a little tighter, I swore I could feel his pulse when my fingers closed around him further down.

For the first time in your life, you've got a man's cock in your hands. How does that make you feel?

It felt nice.

When I let go, he slipped out of his shoes and jeans and retrieved a condom from the bedside drawer, carefully tearing the packet open. I watched, riveted, while he put it on, squeezing out the air from the tip and unrolling it down his length. Not that I was any kind of expert, but I didn't think he had anything to be shy about.

That's going inside me! Despite my excitement, the nerves were still creeping up on me.

'You don't have to worry about hurting me, Steve. I . . .' how was I going to say this delicately? 'I sort of got carried away in the bath one time and . . . well . . . I should be alright.'

He raised one quizzical eyebrow. Maybe he wondered what the hell I'd managed to do to myself but it had just happened; a rush of curious over-enthusiasm and it was all over. It was never my intention for things to go so far, and I didn't realise it would hurt so much, but then the pain quickly subsided and an array of other glorious sensations took its place. I'd never look at deodorant bottles the same way again.

Despite my revelation, Steve didn't begin an awkward interrogation but looked at me kindly.

'That's worth knowing. We can concentrate on what it's like for you instead of worrying about that side of things but I'm still going to take it really gently at first, okay?'

Right at that moment, I think I would have agreed to just about anything. I just knew I wanted him, however it came packaged. Steve knelt in front of me, parting my knees and I found myself balanced on the edge of the chair, exposed, with my legs held wide. I touched his face.

'Just in case I forget to tell you later: thank you!'

His eyes, smiling in reply, didn't leave mine and I could feel the heat and stiffness of him pressed against my opening. I began to tremble slightly.

'We can still stop if you want to. It's not too late.' Steve's voice was earnest yet compassionate. 'Once we go past this point, neither of us can take it back. Are you completely sure you still want this?'

'Yes,' was all I could say. What other words were there?

The tip of his erection rested between the folds of my pussy, opening it up like the petals of some exotic flower. He glanced down, making sure he wasn't going to hurt me, then placing his hands on my hips eased himself smoothly, deliciously home. I wrapped my arms around his neck and clung to him, burying my face in his shoulder and gasping for air. A wave of sensation spread to every part of me, starting between my legs and radiating outwards.

He stilled, and we clung to each other, basking in the glory of the moment. Time froze. We were just two souls entwined in the perfect, never-ending now. I wanted to keep this moment forever like a wildflower pressed between the pages of a book.

Steve touched my face and smiled as if he could read my thoughts. Our lips met in a tender kiss and he began to move, oh so slowly at first but gradually gathering in pace and intensity, filling me over and over again. Waves crested and crashed over us, wind-whipped foam blowing along the shoreline of my mind.

Still rocking his hips backwards and forwards, he shifted position slightly and ran his fingertips along my spine. Electricity tingled up my back and the chair began to rock in tandem with our movements. Every time he pushed forward into me, the sensations altered as the chair tilted.

I leant back and eased my legs up, holding my thighs, instinctively undulating as the urgency of our movements increased. Again and again, he pulled back until he was almost no longer inside me then sank into me again, filling me completely. Looking down between us I could see myself stretched tightly around him, and when I reached down with one hand I could feel how slippery he was. I placed my fingers on either side of him, stroking the junction where his body met mine.

His breathing began to rasp unevenly.

'Whoa, careful! You're going to tip me over the edge

doing that.'

I didn't care. I wasn't going to be far behind him. The pressure from my fingers increased.

'Yes . . . yes!' The words exploded from my mouth, abrupt and insistent.

He couldn't hold himself back any longer. With a final thrust which went deeper than all the others, he fell off the precipice on which he had been so finely balanced. A low groan emanated from the back of his throat and escaped through gritted teeth. Pressing hard with my fingertips I followed him over into the void and we clung to each other, freefalling until our descent slowed and we drifted, light as gossamer, coming to rest in the lush, green blanket of moss that grew thickly over the rocks of the river valley below. Eventually, the rushing waterfall in my ears faded into the distance.

I lifted my head from his shoulder, still trembling slightly, and brushed the hair from his face, looking deep into those gentle, kind, hazel eyes as if I was finally seeing the man behind them for the first time.

'Oh my God!' I sighed.

His expression was questioning, expectant.

'Was that how you thought it would be?'

It was even better.

'Steve, that was . . . amazing. I want more already.'

His eyes danced with a combination of pride, mischief and mirth.

'That can be arranged. If that was the entrée you might have to wait a few minutes for the main course, though,' he chuckled, looking down at his waning glory still sheathed inside me.

Gently, Steve eased himself out and stood me on my

feet. Sweeping me up into his arms he carried me over to the bed and laid me down with gentle reverence, then once he'd dealt with the condom he lay down next to me, spooning, with his arms wrapped around my body, hands cupping my breasts. The sunshine of the clear, late February day filled the room and we lay there for a while in contented silence, luxuriating in the soft warmth of each other's bodies and the cool, clean crispness of the bedclothes. I must have drifted for a while because I suddenly became conscious of his eyes on me. I could almost hear him thinking.

'What is it?' I asked.

He propped himself up on his elbows, his thoughts etched across his face.

'You are full of surprises, you know. I still can't believe you've never done that before. You were just so natural, so instinctive. Are you sure this is your first time?' His eyes were full of humour.

'I think I'd remember if it wasn't. I just feel comfortable with you and I guess that makes all the difference. I know you've taken a big risk for me, but I'm so glad you did.'

'No regrets?'

'No! No regrets. Life's too short.' I turned my head to face him better. 'And don't you dare start feeling guilty on me! I asked you for this and it's not about Jeff either, it's about us. I love Jeff; as far as I'm concerned he's my dad, and I would never want to hurt him, but he doesn't need to know about any of this. No one does, except maybe Linda; she's the one person I tell everything to. I wouldn't worry, though. Believe me; she's very good at keeping secrets.'

He smiled enigmatically, his eyes dancing once again.

'So how do you feel now?'

I wriggled my body against him and gyrated my bottom against his groin.

'Hmm . . . womanly!' I answered.

He bit his lip and inhaled deeply.

'You want to be careful doing that sort of thing. You don't know what it does to a man.' All of a sudden the desire in his voice had returned.

'Oh, I don't know; I've got a good idea.'

Reaching behind me, I wrapped my fingers around his manhood. Signs of life were returning. I rolled over to face him.

'Seeing as you were so nice to me earlier, it seems only fair that I should return the favour,' I hinted.

Steve sucked air in through his teeth when I pushed him onto his back and began kissing down his chest and across his midriff, following the trail of hair down to his groin. Tentatively, I kissed the tip of his cock ever so gently then flicked my tongue across it. He moaned softly.

Getting bolder, I wrapped my lips around him and drew him into my mouth. I could only hope I was doing it right. He started to stiffen and gave a low growl, animal and primal. Holding him at the base, I gently moved my head back and forth, slipping his growing length in and out of my mouth, then shifting position so that I was crouched over him I held his nearly full erection in the hope of giving him my complete attention. Try as I might, though, I could not get it past the point at the back of my mouth where my gag reflex took over.

I wanted to devote myself to his pleasure as

completely as he had done to me, but I'd reached my limit. Judging by the amount of noise he was making, though, my efforts were not going unappreciated. I slipped him in and out of my mouth as far as I dared.

By now he was fully hard again and his hips began to undulate with my movements. Steve swept my hair to one side, enjoying the view for a moment then took charge again, gently lifting my head until my lips reluctantly let him go.

'Oh, Rebecca! You sweet, beautiful, unbelievably sexy young woman!'

Every word sounded so ripe with desire it raised me up, filling me with new confidence. I felt on top of the world.

'Time for the main course!' he insisted, rolling me onto my back and positioning himself between my legs. With his palm facing my crotch, he gently slid both middle fingers inside me. They went in easily.

'Something tells me you're hungry, Miss Taylor.'

'Only for you, Mr Bowes.'

He slipped his fingers out of me and put them into his mouth, removing them slowly like licking honey from a spoon. It was the single sexiest thing I think I'd ever seen; the whole of my insides felt as if they had just turned to liquid. Steve slid his fingers back into the honey pot then leant across to feed me my share. I followed his lead and sucked greedily, licking open-mouthed at his fingers as he withdrew them.

If his burning expression was anything to go by, Steve seemed delighted at my response.

'I think we're ready to serve up if you are.'

'Oh, am I ever!'

He reached for a condom from the top drawer of the bedside cabinet.

'Allow me!' I gently took the packet from him, eager to try.

'Mind out for fingernails,' he said. 'These things tear easily.'

My fingernails weren't very long anyway. The ones on my left hand were kept short for guitar playing and I had a nervous habit of biting the ones on my right when I was frustrated. I'd been frustrated a lot recently for some strange reason. Copying what I had seen him do earlier, I squeezed out the air then unrolled it down him.

I thought for a moment.

'Steve . . . you don't have to be quite so gentle with me this time. I can take it you know; I won't break.'

He stared in amazement.

'Somehow I don't doubt it! Look at you, you're so together. I suppose nothing should surprise me about you by now, but if that's how you want it then who am I to refuse? If it gets too much at any time, though, just say and I'll ease off. Deal?'

'Deal! Now come over here and fuck me, Mr Bowes.'

Fuck: I liked that word. It sounded so dirty, yet felt so right. I loved the way it tasted.

When I lay back down, he pulled my legs up so my knees were raised and wrapped his arms around my thighs, taking control. In one swift movement, he was in me, leaning forwards and pinning my folded legs to my chest, putting his whole weight behind the thrust.

I exhaled sharply, reaching out to touch his chest and looking into his eyes.

'Oh my God, Steve! That's deep.'

'Are you sure you want this?'

I nodded.

He shook his head.

'I need to hear you say it.' His voice was still gentle.

'Do it! Fuck me!' I said, breathlessly.

He eased himself upright, kneeling, and still gripping my legs laid into me with deep, hard strokes. I thrashed my head from side to side, grabbing the edges of the bedcovers in my fists while he ploughed into me.

'Oh, Jesus . . . yes!'

My eyes were wide, my teeth clenched, my back arched.

On he went, lavishing me with his thrusts, settling into a steady rhythm that matched the pounding of the blood in my head. By now I don't think I could have stopped him even if I'd wanted to; it was just as well I didn't. He released my legs and I tilted my hips to wrap my legs around him, my heels pressing into his buttocks, hands clawing at the small of his back, pulling him into me deeper still.

He paused for a moment, bringing his legs out behind him and leant forwards, propped up on his elbows, watching my face as he began again with deep, deliberate strokes, pausing so we could savour the moment each time before entering me hard, grinding his hips against mine.

I was matching him every step of the way, my breathing a short, staccato rhythm. My muscles clenched around him and instinctively I knew what was coming next. So did Steve, but there was no let-up, no mercy.

'That's it. It's your turn this time, Rebecca. Come on baby.'

Holding my breath for what seemed an age, I finally let go. All the air escaped from my lungs with a loud gasp. As my orgasm took hold he powered into me and carried on right through it while I hit the plateau and came down the other side, driving into me with a force that pushed me into the bed, my fingers gripping and clawing at his back until finally, he tensed as he came then collapsed into my arms.

We lay there breathless and spent, with my legs still wrapped around him. Steve's face was flushed, his hair a mess. He looked so damned sexy. I must have looked like a train wreck. He buried his face in my neck and nuzzled my hair then pulled back to look at me.

'Was that what you meant by not so gentle?' he asked.

'Oh, wow!' was all I could manage.

Suddenly aware of how thirsty I was, I reached for the bottle of water I kept on top of the bedside cabinet and took a long swig, then passed it to Steve.

'So now I've made gentle love to you and, for want of a better phrase, well and truly fucked you, which do you think you prefer?' he asked with a glint in his eyes.

'Do I have to choose?'

'No, it's not a one or the other thing but what do you think is more you?'

'I loved all of it, but if it came down to it, I did rather enjoy option two.'

'I had a feeling you'd say that.' He looked across at the clock on the bedside table. 'What time's your mum coming back?'

'About half past three. Why? What's the time?'

'It's almost three.'

'Holy cow! Already?' I lifted myself up slightly.

'Doesn't time fly when you're enjoying yourself? We'd better get tidied up and make sure we've got a good cover story in place.'

He kissed me quickly, slipped off of me and turned to go to the bathroom. Staring, I gasped in horror and put my hand over my mouth.

'Oh Steve, what have I done to you? I'm so sorry.'

There were scratches and reddened weals all over the lower half of his back. Droplets of blood oozed from many of them where my nails had dug into him. When I checked, there was blood on my fingers.

'It's a good job my nails aren't longer than they are. You can't put your shirt back on like that. Let me clean you up.'

I picked his shirt up from the floor and slipped it over my shoulders, then led him through into the bathroom. Taking some cotton wool and antiseptic from the cupboard I began to dab his wounds.

'I am so sorry, Steve. Didn't you notice?'

'Not at the time, no; I had other things on my mind. It's starting to sting a bit now, though.'

He tried to turn and look at me. I turned him back.

'Hold still. I can't have you getting infected. I need you in peak condition.'

'So you're not finished with me yet then, Miss Taylor?'

'Certainly not, Mr Bowes! There, that should do.'

He turned to face me and took me in his arms, kissing me slowly but with impassioned intent. I flung my arms around his neck and cried softly onto his shoulder.

'Thank you for today. It was more than I'd ever dared to hope for and I'm so sorry I hurt you. Can we do it again?'

'It'll be next Saturday before we get the chance. I'll be working in the studio, but the rest of your family will be around until then. It's going to be torture pretending everything's the same as before.'

'I know. I just feel so excited and happy. I can't wait till I can spend time with you again properly. You do want to carry on seeing me, don't you?'

Steve held my shoulders firmly but gently and gave me a lingering kiss.

'Does that answer your question?'

'I think so. I suppose we'd better get dressed before Mum and Rob get home. You'll probably need this,' I said, slipping his shirt from my shoulders, 'although I don't really want to take it off. I'm feeling a little attached to it.'

'You look good in it, but you look even better out of it.' His eyes were doing their mischievous dance again. 'I'd better get my stuff together and go. I can't have your mum seeing me with most of my shirt buttons missing; questions will be asked.'

Standing side by side, we checked ourselves in the bathroom mirror. We both looked flushed and I was quite sure a family of birds had moved into my hair and started nesting. After a quick tidy-up, we dressed again and made our way down to the kitchen.

'Do you want something to drink?' I asked him.

He licked his lips.

'Mm! Something cold, please! I'd better fetch my jacket from the studio and see if I can find my missing shirt buttons.'

Steve disappeared out of the side door. I watched him through the kitchen window, moving with his usual easy grace as he entered the studio, unable to shake the sense of non-reality. I'd just had sex with this gorgeous man. Twice!

Snapping myself out of my reverie, I took two glasses out of the cupboard and poured us some sparkling water from the fridge. I took a sip, feeling its coldness and the bubbles bursting on my tongue, then sat down at the breakfast bar. What was taking Steve so long? He'd been out of the room for two minutes and already I was missing him.

He returned with a slightly worried expression.

'What's up?' I asked, handing him his glass.

He took a deep draught and looked at me.

'I reckon there are four buttons missing but I can only find two.'

'Don't worry. I'll get down on my hands and knees and have a proper look for them later.'

His expression became lustful again.

'Hmm! You on your hands and knees: now there's a thought!'

'Steven Bowes!' I pretended to be shocked.

'I can't help what you do to me.'

'And I like what you do to me.'

'I guess that makes us even then,' he smirked.

My shoulders dropped.

'Do you really have to go?'

'I couldn't face your mum right now. She's got a way of seeing right into people's heads and at the moment I couldn't cope with her rooting around in mine. Sorry to leave you to face the inquisition on your own.'

'Oh, I can handle Mum; don't worry.'

'Come here you!' he commanded, taking me in his

arms and kissing me tenderly while running his fingers through my hair. 'I'll call you later, I promise.'

'It's probably safer to text me. You've got my number.'

'Good thinking as always, Miss Taylor.'

'Why thank you Sir!' I replied in my best 'Southern Belle' accent.

With that, he turned and headed back to his car. I watched through the front window as he waved, blew me a kiss and pulled away.

It was a good job he went when he did. Within ten minutes Mum and Rob were back, breezing into the kitchen. Rob dumped his sports stuff down with a clatter.

'Uh . . . not in here!' Mum reprimanded him. 'Take your stuff up to your room and sort it out from there.'

He huffed and disappeared out of the door again to go up the main stairs.

Mum put the kettle on and reached for the teabags.

'So how's your day been?'

Here we go! The interview!

'Oh, alright,' I said noncommittally. 'We've been working on ideas for another couple of songs. One's sounding pretty good and I think I've got a bit more inspiration for the lyrics to the other one.'

'That's nice. I don't know what we'd do without Steve. He's so helpful and accommodating.'

My stomach began doing somersaults.

'Mm, he is.'

She handed me a mug of tea and began unpacking a bag of shopping.

Awkward moment avoided.

'Thanks, Mum. So what's for dinner?' It was dawning on me how hungry I was. I hadn't eaten since breakfast.

Strangely enough, I'd had other things on my mind.

'I'm doing a beef casserole. It'll be ready about six. Jeff should be home by then.'

I helped myself to an apple from the fruit bowl on the worktop and biting into it, took my tea out to the studio and began my search for Steve's buttons. Eventually, I found one that had rolled into a corner, but the last escaped me. I consoled myself that one button could be easily explained, four could not. The computer was still on, the screen awaiting its first instruction since mid-morning.

Where did the day go? This morning I had been a girl I no longer knew. Now I was me. I shut everything down just as I had seen Jeff and Steve do so many times, turned off the lights and locked up.

Upstairs in my room, I put down the nearly empty mug of tea and lay on the bed looking up at the ceiling. When I closed my eyes I could still feel Steve lying beside me if I tried hard enough.

My mobile phone beeped on the bedside table. There was a text.

Shit! There have been two already.

Steve
Hope you are still feeling good about today. How's it going with your mum? ;-)
3:54 pm

I texted back quickly, to put his mind at ease.

Within a minute the phone rang.

'Rebecca?'

'Hi, Steve! It's okay. Everything's okay.' I could hear the relief in his exhalation of breath on the other end. 'It's all fine. I'm fine; in fact, I'm more than fine, I'm . . . glowing. Anyway, I thought you weren't going to call me and we'd stick to texts.'

'Is it okay to talk?'

'It's alright; I'm in my room.'

'I was worried you'd had a change of heart,' he said.

'About what? Having the best day of my life? Don't be so soft. I can't wait for next Saturday. I know I won't be able to show it during the week, but I'll be thinking of you.'

'Thinking of me how?'

Now I had his interest.

'I'll be thinking of you when I'm in bed, and when I'm in the bath, in fact, most of the time.'

There was a pause.

'Go on.'

'Come to think of it,' my voice became soft and seductive, 'I'm thinking of you right now.' I slipped my free hand up my leg and under my skirt. There was already a slight dampness seeping into the thin cotton of my underwear.

'And what do you do when you think of me?'

I liked this game.

'I've got my hand on my pussy. I'm caressing myself through my panties. It's so nice, but I wish you were here to do it for me.'

'Oh, believe me, so do I.'

I might have been feeling a bit sore from earlier, but I still wanted him.

'I can't wait to feel you inside me again.'

'Miss Taylor you are unstoppable. I think I've created a monster.'

'You didn't create it, you just unleashed it. Anyway, I like that monster.'

'Rebecca!' Mum's voice carried up the stairwell.

'Shit! Mum's calling me. I'd better go,' I said in a hoarse whisper.

'Okay, text you later,' said Steve.

'Okay, bye!' I rang off. 'Coming, Mum!' I called down the stairs.

If only.

Down in the kitchen, Mum was putting the casserole in the oven.

'You couldn't be a darling and help me get these ready could you?' she said, pointing at the pile of broccoli, carrots, and green beans on the chopping board. 'I need to put Rob's sports kit in the wash.'

'No problem, Mum.'

'Oh, and the animals need feeding too.'

By the time dinner was ready, Jeff had come back. We all ate at the breakfast bar in the kitchen as usual; the dining room only usually got used when we had guests. I was famished, but by the time I had polished off my second helping I was beginning to regret overdoing it.

After I helped clear up from dinner, I retreated to my room to call Linda.

'Hiya, sweetie!' she said.

'What're you doing at the moment?'

'I'm out with Dean.'

'The guy in our year you had your eye on?'

'The very same!'

'Listen, are you free tomorrow morning? I've got some stuff to tell you.'

There was a pause before Linda replied.

'That sounds intriguing. Yes, come over in the morning. I wish I could talk now but I've got my hands full.'

I could hear Dean's whispered voice in the background and what sounded like a hand being slapped.

'Well, you have a good evening then,' I said, smiling to myself.

'Oh, don't you worry. I will.'

I rang off. It sounded like we would both have some confessing to do tomorrow.

Downstairs I tried to watch some comedy programmes on the television in the snug while Fluffy lay curled up on my lap but I was just too tired. I turned off the telly and decided to head to bed early. Not forgetting my earlier promise, I retrieved my phone from the back pocket of my skirt and sent Steve a text.

> Me
> Really tired for some strange reason. ☺
> Going to bed now. Good night Mr Bowes.
> Xx
> 9:02 pm

Mum and Jeff were snuggled on the sofa in the main lounge with their obligatory bottle of wine. The faint sounds of Rob's game could be heard coming from his room. Everything was exactly as normal.

My phone beeped.

> Steve
> Good night Miss Taylor. Sweet dreams. Xx
> 9:05 pm

The clock on the kitchen wall still ticked as it marked each passing second. The fridge still hummed when it cut in and out. Nothing had changed and yet everything was different. I was different. Some hidden part of me had been unlocked, and what lay within had been awakened and set free. Now it was pacing anxiously and licking its lips in hunger.

CHAPTER SIX

'So? Did you get to talk to him?' Linda asked as soon as I came through her bedroom door.

'And a good morning to you too!' I replied.

'Come on, don't keep me in suspense. What did he say?' She patted the bed and we sat down cross-legged on the duvet, facing each other.

'It's more what he did that's the point.'

Her jaw dropped. Her eyes widened.

'You didn't!'

'We did, and it was . . . amazing!' I brimmed with excitement, still unable to quite believe it myself. Despite her apparent shock, Linda looked fascinated, impressed even.

'I said talk to him, not fuck his brains out! I don't believe it. What are you like?'

'Actually, if anybody got their brains fucked out it was probably me. Besides it wasn't really like that, not at first, and anyway,' I poked her with my finger, 'you sounded pretty busy when I spoke to you last night.'

'Oh, I held Dean off at third base.' She was doing her dismissive wave. 'Not that I don't intend to deliver on my promises, but it's nice to keep him dangling just a little bit longer. Treat 'em mean, keep 'em keen, that's what I reckon. Anyway, never mind me, what about you? Somehow you look different. Even the way you carry yourself has changed. I noticed it the moment you walked in.'

'That's probably just because I'm a bit sore today,' I quipped.

Linda grinned.

'Seriously, though, how was it?'

'It's hard to find the words to describe it. It was like some other 'me' took over, almost like an out of body experience. It made me feel so . . . I don't know . . . alive.'

'Wow! You did hit the jackpot. Steve . . .' She rolled his name around her mouth as if trying to place some unknown flavour. 'I never would have thought it.'

'How come?'

'I guess laid back, soulful musicians aren't my type, but he's clearly yours.'

I shrugged my shoulders.

'I don't think I've had enough experience to know what my type is yet.'

'Further research required, eh?'

'Eventually, maybe! Right now, I've got a lovely, kind, fun, sweet man I enjoy being with, who knows exactly what he's doing and wants to share that with me. What's not to like?'

'What indeed? What's the score with his estranged wife?'

'Valentina? I haven't met her so I don't know what she's like. He moved out a couple of months ago and he's been renting a small flat for the time being. He doesn't talk about it much.' Linda nodded thoughtfully.

'Anyway, another thing: the stuff I was saying. I can't believe the words that came out of my mouth while we were . . . you know.'

'Oh, I can! I'm not sure you realise what a potty mouth you have when you get going. You've got the vocabulary of a navvy sometimes.'

I gave her a look of mock disdain.

'There's something else I was going to ask you about,' I added.

'Yeah?'

'Oral sex.'

'Okay, don't you beat about the bush now; just get straight to the point.'

That struck me as rich. Sugar-coating things was hardly Linda's style either.

'He seems so good at it, I mean *really* good at it, and I want to please him back. I don't think I did badly but I want to, um . . . go further.'

'You mean let him come in your mouth? It's nothing much; it's like swallowing an oyster.'

I didn't like to tell her I had no idea what oysters were like. We generally never ate shellfish, apart from prawns sometimes.

'No, not that! I mean,' I took a deep breath, 'get it all in. He's not exactly small and . . .'

'Ah, I see.' Her voice became throaty. 'Patience, my young Padawan. Learn to use the force, you must. Find something to practice on until you re-train your gag reflex, you should.'

I punched her playfully on the arm.

'Alright, Yoda! I don't remember blowjobs being part of a Jedi Knight's training. Besides, who am I going to practice on?'

'Not someone, something! I'm sure with that vivid imagination of yours, you'll think of something suitable. Be creative.'

The cogs in my mind were already turning.

Hmm . . . ! Food for thought!

-0-

That week dragged interminably. In school, even the normally genial Mr Travers, who took us for English Literature these days, lost patience with my daydreaming and became uncharacteristically surly.

'Rebecca! When you're ready to come back to planet Earth there is work to be done. Honestly, I don't know what's got into you this week.'

I did.

Linda lifted her head from her writing and glanced knowingly across the classroom at me. Sometimes I swear she could read my mind.

On the days when I wasn't at Linda's after school, Steve and I would cross paths at the end of the day. It was so hard not to let anything show, but Jeff didn't seem to notice. Sometimes Steve shot me a wink when he was sure no one was looking and I would blush. I just wanted to grab him and kiss him, and he knew it. Every night he would text me before bed to wish me sweet dreams or something similar, and although my dreams might well have been sweet, they certainly weren't restful. I couldn't wait for Saturday to come around. If I didn't get my fix of Steve I was going to burst.

Thankfully, Saturday morning arrived without any major explosions. Jeff left early to go into London. Mum and Rob were heading off at about half past nine for a team meeting before the football match. They weren't due back until four. Inside, I was doing a little victory dance.

I showered early and took extra care with my hair before putting on light make-up and dressing in a pair of close fitting blue jeans and a short, white top with my usual slip-on pumps.

Venus, eh? Let's show him some curves. If it was a goddess he saw, then a goddess he would get.

Down in the kitchen, Mum was making toast. She handed me a mug of tea as I walked in.

'You look nice, honey. Are you going out somewhere today?'

'Maybe later on.'

'If you do, I'd put something warmer on. It's cold this morning.'

I wasn't going to tell her my clothes probably weren't staying on that long and that I had my own ideas about keeping warm. Despite the butterflies in my stomach, I made myself finish a good bowl of cereal and a couple of thick slices of hot buttered toast washed down with a second mug of tea.

Steve arrived about nine o'clock to set up ready for Monday's recording sessions. Jeff liked to keep everything ship-shape, particularly when new clients arrived for the first time. Whispered Scream would be coming in for pre-production on their second album. They were a band on their way up in the rock world after the success of their debut, and the plan was to work on the arrangements and record demo versions in the barn before moving on to a bigger studio in London to record the actual album. Jeff had been pencilled in for the whole job.

Steve poked his head round the kitchen door and seeing that Mum was there, kept himself in check.

'Morning all!' he breezed as he came in to pour himself some tea. He was wearing a different shirt today. This one was deep mustard yellow in colour. For some reason it made him look like a hot dog. I wanted to eat him.

'Do you want some toast, Steve?' Mum asked.

'No thanks, Avril. I've already eaten and there's a lot I want to do today.'

He glanced across at me while Mum was looking the other way. My butterflies were doing their dance again.

'I'd better go and make a start,' he said and taking his tea, headed outside.

I wanted to follow him straight out there but I had to play it cool. I finished my tea and cleared my breakfast stuff away before telling Mum I would go and give Steve a hand.

'That's sweet of you, darling,' she said. 'He'll appreciate that.'

I found Steve in the performance area, whirling around like a dervish, straightening everything up and moving microphone stands to one side.

'Can I help?' I asked him. 'Maybe we can get this stuff done quicker.'

He stuck his tongue in his cheek and looked at me, a smile beginning in his eyes.

'Well, if you fancy helping out then maybe we can move on to other things.'

That sounded good to me.

'What can I do?'

He was all business.

'We're going to need male to female XLRs, one over each stand ready to go, plus microphones. I think we'll want about half a dozen Beta 57s, the full set of drum mikes and a stereo overhead pair: the Sennheisers I reckon. We can put them on the stands ready but they won't go in place until the band's equipment is in on Monday. Are you okay with that?'

I'd spent long enough around the studio to know exactly what he meant. We headed straight for the storeroom to retrieve armfuls of neatly coiled cables from their hooks on the wall and were busy distributing them along the row of stands when Mum put her head around the control room door.

'See you later. We're off. Don't worry if we're not back bang on time. We're taking Rolo with us. There's plenty of food in the fridge; help yourselves.'

'Thanks!' we chorused.

'See you later, Mum.'

She smiled and left.

Now we were on a roll. We finished with the cables and went back for the microphones, taking them out of their cases, carrying them through and attaching them to the correct stands. When we had finished I stood back to survey our handiwork. It dawned on me after a few moments that Steve was surveying me instead.

'What?' I asked him.

'You!' He seemed amused. 'Even when I know you've got other things on your mind you're still so . . . committed.'

'No different to you.'

He nodded his head.

'True, but then it's my job to be. What I mean is you throw yourself one hundred percent into everything you do.'

'Everything?' I was creeping closer to him, getting ready to pounce.

His voice became heavier, silkier.

'Everything!'

'So, does that mean we're free for some more 'everything' now?' I asked, slinking towards him slowly, one step at a time.

'If that's what you'd like to do today, Miss Taylor, then who am I to refuse?'

I was now close enough to wrap my arms around his neck while he rested his hands on my hips. Fixing his gaze with mine, I concentrated all the week's pent up frustration and longing into my stare and bit softly into my lower lip. He swallowed hard, unable to tear his eyes away from me.

'How do you do that?'

'Do what?'

'That! That look! If you could bottle it and sell it you'd make a fortune. I'm almost ashamed of the thoughts it puts in my head, not ashamed enough to stop me doing most of them, though.'

'Good, then you'd better take me to bed, Mr Bowes; take me to bed and show me.'

His lips brushed against mine and made their way down to the soft skin of my neck. Taking a handful of my hair he bent my head gently but firmly back and nipped at my skin, rasping his teeth across my throat.

He pulled back to look at me, amusement spreading

across his face.

'I'd like to carry you up there but I think that back staircase would be the death of both of us. I think we'd have a hard time explaining away the injuries.'

I grinned and took him by the hands.

'We'd better be careful then. I want you in one piece.'

'Then get thee up to thy chambers wench, for I would have my wicked way with you.'

'Oh, please sir, not that! Anything but that!'

He chased me out of the studio and across the courtyard, playfully slapping my behind as we went. Once we were at the top of the stairs he picked me up, carried me in giddy and giggling and dropped me gently onto the bed. Thankfully, I had managed to keep my room tidy for a change. Knowing I would have Steve for company prevented me from allowing it to relapse into its usual chaotic state.

He removed my shoes and tossed them aside. Resting my feet against his chest I lifted my behind off the bed and undid my jeans, wriggling them down over my bum along with my underwear. He grasped hold of the legs of my jeans and with a little help, slid them off and sent them to join my shoes. I lifted my top over my head then made a big show of unclipping my bra, ceremoniously allowing it to dangle from my fingers before dropping it to the floor.

'Come on Mr Bowes, you're still dressed. How are you going to have your wicked way with me like that?'

Rubbing the soles of my feet against the crotch of his jeans I slid one hand between my legs, cupping myself. I could feel the heat and dampness already. I watched him slip out of his shirt and then sat up to help him out of his jeans. Finally, I had him naked and right where I wanted him . . . almost. A plan was beginning to formulate in my mind.

'Maybe . . .' I was thinking out loud now. 'Maybe I should have my wicked way with you instead.'

'Oh, it's like that is it? You want to take charge? Well I'm here and I'm all yours, so where do you want me?

I gave him 'that look' again.

'There!' I ordered him, pointing behind me to the bed, 'On your back!'

I could tell by the look on Steve's face he knew where I was going with this. He took one of the condoms from the bedside drawer, quickly rolled it on and lay back with his hands behind his head, grinning.

'Ready when you are!' He was enjoying this game.

I positioned myself over him and slipped a finger inside me. I was so ready for this. I'd been ready all week, but when it came to the crunch I wasn't sure how to guide him in. His hands remained behind his head and he looked amused.

'You're in charge, remember?' he teased.

I was just going to have to busk this. Instinct took over. I brought one leg forward to steady myself and hovering over him, reached down to locate the tip of his erection at my opening. After a few moments, I found the sweet spot.

Oh yes, that's it. Right . . . there!

Slowly, smoothly, I eased myself down onto him and the feeling washed over me again, a warm wave of overwhelming fullness that tingled to the very tips of my fingers.

'Oh, hello again. I've missed you,' I cooed, my voice

soft and beguiling.

'Are you talking about me or him?' he asked, looking down at where his body met mine.

'Both!'

I brought my leg back so that I was kneeling astride him and he put his hands out, palms outstretched, fingers splayed. I didn't understand at first, furrowing my brow at him.

'To steady yourself,' he explained.

Now I got it. I placed my palms against his, and we locked our fingers together, then leaning forwards I began to rock myself up and down on him. It felt so nice, so natural.

'Don't be afraid to experiment,' he encouraged. 'Find out what works for you.'

I started to vary things a bit and soon discovered there was a lot more I could do. I could gyrate my pelvis and grind into him; I liked that one. I could lift my whole body up then plunge down hard on him. He really liked that one; I could tell by the heat in his eyes and the growl that came from the back of his throat every time I did it.

'Try leaning back,' he suggested.

I let go of his hands and worked my way backwards, keeping myself supported by resting my palms on his legs. As it bent backwards, his erection pressed deliciously against the front wall of my vagina. I kept up what movement I could.

'How's that?' he asked.

'Fucking amazing!' I panted.

'Go further back.'

Now I was concerned for him.

'Won't it break?'

He shook his head.

'No. Just don't make any sudden movements,' I started to giggle, 'or laugh,' he added with a wry smile, 'or you'll shoot me across the room like a wet bar of soap.'

I convulsed with laughter, a whole array of unexpected muscles going into spasm.

'Stop it! You're not playing fair. You knew exactly what that would do.'

'Did I?' A wicked grin had spread itself across his face.

I slid right back until I was almost horizontal. Neither of us could move very much, but the pressure, oh my God, the pressure!

'That's a hell of a sensation isn't it?'

'Mm-hmm!' I replied, finding it difficult to speak.

He reached out and hooked my outstretched fingertips with his, flipping me forwards until I was right over him, my hair cascading over his face.

'The trouble is, neither of us can move much like that, whereas when you lean forward,' he added, 'I can do this.'

He pulled me in close, his fingers tightening in my hair and kissing me deeply, bucked his hips hard and fast, pummelling into me. I was rooted to the spot. I couldn't even breathe. It wasn't long before he slowed down and released me but my head was still spinning.

'Oh fuck, Steve!' I panted. 'Do that again!'

He did, harder still and more sustained than before. This time it took me even longer to come down off my cloud. I took a moment to halfway recover myself.

'Again! I'm almost there.'

This time he kept going, powering into me again with

short, hard strokes, his vice-like grip on my hair keeping me captive. I cried out involuntarily, my orgasm suddenly overtaking me, spinning me off into outer space amongst the stars. Steve released his hold on my hair and held me close with his arms wrapped around me while I slowly returned from orbit. For a moment he must have thought I was crying but I was laughing, delirious with joy.

'Oh my God, Steve! Just when I thought it couldn't get any better.'

But he wasn't finished with me yet.

Steve sat up, bringing me with him so I was kneeling in his lap and slid his hands up to my breasts, spreading his palms across them and kneading at the taut, rounded swell then pulling at my already stiffened nipples with dexterous fingers. He began a gentle rocking motion with his hips and kissed me tenderly. I undulated in his lap, meeting him in the middle every time he pushed forward. I could feel every movement deep inside me.

His hands snaked their way down over my hips to caress my buttocks then gripped them hard as the roller coaster ride continued, gathering pace, becoming ever more breathless and intense. Steve's expression began to tighten, teeth clenched, eyes rolling back in his head.

'I want to see it. I want you to come on me,' I sighed into his ear.

I slid off him and lay back on the bed, hands cupping my breasts and pushing them together. Removing the condom and tossing it aside he knelt beside me and wrapped his hand around himself, massaging his cock with long smooth strokes, his breathing becoming increasingly fitful.

'That's it, come on me. Come on my tits. Show me.'

I didn't know where the words were coming from, but I was enjoying this whole new brazen me. His whole body tensed, his face tightened and with a low groan, he finally let go.

'Yes!' I hissed as a creamy jet of semen arced into the air and splattered across the smooth skin of my breasts, followed by a second which landed alongside it.

I watched in fascination as the thick, pearly droplets pooled on my skin. A string of it still hung from the tip of his cock. In the wake of Linda's comments, I couldn't help wondering what it would taste like. Gingerly, I ran one fingertip up his length, collected it up and put it to my lips, testing it with my tongue. It tasted salty and slightly soapy, but not bad at all. With two fingers I scooped up as much as I could from my breasts and making a big show of it, licked them clean. Two could play at the honey pot game.

Steve sat back on his heels, watching me open-mouthed.

'I think it's your turn to come again now, you saucy minx.'

In a sudden move, he dived between my legs, lifting them up in the air and burying his face in my pussy, his tongue lashing hard at my clitoris. I grabbed at my breasts, massaging the rest of his cum into my nipples and arched my back, lifting my bum off the bed and pushing myself onto his face. His glorious tongue probed and teased until my orgasm exploded upon me so hard I thought the top of my head was going to come off.

I was still shuddering from the force of it when Steve slid up my body to cradle me and I parachuted back down to Earth again. We were giggling and breathless, still reeling from the intensity of it all.

'Holy shit, Steve! What was that?'

He held up his hands in surrender.

'I can't take the credit for that one. You were in charge, remember?'

'By the end of that, I think we were fairly even. Whatever, I still think we make a pretty good team.'

We threw our heads back against the bedclothes, looking into each other's eyes in disbelief while the pounding of our hearts slowly returned to normal.

'Is it always like that?' I asked him.

Steve shook his head.

'To be honest: no. On a scale of one to ten, that was at least an eleven.'

I smirked and put on a London accent.

'That's one louder, innit?'

He grinned at me.

'So you've seen 'This is Spinal Tap' then?'

'Of course, what musician hasn't? It's one of Jeff's favourite movies. I must have seen it about a million times.'

I snuggled into his chest and for a while, we just lay there watching each other, basking in the warm glow of post-coital bliss.

'Are you hungry?' I asked eventually.

'Starving!'

'I couldn't believe how hungry I was last week after you'd gone. Mum was cooking food and standing guard over the fridge, so all I had until dinnertime was an apple. I didn't want her to realise I hadn't eaten anything.'

'I know what you mean. I think I emptied the

cupboards when I got home.' He glanced across at the clock. 'It's just coming up to twelve, as good a time as any for some lunch. What do you fancy?'

'Apart from you, you mean?'

'Miss Taylor, you're insatiable! What does a man have to do? I was talking about food; after all, we have to keep our strength up. Come on. Let's get creative.'

He sprang up from the bed and held out his hands to help me up but I dived straight off the edge and onto the floor to stake my claim on his shirt.

'Mine!' I declared. 'You'll just have to go bare-chested.'

'I'd borrow your top but I don't think it would suit me.'

I smiled to myself at the thought of Steve trying to shoehorn his torso into my little crop top. It stood little chance of surviving the process. I slipped his shirt over my shoulders but I didn't want to do it up yet. There was a little bit of tidying up to do first.

'How come you look so damned sexy in my clothes?' Steve asked. 'Mind you, you'd still look sexy in a grain sack.'

'You don't have to sweet-talk me now, you know; you've already won me over.' I located my knickers amongst the discarded clothing. 'I'm just going to freshen up a minute,' I informed him as he slid his jeans back on, minus the underwear. 'I'll see you downstairs.'

By the time I got down there he was busy taking ingredients out of the fridge and lining them up on the worktop. A pan was already warming up on the hob. He was humming to himself.

Steve looked round.

'Omelette do you?'

'Sounds lovely! I would have made something for us, though.'

'It can be your turn next time. Ladies like a man who can cook, don't they?'

I sat at the breakfast bar wondering how many 'ladies' he'd cooked for and watched him work, setting chopped chorizo and sliced mushrooms in a pan to fry then grating some cheese. Thankfully his back was healing nicely from the abuse it had sustained the week before. I must admit I was enjoying the floor show as he busied himself at the stove, wearing nothing but a pair of jeans. Some women would pay good money for this kind of entertainment and I was getting it for free. Now that would be a cookery show I'd bother to watch!

He placed two glasses on the counter and poured orange juice into them, topping it up with sparkling water. He held one glass out to me. I took it gratefully. I was thirsty.

'Poor man's Bucks Fizz!' he explained. 'Your mum might ask questions if the Prosecco disappears.'

Steve drizzled olive oil into a frying pan and placed it on the hob, cracked a handful of eggs one by one into a bowl, seasoned and whisked them up then poured the mixture into the hot frying pan with a satisfying sizzle.

'Don't you add milk?' I asked.

'Nope! Better texture this way. You'll see.'

As soon as it started to go firm, he sprinkled the other ingredients on top along with the cheese and put the pan under the grill until the cheese melted. By now the whole thing had puffed up. He divided it onto two plates and placed them on the breakfast bar along with the cutlery.

'Bon appétit.' He looked at me expectantly, waiting for

me to try it.

I took a forkful, blew on it and tucked in.

'Mm, this is lovely. It's so fluffy.'

'Told you,' he said smugly.

I finished the first half of my omelette before I spoke again. I was turning something over in my mind.

'Steve?'

'Yes.'

'You know I tend to, um . . . say things when we're doing it?'

'Mm-hmm.'

'You don't mind, do you? I mean, Linda reckons I talk like a navvy and . . .'

He shook his head.

'Mind? Why should I mind? I wouldn't worry about that if I were you. For me, it's wonderful to know you are so caught up in the moment that you lose all inhibition. What might seem crude out of context can be a huge turn on at the right time. Believe me, there's nothing worse than feeling like the other person's just not into it.'

'I've got to admit I like it too. It makes me feel . . . I don't know . . . liberated.'

'There you go then. Don't ever be ashamed or embarrassed about your sexuality, Rebecca. It's a beautiful thing; one of life's great pleasures. Can't you tell what it does to me when you get carried away with it all?'

'When you put it like that, yes. Did . . . did Valentina do the same thing?'

I could see him thinking it over.

'Not so much. But then English isn't her first language. She tended to lapse back into Spanish in the heat of the moment and my Spanish isn't brilliant, so I was never too sure what she was saying when she started to babble. It sounded good, though.' His expression saddened. 'Later on, it didn't happen so much. All the fun and the passion had gone out of things.'

Suddenly he was bright and breezy again.

'Anyway, let's not spoil today by dwelling on the past. Eat up; we've still got dessert to come,' he added with a wink. I liked the sound of it already.

We finished our omelettes and stacked everything in the dishwasher.

'So,' I made big eyes at him and rested my hands on his upper arms, nudging the dishwasher door shut with my hips, 'how about that dessert you promised me?'

Steve turned and opened the fridge door.

'Oh!' I was surprised. 'I didn't think you meant actual dessert.' The self-satisfied smile that was beginning to spread from one corner of his mouth told me maybe I wasn't going to be too disappointed. What was he up to?

He took a large glass bowl of fruit salad and a pot of cream off the shelf. Inside the bowl was a mixture of strawberries, grapes, chunks of kiwi fruit, and what looked like mango.

'When did you make that?'

'While you were upstairs, freshening up. It was the first thing I did. Nothing planned, I just had to improvise. Come on. We'll have this upstairs.'

'I'll get us a couple of bowls and spoons.'

He shook his head and gave me a look of fierce intent.

'We won't need those where we're going.'

'Oh!' I said again. Now I was intrigued and excited at the same time. The dancing butterflies were back.

'Now up those stairs with you!' he ordered, his voice

suddenly commanding.

I complied meekly while he followed behind me into the room and placed the fruit and the cream on the bedside cabinet.

'I'll be straight back. Stay right where you are.'

I did as I was told and stood in the middle of the room with my hands by my sides, hardly daring to move. Within seconds, Steve was back from the bathroom with a couple of fresh towels from the rack. He spread them over the bed, smoothing them out carefully.

'It's better to be safe than sorry. This could get messy.' His voice was dark with promise. My insides were going into meltdown.

'I'll take this off you,' he said, undoing his shirt and slipping it off my shoulders. 'I can't afford to lose another good one.'

'You'd have to go bare-chested all the time. What a shame!'

He circled around behind me like a predator stalking its prey then slapped me on my behind and bit softly into my shoulder.

'I'm going to eat you up,' he informed me, speaking softly into my ear.

'Please!' I had a vague inkling where this was going. Since my legs were turning to jelly, we could make this into a trifle. All we needed now was some sponge cake, sherry and custard.

'I want you to lie down on the bed.'

I started to peel off my underwear.

'Uh-uh!' He waggled his finger at me. 'Not yet. Keep those on until I say. Lie on your back, hands by your sides.'

I lay flat out on the bed while Steve picked up the bowl and looked the fruit over carefully. He was enjoying keeping me waiting. Although he was trying to remain stern I could see the mirth in his eyes.

He selected a ripe, juicy strawberry and held it just above my mouth. I parted my lips in anticipation, my tongue questing against my lower lip, waiting for the first bite. Instead, he took it away and kissed me hard then bit into one side of the fruit and descended again to feed it to me, pushing it into my mouth with his tongue.

Mmm! Strawberries and Steve: now there's a flavour combo I could get used to!

Returning to the bowl he selected another piece of fruit, mango this time, and balanced it carefully on my left nipple. The coldness of it against my skin made me gasp and I flinched slightly.

'You're going to have to hold still,' he said. 'Think you can do that?'

'I'll try,' I replied.

Steve placed a grape between his teeth and fed it to me, just like he did with the strawberry. The juice exploded onto my tongue when I bit into it. Meanwhile, he positioned a piece of kiwi fruit on my other nipple. He carried on alternating between dotting fruit down my body and feeding it to me, until finally, he balanced a grape on the pink cotton of my knickers, right above my pubic bone. I started to laugh and a strawberry rolled off my midriff.

'Hold still!' he admonished, his eyes sparkling. Replacing the strawberry, Steve stood back to admire his handiwork and smacked his lips. 'There! Good enough to eat!'

'I was hoping you were going to say that, Mr Bowes.'

Looking down my body I could see that there was a gap in the line of fruit at my navel. A grape would have fitted perfectly, like spotting a rugby ball. Surely he hadn't missed it by accident. What was he thinking?

'There's just one more thing this fruit salad needs,' he announced. 'Cream!'

The way he shaped the word made it sound delicious all by itself. If Steve didn't eat the fruit soon, my body heat was going to cook it. He took the pot from the bedside table, peeled back the lid and drizzled a little of it over the kiwi fruit on my right nipple.

I inhaled sharply.

'Fuck, that's cold!'

Tucking his hair back he closed his lips around it, drawing the fruit into his mouth and swirling his tongue around my nipple to remove the cream. The combination of heat and cold was electric. My mouth fell open, my whole body responding to the touch of his lips and hands.

Switching his attention to the other side, he poured cream over the piece of mango. A thick, white rivulet of it ran over my breast and down my side. He chased it with his tongue, following it up and over the smooth contours before closing his lips around the fruit topped nipple, the tip of his tongue circling around the deeper pink of my areola.

Steve added little dashes of cream on his way down the line until he reached the gap at my navel. By now he could barely contain his self-satisfied smirk, pouring a deep pool of cream into it, then diving in with his tongue. Squealing and giggling uncontrollably, I lifted my knees and drummed my heels against the bed. The last, delicately poised grape rolled off between my legs.

'Now look what you've gone and done. I'll have to retrieve it by any means possible.' He licked the cream from his lips but there were still little smears of it across his face and down his chin.

Steve's eyes were dancing. I was melting. He finished the last couple of pieces of fruit before reaching the line at the top of my panties, parted my knees and ran one fingertip slowly up the damp fabric, tracing the line of what lay beneath it in silent veneration. Hooking the material aside with one hand, he slipped a finger inside me and gave a low, appreciative sigh.

'Oh my God, Rebecca! You're so wet!'

'No shit, Sherlock! What did you expect?' I wasn't sure if I wanted to kiss him or hit him with a pillow for keeping me waiting. I was fit to explode.

Steve retrieved the grape from between my thighs and held it up in triumph.

'I'm not ready to let you off the hook just yet. I've got plans for this little fellow.'

What now? I didn't have to wait long to find out. Still holding my knickers to one side, he rubbed it up and down the lips of my pussy then slipped it just inside me. I gasped at the strange sensation. It wasn't that big, it was just . . . there.

He moved the fabric back into place and massaged me through the thin material, caressing me in a circular motion which felt like it was rolling the little invader around inside me. Pulling the material aside again, he poured out a long trail of cream which mingled with my pubic hair then ran down the lips of my pussy and between my buttocks. He plunged his tongue into the honey pot and hooked out the grape, gathering it up with his lips. It popped between his teeth.

'Mm, Rebecca flavour. My favourite! Now that's the kind of cream I like.'

'Enough! Enough teasing, Steve! Finish me!' I panted, now consumed by the aching need to feel him inside me again, my hips grinding against thin air.

Finally, he took pity on my desperation, tore off his jeans and reached for a condom. The few seconds it took him to put it on felt like an age of waiting. By the time he turned his attention towards me again I had grabbed my knickers to one side and slid two fingers inside me. I slipped them back out and parted the lips of my pussy with my fingertips. It had exactly the effect I'd hoped for. He plunged himself into me, deep and hard.

'Oh, yes. That's what I'm talking about,' I breathed into his ear.

All finesse and delicacy thrown to the four winds, Steve no longer made any attempt to hold anything back. I bent my legs almost double, tilting my hips back, and reached behind my head to grip the edge of the headboard as he slammed into me full force, our thighs making resounding contact every time he drove into me. Soon I could feel my impending release, so long awaited. My muscles clamped around him, gripping hard, and my orgasm exploded like a supernova. I tipped my head back, crying out at the top of my voice. With one final, driving thrust he reached his own point of no return and collapsed on top of me with our hair mingling, splayed out on the pillow.

We were both shaking like leaves. Steve's breathing

felt hot and fitful against my throat as we both waited for the room to stop spinning.

'Now wasn't that worth waiting for?' he sighed.

I said nothing but with one arm around his shoulder and the other caressing the back of his head, held him close.

Oh, Steve! My Steve . . . ! Mine.

I wanted to keep him there inside me forever. Eventually, though, we had to move; the stickiness on our skin was beginning to weld us in place.

Carefully, Steve peeled himself away and lay back against the pillow.

'I think maybe a bath would be a good idea.'

'You could be right there. I've got stuff in places I didn't know I had.'

Steve grinned.

'Fun, though, wasn't it?'

I feigned petulance.

'I still haven't forgiven you. It isn't polite to keep a girl waiting, you know, but if I don't soak this off I'm going to be finding bits for weeks. Look at this!' I ran my fingers through my long, wavy tresses. 'There's even mango in my hair and I haven't a clue how it got there.'

'Did you know you still look gorgeous annoyed and covered in fruit salad? Come on, let's go and clean up our act. I seem to remember you telling me you enjoy a good bath.'

I reddened. Why should I find it embarrassing after what we'd just done? It didn't make any sense.

Steve picked up the bowl with the remaining fruit from the bedside cabinet and disappeared into the bathroom. I could hear him humming to himself as he turned on the taps and began filling the tub. It was a big corner bath so there would be plenty of room for the two of us. The sound of the water began to drown out his soft, musical voice but I was certain it was 'Drifting', the song I had been singing to him the week before.

Was that only a week ago? It seemed like another lifetime, another world.

I stood up and lifted the towels off the bed. They might have stopped the worst of it, but I would still have to change the bedclothes. Deciding I'd have some trouble explaining away the large damp patch in the centre of the bed, I stripped the duvet cover off and threw it into the wash basket along with the towels then headed into the next room. The corner bath was already half full and there was a deep layer of bubbles on top. The air filled with the heady scent of essential oils.

'I took the liberty of adding a bit of bath foam. Is that alright?'

'Just the way I like it: hot and steamy.' I couldn't resist.

'Really? I can't say that I'd noticed.' He had that smirk on his face again and his eyes had come alive. I couldn't believe what it was doing to me inside . . . again.

Steve turned off the taps and held out his hand to me. I took it, stepping over the edge of the bath and into the middle. He followed me in and sat down with his back against one corner, gesturing for me to join him.

'Come!' he entreated.

I raised one eyebrow at him.

'I thought I already did.'

'You know what I mean.'

I eased myself down into the bubbles with my back to him. Now the two of us were in there the water came up much deeper, thankfully not deep enough to overflow or we'd have had an even bigger mess to clear up. I sank back into Steve's embrace with a soft sigh, revelling in the warmth and the bubbles.

Picking up a flannel from the edge of the bath, he dipped it in the water and gently leant me forward to wash my back and down my arms. He lifted my hair and brushed his lips against the back of my neck then brought his hands around to wash my front. Rivulets of warm soapy water ran down over my breasts.

'Mm . . . That's nice.'

I was drifting on an azure blue, tropical sea. The palm trees standing sentry along the white sandy beach swayed gently in the salty breeze that carried the scent of coconut and exotic flowers. Occasionally a small fish would momentarily leap out of the water before disappearing again beneath the surface to become a shadow in the crystal waters. The sound of a calypso band playing in the distance carried across the bay, coming and going with the lapping of the waves at my head. A soft voice whispered in my ear.

'Hey you, come back. You were gone there for a minute or two.' Steve's fingers gently massaged my scalp. 'Would you like me to shampoo your hair?'

'Yes please,' I murmured, still half in and half out of my trance-like state.

He took a bottle from beside the bath and squeezed some into the palm of one hand then rubbed it onto my hair, working it in with his fingertips.

A dark-skinned boy made his way down the beach with a basket of ripe mangoes, his bare feet leaving a trail of impressions in the sand. He was calling and waving, holding up one of the fruit towards me.

'No thanks! I've already got some.'

'Hmm?'

'Oh! Sorry, Steve. I was miles away; that's so nice and relaxing.'

He took the hand shower and rinsed away the shampoo, warm droplets of water raining on my head and running down my back, then reached for the conditioner and began smoothing it through my hair from root to tip.

'So, how's your day been so far?'

I was back in Steve's arms, the fruit seller forgotten.

'Well, until today, last Saturday was the best day of my life. Today's been heavenly. Thank you. I tell you what, though: I'm going to sleep well tonight.'

'So you're still enjoying your education?'

'Every second of it! It's like every new thing we do together opens up a hundred new possibilities, and I want to try all of them.'

His hands stopped.

'We can't possibly do everything at once, so I need you to say what it is that you want. Just be honest with me. Promise?'

'Promise!'

Steve took the hand shower again and rinsed the conditioner out, running his fingers sensuously through my hair.

'Make love to me again,' I said. I was feeling all warm and fuzzy. I wanted to feel him inside me in the water.

He reached into the bowl of fruit and fed me a strawberry.

'I'll have to go and get another condom.'

'I wish we didn't have to use those. I'd love to know what it feels like without them: when you come inside me.'

He turned my head towards him slightly and kissed me on the cheek.

'Well, that would have to be your choice. Take the time to think about it. If you still want to, then you'll need to see your doctor about the alternatives. I would go with you for support, but it might look like I was pressuring you and that's not something I would ever do.'

'I know. Thank you.'

He smiled.

'You do realise that if we go for a third time we could be here for hours, don't you? We don't have all that long before your mum and Rob come back.'

'Why would it take hours?' I probably looked a bit confused.

'Each time it usually takes longer before I orgasm, so if we do, don't wait for me.' He chuckled. 'We could be here all night otherwise.'

'Right now, what I want is the closeness. I want it to be gentle and tender like it was the first time.'

'See! Now I know exactly what you want and that's good.'

I moved forward in the water then turned to face him and he slid up so that he was sitting on the side of the bath. His erection was growing by the moment, but I figured a little encouragement wouldn't do any harm. I caressed him gently with both hands and looking up into his eyes, ran my tongue up his length then slid my lips around him. He moaned softly.

Suddenly there were voices reverberating down in the

hallway. The front door closed with a dull thud. We froze, eyes wide with terror, hardly daring to breathe.

Shit! Shit! Shit! What now?

I spoke first, half-whispering the words and gesturing exaggeratedly with my hands.

'You throw your clothes on and go out the side door to the studio. I'll delay them from the top of the stairs. Go!'

We both moved like lightning. I launched myself out of the water and grabbed a bathrobe from the back of the door on my way out. Slipping it around me, I headed for the top of the main stairs, still dripping water onto the floor as I went. My heart had clawed its way up from my chest and was trying to escape through my mouth.

'Hi! You're back early.' I was trying to be as cheery as possible.

Mum looked up the stairs at me. Rob was just behind her with Rolo milling around them in the hallway.

'Only by about half an hour. I thought we'd have to stop off for something on the way home but we didn't need to in the end,' she said.

'I was just in the bath.' Talk about stating the obvious, but I needed to keep them there talking long enough for Steve to make his escape. It was all I could think of.

'Didn't you have a shower this morning?' asked Mum, her head cocked slightly to one side.

Damn!

'Not me. It must have been Rob,' I replied.

Stupid! Stupid! He's standing right there.

Rob opened his mouth as if he was about to say something, then thankfully thought better of it but shot me a look that told me I owed him an explanation.

'How did the match go?' I never asked that. Try as I

109

might, sport never really interested me that much.

Rob chimed in.

'We won of course. I got the second goal.'

'Cool.'

Mum reached for the door that led into the kitchen. I had to buy more time if I could.

'What were you going to stop off for, Mum?'

She turned back to face me with a look of mock annoyance and crossed her arms.

'Oh, that's what all this is about! I wondered why you were acting so strangely. Fishing, are we? Just because you've got a birthday coming up in a few weeks you think you've got a right to know everything that's going on. Well let me tell you,' she tapped her nose and raised her eyebrows at me, 'there are some things you don't need to know.'

I'd hit pay dirt! I could play for time with this.

'You could give me a clue, Mum,' I pleaded.

She shook her head.

'Nice try young lady. No dice! You'll find out soon enough, just don't make any major plans on your birthday, okay?'

Rob was looking smug. What were they up to? Now it was my turn to be suspicious.

'This isn't fair. You're sneaking around behind my back,' I pouted. The irony of this comment wasn't lost on me.

'All will be revealed in good time. For now, though, I'm in dire need of a cup of tea. Go and dry yourself off and I'll put the kettle on.'

With that, Mum turned, opened the kitchen door and disappeared. I just hoped I'd been able to delay her for long enough. My stomach was still doing somersaults. Rob picked up his sports bag and followed up the stairs to his room while I made for the bathroom to cover my tracks.

By the time I'd cleared up, dried my hair, dressed and put fresh bedcovers on, Rob had come out of his room and was waiting for me on the landing.

'So, Sis, are you going to tell me what all that was about?'

How was I supposed to handle this one?

'I know you're up to something. Why lie about the shower?' he added.

I decided to be honest, at least up to a point.

'I know you covered for me back there. Thank you for that; I owe you one. One day you'll need me to keep quiet about something and then it will be payback time. You're just going to have to trust me on this one. It's nothing terrible, just something I didn't want to have to confess to Mum about.'

He tipped his head to one side, giving me the same quizzical look as Mum had. Sometimes he could look so like her.

'Have you had a boy up here with you today?'

'No.' It was almost the truth. 'Like I said, it's nothing major, just some awkward girl stuff that I'd rather not talk about.'

That was enough to put him off the scent. He recoiled at the thought of intruding any further. My period would be due soon anyway, so I could play that card if I needed to; he'd run a mile. For all his macho, sporting competitiveness he was a pussycat underneath the skin. He was so shy about that sort of thing, so easy to embarrass. Rob said no more and retreated to his room, busying himself with his sports kit.

Another hurdle overcome, I checked over my room again. I would have to do some washing tomorrow to deal with the evidence. I ate the last few pieces of fruit, drank the bit of cream that still lingered at the bottom of the pot and threw the container into my waste paper basket. Those would need dealing with too. I could hardly take the bowl back down to the kitchen right now.

Downstairs, Mum was clattering around the kitchen as usual. Mugs of tea had already been prepared. She placed two of them on a tray and held it out to me.

'There's one for you and one for Steve. He must be here, his car's still out front. He's obviously had his hands full today.'

Oh, Mum! You have no idea!

I took the tray from her and headed outside, not knowing what state I would find him in. He was busily trying to occupy himself around the studio but looked round as soon as I came in through the door. His worried expression softened when he realised it was me and that I was smiling. His hair was still damp and the shirt clung slightly to his skin. He'd obviously put it back on without any attempt to dry himself.

'Are you alright?' After everything, he was still concerned for me before himself.

I put the tray down.

'I'm fine. I had to cover my tracks a bit. I take it you had enough time to get out.'

'Just about! It was only seconds after I went out through the side door before your mum came into the kitchen. I had to sneak back in here without her noticing me through the window.'

We looked at each other in relief and amazement then burst out laughing.

'Holy shit, that was close!' Steve's eyes were still wide but he was visibly calming down now.

We held each other tightly and our lips met in a tender kiss. I rested my head on his shoulder.

Steve puffed out his cheeks.

'We're going to have to be really careful you know.'

'I know, but I don't want us to stop. I feel like I'm just getting started on this voyage of discovery I'm sharing with you. I'm not ready to give that up; I'm enjoying myself too much. What about you, though?'

Steve held me close.

'I'm addicted to you, Rebecca. I don't think I could give this up right now, even if I wanted to. You make me feel more alive than I've been in a long time.'

He kissed me again, this time deeply, passionately, and I knew he meant it.

'I'm going to have to go soon. There's stuff I need to sort out and I promised a friend I'd meet him for a drink later. He's going through the mill a bit and wants to talk. What about you? Aren't you seeing Linda this evening?'

'Not tonight. She's seeing her latest beau. I'm not even sure which one, to be honest; she likes to keep her options open. I've got revision to do anyway. The exams are only just over two months away. I was supposed to be revising today but I was a bit distracted. I can't think why!'

Steve grinned, his eyes sparkling.

'I guess you'd better go and do what you've got to do. I don't want to be responsible for messing up your exams, glittering music career or not.'

We downed our tea and headed out of the studio, turning off the lights and locking the door behind us. He opened his car door and winked at me.

'Until next time then, Miss Taylor!'

'Promises, promises, Mr Bowes!'

It was getting dark and starting to rain slightly. I was becoming aware, on account of the goose pimples on my arms, how cold it was; I hadn't noticed up until then. Steve started the engine, turned on the lights and conscious that Mum might see him through the kitchen window, gave me a surreptitious wave before pulling away.

CHAPTER SEVEN

The room was a blur when I opened my eyes, blinking in the light that streamed through the window. Someone had opened the curtains. I rubbed the sleep away and tried to focus on the tall, willowy figure beside the bed.

'Morning, Rebecca,' soothed a familiar, soft voice.

'Morning, Linda. How come you're here so early?'

'I'm not. You're late. It's almost ten.'

'Is it?' I rubbed my eyes again and sucked a lungful of air in through my nose. 'I must have slept like a brick.'

'Busy day yesterday?'

'You could say that. I've got aches in muscles I've only just discovered.'

I sat up and peeled back the duvet, levering my legs over the edge of the bed and placing my feet carefully on the floor. Linda chuckled when she saw the baggy tee-shirt I was wearing which read: 'Yes please . . . I'll have a cup of tea'

'It's a good thing I brought you one up, isn't it?'

'Thanks, Linda. You're an angel,' I sighed as she handed me a steaming mug.

'I've been called a few things in my lifetime so far, but I'm not often accused of being angelic.'

I took a sip. It was still a bit hot for me.

'Speaking of which, how was your date last night?'

She grinned but her tone remained surprisingly even.

'Fucked him!'

'Who? Dean?'

'No, Scott. Scott Maybury!'

'What happened to Dean then?'

'Oh, I'm still seeing him too.'

'And they know about each other, do they?' It was my turn to interview her for a change.

'Yes, of course.'

'And they're okay with that?'

'Of course they are; I'm not playing them. I've been honest with both of them that I'm not really interested in committed relationships and that I just want to have some fun. I've been upfront about everything from the word go so there are no misunderstandings.'

She sat down beside me on the bed and continued in a matter-of-fact tone of voice as if she was explaining something blindingly obvious.

'Nobody has to pretend to anybody else about emotional involvement and both of them are quite happy to come along for the ride, as it were. Everybody has a good time and nobody gets their feelings trampled.' She shrugged her shoulders. 'It works for me and I've not had any complaints from them.'

'It's not always easy to separate your emotions, though, is it?'

'You speak for yourself, little miss hot and passionate. I don't have a problem with it.'

Sometimes I wondered why our friendship worked the way it did. On the face of it, we were like fire and ice, yet somehow we completed each other, one a yin to the other's yang.

Linda sprang to her feet.

'Come on, let's get going. Your mum said she wanted you to take the dog for a walk and your mother is one woman I wouldn't want to mess with.'

'How do you mean?'

'Well, she may come across all warmth and domesticity, but underneath the skin she's made of steel. She doesn't take prisoners.'

I snorted.

'I think you may be right there.'

'Come on then, get yourself ready to go out. I'm waiting to hear all the juicy details about yesterday. You'll be able to tell me on the way round the park.'

Downstairs in the kitchen, Jeff was making toast. Mum looked up from her shopping list.

'Good morning, sleepyhead. Glad you could join us.'

'Morning!' I was trying not to be sheepish and failing. 'We're going to head off up the park with Rolo.'

'Before you go, can you think of anything we need from the supermarket?' Mum enquired.

'Teabags are running a bit low. We do go through them.'

'Got that one! Oh, and the fruit's running out.' Suddenly she had a brainwave and began scribbling on the pad. 'Bananas! We're almost out of bananas. We had lots a few days ago. I don't know where they all went.'

Jeff handed me a slice of hot, buttered toast.

'Do you want any, Linda?'

'No thanks, Mr Taylor. I've already eaten.'

He rolled his eyes. Linda would still insist on being

formal with him.

Gripping the toast between my teeth, I grabbed my coat from the utility room, along with Rolo's lead. As soon as he saw it he padded over to join us.

'See you later!' we chorused on the way out.

Thankfully, the overnight rain had stopped and the weather was clearing, although everything still felt a bit damp. We were almost at the end of the driveway and I'd already put Rolo on his lead ready to go out to the main road before Linda spoke.

'So, now they're out of earshot you can dish the dirt. I want to know all about yesterday.'

She listened intently to the whole story while we walked along. When I got to the part about Mum and Rob arriving home she roared with laughter, bending forwards and clapping her hands on her thighs in sheer delight.

'Fellatio interruptus: that sucks, or doesn't as the case might be. What a classic! How is your training going by the way?'

I spread my fingers out and rocked my hand from side to side in a gesture of ambivalence.

'Okay. I'm not ready for the grand unveiling yet. I need a bit more practice first. Getting there, though!'

'Well, I think it should go down well.'

I shook my head but couldn't help smiling at the same time.

'I can't believe you just said that. There are small dictatorships where you can be shot for making a pun that bad. You're incorrigible.'

Linda looked very pleased with herself.

'That's me alright; I cannot be 'corridged'.'

When we rounded the corner and passed through the park gates, I let Rolo off his lead for a run. He bounded off across the grass in the direction of another dog he knew. We continued along the path.

'Linda?' I asked thoughtfully after a few moments, looking down at my chest. 'Do you think my boobs will get bigger? There was something I thought of doing yesterday only I don't really have the cleavage for it.'

'Oh, that! Give it time. I should imagine they'll get plenty bigger yet. Besides, you've got more chance than me,' she said, trying to push her breasts together. 'Girls my shape make clothes look good. Girls your shape make not wearing clothes look good. You've got curves in all the right places. Men like that. Trust me; you might not be able to do that sort of thing yet, but you will sooner or later.'

Rolo came over with an expectant look on his face and sat in front of me. I produced a doggy treat out of my pocket and he took it from my hand before chasing off again.

Linda fixed me with her emerald stare.

'Has he fisted you yet?'

'Has he f . . . ? No!' It had taken a couple of seconds for the shockwaves from that particular F-bomb to reach my brain. 'No, he hasn't!' I must have been raising my voice because Rolo stopped what he was doing and looked at me. I reined in the volume. 'I didn't even know what that was until I sat and read a bit of one of your books while you were finishing your homework one time. God no! To be perfectly honest it sounds painful. Why on earth are you bringing that up?'

'I'm just curious.'

'Have you had it done to you?'

'No. Not yet. I just wondered if you had.'

I was calming down a little now.

'A bit over a week ago I was still a virgin. I think I'm still getting used to the basics. I know there are lots of things I'd like to try but maybe that's pushing the boat out too far too soon. I mean,' I bunched my fingers together and looked at my hand, 'that's gotta hurt.'

'I'm not so sure. Not if it's done right. Let's face it; us girlies are pretty elastic down in that department. We have to be able to cope with childbirth after all.'

'I know, but I wouldn't class giving birth as a pleasurable experience.'

'And I'm not talking about trying to get anything past the cervix, so I can't see it being so traumatic.'

I shook my head and began to laugh at the bizarre turn this conversation had taken.

'Honestly Linda, you can be so . . . graphic sometimes. I swear you do it just to shock people.' Her fascination with people's sexuality seemed almost scientific. I could imagine her in a white coat, measuring their responses, as if they were animals in her own personal laboratory. 'If we're going to be totally honest it's not high on my list of what I want to try next.'

'What is, then? There must be stuff you want to experience, even if it's just so you can tick a box to say you gave it a go.'

'Yeah, well, I'm already in training to overcome my next hurdle, aren't I? Beyond that, I haven't decided. It's more like an unfolding experience than a checklist of things to do before I die. I know what will help put some ideas in my head, though.'

'Go on.' Now Linda looked intrigued.

'There are parental controls on the internet in the house, but I know where Jeff keeps some porn movies. I found them behind a bunch of other DVDs in a cabinet in the lounge. I haven't actually watched any yet but they've got to be full of ideas of stuff to try. How do you fancy getting some popcorn and having a movie night later on?'

'Now that sounds like a plan to me.'

'Deal! We can see what inspiration strikes.'

'And probably shock the hell out of the men in our lives,' added Linda.

'Oh, can you imagine? They won't know what hit them.'

I called Rolo over and put him back on the lead. It looked like we needed to hit the shop on the way home for supplies. This was going to be interesting.

-0-

When we arrived home with a carrier bag of cola, popcorn and crisps, Mum and Jeff were discussing the building of the new gym. They had decided to put one at the far end of the house, mostly for Rob's benefit, but we'd all be able to use it. Construction was due to begin in the last week of April, a couple of weeks after my birthday. I couldn't help wondering where Jeff got the energy and the time to organise everything, including all the stuff he was doing on my behalf.

Jeff uttered a quick 'Hi!' when we walked through the door, before turning back to Mum.

'At least it will be down the far end so any noise won't

affect Rebecca's revision too much. We need to get it underway because things are getting serious with all of Rob's sporting commitments. Plus, the workmen will be making the most noise at a time when Steve and I will be in London for the recording of the album. It won't interrupt any recording going on here. I know the studio is soundproofed to a great extent, but it's not perfect, and nobody wants the sound of diggers and angle grinders on their records . . . well, almost nobody anyway.'

Jeff waved me back before Linda and I could leave the kitchen.

'Oh, Rebecca, while I'm thinking about it,' he continued. 'The Saturday after next, we're going into London to meet Mitchell Sacker. I'm hoping he'll take on the management side with you. Things are getting interesting now and it's going to need someone who can give your career their full attention. I don't want to take you out of school, certainly not this close to the exams, and the following week while you're on school holidays he's got a big album launch going on so he's agreed to meet us on the Saturday, okay?'

'Okay.'

This is it then. It's getting serious.

I sounded hesitant. That and the look on my face must have betrayed my apprehension.

'Don't worry! Mitchell's a good guy. He specialises in developing new talent and he's got a good track record. He builds careers instead of exploiting them, unlike a few notable music industry figures I could mention. I've known him for a long time and I trust him; you should too. He knows what he's doing.'

'But I thought you would . . .'

Jeff shook his head.

'I'm a record producer, not a manager. Pretty soon I'd be out of my depth and away from what I do best, which is making records. Don't worry; you'll be in safe hands.'

The reality of the future in front of me loomed large. Although I felt both excited and daunted at the same time, it was now or never. I had to grasp every opportunity I could.

'What time's the meeting?'

'Ten o'clock. We'll have to drive in and park up then catch the tube, so it means a fairly early start. His office is in the West End.'

'Cool. Well, for now we've got some revision to do and then we're going to have a movie night up in my room.'

'What are you going to watch?' asked Mum.

'We haven't quite decided yet, but we've already got the snacks,' I announced, holding up the carrier bag of goodies.

'Well, enjoy yourselves but don't start on the nibbles just yet. Lunch should be in about half an hour.'

We took ourselves up to my room, dropped the bag off and sneaked down to the big lounge via the main stairs to rifle through the DVD stash. We selected a handful of promising titles and hurriedly retreated to my room to take a better look.

Linda turned one of them over in her hand, examining the photograph on the cover.

'I'm not sure which way up this photo should go. I think it works both ways. This one could be interesting.'

'That looks . . .' I tilted my head to one side. 'Hmm, I don't think I'm double-jointed enough to pull that one off.'

We looked at each other and burst out laughing, then slid the DVDs under the bed for safekeeping.

'Revision first,' I insisted.

'Oh, you were actually serious about the revision?' Linda seemed surprised.

'Of course I was! Not everyone is as effortlessly clever as you. I need all the help I can get.'

Linda lay down on the bed with her feet crossed and one hand behind her head, looking up at me.

'You underestimate yourself, you know. You can do things I could never dream of, and you don't seem to see it. You needn't be so modest. There are different sorts of intelligence. I have one kind in particular; you have several.'

I'd never thought of it that way, but then Linda was the one taking A-level Psychology, alongside English Literature and Sociology. I wasn't sure if I would be staying on past the AS exams. It depended on how fast everything moved, and a lot of that would be down to this manager bloke that Jeff was bringing in.

Once lunch and revision were out of the way, we picked a DVD and settled ourselves on the bed. Turning the volume down low to avoid any embarrassment, we curled up together with a big bag of toffee popcorn to watch the show. It was certainly educational. We ended up watching all of them: some bits twice!

After Linda had gone home and I was getting ready for bed, I picked up my clothes and made for the wash basket, remembering on the way that I still had some washing to do from the day before. I could put them on to wash overnight and take them out first thing in the morning without arousing any suspicion. When I lifted the lid, my basket was empty. Mum must have cleared it in the morning while we were out.

Shit!

I could only hope that she hadn't noticed the state of the towels and bedding and just put it all in without looking too hard. There was nothing I could do anyway; it was too late now, although it didn't stop me from lying in bed, staring up at the ceiling and turning the possibilities over in my mind. The last thing I wanted to do was make things awkward for Steve but the thought of not being able to see him was even worse. I turned out the light and tried to put it out of mind.

CHAPTER EIGHT

When I got home from school on Monday there were two large vans on the driveway. It was only when I rounded the corner of the house by the studio that the sound coming from within hit me and the penny dropped as to why they were there.

Of course! The band!

I always enjoyed it when there were other people recording in the barn. It fascinated me to watch them work, and these guys were no exception. A couple of times after school I sat on the sofa and listened at the back of the control room, although Jeff became a little irritated at times at the lack of focus from one or two of the band; they seemed distracted somehow.

Although their brand of musical rage interspersed with more melodic passages and use of unusual time signatures was very different from anything I did, there was no denying their technical skill. The drumming, in particular, was off the scale, and how the vocalist did what he did without shredding his vocal chords I'll never know.

On the Thursday of that week, my period arrived with a vengeance. It wasn't usually like that. It was as if my body had come out in protest at everything it had experienced recently. I spent the evening curled up with a hot water bottle to ease the dull ache, but at least I could console myself with the fact that I wasn't pregnant, not that I expected to be. Still, I had to be thankful for small mercies.

Steve was really sweet about it when I texted him, sending me back a hug. It brightened my evening somewhat, only to have my mood darkened again the following morning by the news that Rob was going down with a bug and wouldn't be playing on Saturday. Mum and Rob would both be at home. That ensured my hopes for the weekend had gone up in smoke. It looked like Steve and I would have to stick to making music of the conventional kind, but at least I'd still get to spend some time with him. He assured me he was going to be coming over.

When I woke on Saturday morning I was still on quite heavily. The worst of the discomfort had subsided by Friday night but it still looked like rain would be stopping play. As I sat and munched absently on a spoonful of cereal a thought occurred to me. Maybe it wasn't a complete loss. I could still give Steve a surprise he wouldn't forget in a hurry.

There's no time like the present.

Upstairs Rob was still in his room, feeling sorry for himself. While I was brushing my teeth, the bottle of perfume on the bathroom shelf caught my eye. I didn't normally wear much perfume but it seemed like a good idea today, so I applied a little dab to my throat just beneath each ear then my wrists and finally, as an afterthought, just above my breasts before tidying my hair in the mirror. Feeling ready to face the day, I took my guitar from its stand in my room and made my way back downstairs.

Mum was sitting at the breakfast bar with a look of concentration and her glasses on, trying to get to grips with her new tablet. She only wore her glasses when she was serious about something; most of the time she didn't bother. She looked up.

'Hey sweetheart, are you going into the studio?'

'Yes. I want to play around with some new stuff today, some more ideas I've been working on.'

'Steve must already be in there. I saw his car arrive a few minutes ago, but he hasn't been in here. Try some of your new ideas out on him and see what he thinks.'

I nodded thoughtfully.

'Good. I will.'

Too bloody right I will!

Steve looked busy in the performance area when I went in. The band's equipment was still set up from the week's recording sessions. A shiny, black drum kit surrounded by an array of microphones had filled up the drum booth, and in the main performance area, a variety of amplifiers and racks of processing equipment jostled for position with each other. It made what used to seem like an enormous space look very small. By the time the musicians were in there too, there wouldn't be room to swing a cat.

I quietly slipped the lock on the main door as it closed behind me and put my guitar down on a stand. Sensing movement on the other side of the glass, Steve looked up from what he was doing and smiled. I liked what it did to me. I can't help it; I'm a sucker for a good smile. He threaded his way over the assault course of cables on the floor and came through the control room door.

'Good morning, Rebecca,' he breezed.

'Good morning,' I replied with silken promise.

Steve stopped for a moment, eyeing me carefully.

'You're looking very pleased with yourself today. What have you been up to?'

'Oh, nothing much,' I lied.

He took me into his arms and kissed me, then bowed his head to my throat and inhaled deeply.

'Mm, you smell especially nice today. Rebecca mixed with . . . what is it?'

'Trésor. Anyway, I didn't know I had a smell.'

'Everybody has a smell, albeit faint after they've just come out of the shower. You can't beat the scent of clean skin. It's just so . . . intimate.' He made the word sound so inviting.

He was right of course. Steve's skin had its own signature too. I took hold of the front of his shirt in my fists and pulled him close, taking it in. A smile spread from one corner of his mouth and his eyes sparkled.

'So you're feeling 'intimate' are you? I thought we were out of action for today.'

'The way I'm feeling, I don't think I'd have let it stop me so long as you didn't mind.' I scrunched my face. 'But it's not good down there right now and besides, Mum and Rob are both here. It's really frustrating,' I continued glumly.

'Never mind! You've brought your guitar down. We can work on some of your song ideas.'

It's now or never.

'Maybe later,' I hinted, pushing him back towards the

mixing desk until he had to steady himself against its padded front rail. 'Right now I want to finish what I started last week before we were so rudely interrupted.'

Realisation dawned across his face as, biting my lip, I knelt down in front of him and began unbuckling his belt. He didn't resist. One by one I undid the buttons at the front of his jeans, stroking his growing erection through the denim then peeling them slowly down to his thighs. I could already feel the heat through the thin material of his underwear when I touched him. His cock strained against it, threatening to burn its way out.

I looked up, making big eyes at him. I already knew what kind of effect that would have.

'Mm, he looks pleased to see me.'

'We both are.' The hunger in his eyes matched my own.

I slid his underwear down, releasing his erection from its confines. Wrapping the cool fingers of one hand around his incendiary heat I stroked him reverentially then slipped my mouth around him until I was halfway down his length. Steve gave a deep, satisfied sigh.

Just you wait, Mr Bowes. You haven't seen anything yet!

I pulled back slightly and swirled my tongue around, coating him with saliva, then opening my mouth wide I moved smoothly forwards again, holding his gaze. I didn't want to miss his reaction, not one bit of it. This time I just kept going until I had enveloped him completely and clamped my lips around the base of his cock. It was like trying to swallow an iron bar, quite unlike what I'd been practising on, but I managed it.

Steve's eyes opened wide with a combination of shock and delight. It was just the effect I'd hoped for. His lips formed a perfect 'O' as if in imitation of my own and I began to move my head back and forth slightly, still getting used to the feel of him deep in the back of my throat. I pulled back to catch my breath, a self-satisfied smile breaking across my face.

I did it!

'Is that nice?' I asked, the words dripping from my mouth, exaggerated, half-whispered. I caressed his stiffness with my fingertips.

Steve remained dumbfounded. Unable to speak, he opened his mouth to reply but the look on his face had already told me everything I needed to know. I was too turned on to wait. I wanted to drive him as wild as he'd driven me that first day, to take him to the same heights he had taken me to and share the view from the top.

With a wet, satisfying squelch, I closed my mouth around him again, not stopping until the scent of his skin filled my nostrils and I had swallowed him whole like a snake consuming its prey. I began to rock my whole body backwards and forwards, gripping his thighs with my fingers and drawing back until only the tip of him remained poised between my lips then plunging forwards to engulf him again.

His fingers were in my hair now, caressing my scalp while I fucked him with my mouth.

'Oh, Rebecca . . . Oh my God!'

I needed to catch my breath. Lack of oxygen was making my head spin. I pulled back momentarily to fill my lungs again, still connected to him by a thread of saliva which I wiped delicately away from the corner of my mouth.

'You want some more?' I panted.

Steve nodded, his lips parting slightly.

'Mm-hmm!'

'That's just as well because I'm not finished with you yet, Mr Bowes.'

I had no intention of stopping until I'd claimed my reward. This time I attacked with renewed intensity, repeatedly going at him hard then drawing back slowly only to devour him again with a ferocious hunger. Steve's breathing was becoming more ragged and he gripped the edge of the mixing desk, his knuckles turning white.

'Fuck, Rebecca! I'm going to come. I'm going to . . .'

There was no let up in pace; if anything I redoubled my efforts. I was taking this all the way, and now he knew it.

'Alright . . . have it your way . . . if you insist.'

I did.

With his breath now coming in short stabs, I drew back slightly so the tip of him pressed against my tongue, cupping his balls with one hand and wrapping the other around the base of his cock. With a final cry, he came, pouring himself into my mouth with wild abandon, the hot flood spreading across my tongue, his hips bucking and heaving. I kept my lips clamped around him, refusing to let go until I knew I had claimed every last drop.

Eventually, his frantic climax subsided. The twitching of the muscles in his thighs abated and I felt him begin to soften. Carefully, I slipped his waning erection from my lips and making sure I still had his full attention, opened up to show him the big, slippery present he had just given me. I closed my mouth, savouring the sweet taste of victory, swallowed down my medicine like a good girl, then opened up again with a deliberate smack of my lips. Licking around the corners of my mouth I smiled at him, eyes shining with triumph.

'Gotcha!'

Finally, I understood why Steve took such delight in my pleasure, such joy in the effect he could have on me. It felt so liberating, so powerful. Although physically I was kneeling in front of him, it was really Steve who was at my mercy. It was he who metaphorically knelt at my feet. Disbelief still registered on his face.

'How the hell did you learn to do that?'

I pursed my lips and smiled coquettishly, wriggling my shoulders.

'Bananas! It seemed like the best way to practice. Did I do alright?'

'Alright? Are you serious? That was . . . incredible. You totally blow my mind.'

'As opposed to just blowing you?' I chuckled. 'I'd hate to think I didn't know how to please you.'

He was still looking at me wide-eyed.

'There's no fear of that.'

I kissed his now softened manhood, tucked him back into his pants and gave him a wink.

'So, have I been naughty?

'Very! Deliciously naughty!'

'Oh good, I was hoping you'd say that.'

'How so?' He looked intrigued.

'Well, naughty girls get spanked, don't they?'

Now we were on the same page; I could tell by the look in his eyes.

'You think I should spank you, Miss Taylor?

'Maybe you should, Mr Bowes.' I was doing my best

to look coy.

Steve sat down on the swivel chair in front of the mixing desk and patted his knees.

'You'd better get that sweet little arse over here then, so I can chastise you appropriately.'

I sighed and stepped closer.

'I love it when you're all masterful with me.'

He took me gently but firmly by the wrist pulling me in towards him and stroked my behind through the taut material of my jeans.

'I can't spank you through these; it just wouldn't do.' He paused for a moment. 'And we'd better lock the door; we can't have your mum interrupting us.'

'I did that earlier when I came in.'

Steve's jaw dropped in amazement.

'You really do think of everything, don't you? You clearly are deserving of a good spanking.'

I undid my jeans and wriggled them down to my thighs before leaning decorously across his knees, propping myself up on my elbows.

'I hope you realise I'm not going to show you any mercy,' he said. 'You've got me too turned on for that.'

I looked round at him.

'I should hope not. I expect nothing less than your best.'

'Well . . . you asked for it.'

Gentle hands softly stroked the cheeks of my behind through the thin cotton of my underwear. It wasn't what I'd expected.

'I thought you were going to . . .'

'All in good time, Miss Taylor.'

I should have known he was going to torture me

slowly by now. He slid the material down over my buttocks and continued caressing the taut roundness with both hands, kneading me in a circular motion with both palms and I sighed softly, thrilling to his touch. I found myself back on the sun-kissed beach, waves lapping at the shore. They rolled up the sand, dissolving into foam.

The first slap arrived without warning, his palm making contact with my left buttock with just enough force to shock me out of my swoon. It was followed almost immediately by one to my right. A sharp, breathy 'aah' escaped from my lips, more from surprise than any pain, and then the caressing hands were back. Palm trees swayed gently in the warm tropical breeze. Soft hands were rubbing sun lotion into the cheeks of my behind, following the line of my bikini.

A stinging slap landed across both buttocks, catching me off guard again. I looked round, but Steve's expression was focussed, giving nothing away. More slaps arrived, first on the right, then on the left and back again, between which he caressed me tenderly, mitigating the hot tingle which was building each time his hands made contact.

By now I was slumped over his lap, the tips of my hair almost scraping the floor. The striking of his palms was becoming harder now and more frequent, jolting my whole body, and as the tingling sensation spread, the muscles inside me clenched as if they were trying to tighten around him.

The door handle of the studio gave a clunk then rattled as someone on the other side tried to enter. Red-faced and panting, I looked round at Steve through the curtain of hair that had fallen across my face.

'I don't believe it! It's a good job I remembered to lock the door,' I whispered, gyrating my hips so my buttocks brushed against the flat of his hand.

'Shh!' Steve touched his lips then reached out and put one hand over my mouth, still stroking my bum with the other.

I scraped my teeth against the flesh at the base of his thumb. Whoever was at the door appeared to have given up because the handle returned to its normal position, then stopped moving. I bit harder into his hand but let go in surprise when a resounding smack struck me across both cheeks.

'You really are in a very naughty mood today, aren't you? If I didn't know better I'd say the danger turns you on. I can see I'm going to have to thrash that out of you.'

I removed a strand of hair that had wandered into my mouth and brushed the rest of it back from my face.

'You better had.'

A smile crept up from the corners of his mouth.

'I do believe we've just discovered another of your erogenous zones judging by how flushed you are.'

Another stinging slap landed on my right buttock making my whole body quiver.

'You think?' I gasped. 'Now spank my naughty little arse until I come, Mr Bowes.'

It wasn't a request, but even so, he needed no further bidding. While he rained blows on first on one cheek then the other I reached down to touch myself and felt the heat rising within. By now, my buttocks were the glowing red hot embers of the fire that raged inside me. The bombardment continued with me bent almost double over his knees. That and the tide of release that was threatening to wash over me meant I was finding it hard to breathe.

'Yes baby, come. Come for me,' he implored, slamming his palms against the cheeks of my arse, pleasure and pain melding onto one exquisite cacophony of sensation.

I held on as long as I could then exploded, pressing hard against my clitoris with my fingers, and collapsed, whimpering, unable to speak or move. Steve gathered me into his arms, lowered us both to the floor and held me close while I recovered myself, returning slowly from my little death to the land of the living. He gave me a sweet, simple, tender kiss that spoke more than a thousand words could ever do.

'You amaze me,' he said eventually. 'You remember what I said about how completely you give yourself to everything you do? I noticed it the first time I heard you sing and that seems like a lifetime ago now.'

'I guess I'm not that same young girl anymore.'

'Yes and no. You're still as extraordinary as you've always been, but 'girl'?' He raised one eyebrow. 'Not anymore you're not! You're a woman now, no doubt about it.'

'And I'm enjoying every minute of my new found womanhood, thanks to you.'

We picked ourselves up off the floor and began straightening our clothing. He shook his head slightly.

'I don't think you realise the effect all this is having on me. You probably think I know everything about sex, but in reality, I'm learning as much from being with you as you are from me. It's been years since I've experienced anything remotely like this.'

'With Valentina?' I asked him over my shoulder as I crossed the room and flipped the lock on the studio door so it would open again.

'Yes. The early days were pretty adventurous, but the magic went out of things eventually.'

'How did the two of you meet?' My curiosity had been pricked now. I wanted to know more.

'Just on a night out, like people often do. She was an exchange student at the time. After we got together she decided to stay. The rest, as they say, is history.'

We sat ourselves down on the sofa at the back of the control room, now deeply engrossed in our conversation.

'How old were you when you met her?'

'Twenty-two?' He looked upwards for a moment as if the answer was written on the inside of his eyelids. 'Yeah, twenty-two. So, I've not exactly been around all that much if that's what you're getting at.'

'What about before then?' I asked.

He probably thought I was giving him the third degree but I was just interested. Steve shrugged his shoulders.

'A handful of girlfriends, some long term, some not, and a few one night stands. After all, who doesn't do that these days?' Maybe he thought I would be uneasy about the flings but I wasn't judging, certainly not after all of Linda's revelations. 'I haven't exactly been prolific, but then I've always been more interested in quality rather than quantity.' He gave me a sideways look of amusement before his expression became more earnest again. 'If you're hoping, with your thirst for knowledge and experience, that I know everything there is to know on the subject then I'm afraid you'll be disappointed.'

'Disappointed? How could I be disappointed? I'm having the time of my life. In fact, I wish I could capture how the things we do make me feel, musically.'

'In what way?'

'Well, I want to write something intensely sexual. I want it to have the same feeling of being without boundaries, of being completely liberated, of running wild. Does that make sense?'

He nodded in recognition.

'It does. It's not easy to do well in a song, mind you. Various people have tried it over the years in different ways. Back in the eighties, you had Billy Idol and Prince. Before that, there was Marvin Gaye and even Barry White, although his stuff was pretty cheesy even by seventies standards. Then, of course, there has been a whole slew of female artists, Madonna, Britney Spears and Christina Aguillera to name a few, all of whom have gone at least some way down that road. Others have done it more recently still, some more successfully than others. The thing is: it's easy to make a song about sex, not so easy to make it genuinely erotic. I know it's before your time and even a bit before mine and the production sounds kind of dated now, but Billy Idol's 'Rebel Yell' album has some of the most erotic rock music I've ever heard on it. 'Flesh for Fantasy' has some of the sexiest rhythm guitar playing ever recorded, and if you want to try to match Billy Idol's vocal delivery then the only way to do it is to be constantly thinking about the wildest, hottest sex you can imagine.'

'I don't know.' I looked at him, raking my top teeth against my bottom lip. 'Right now my imagination isn't finding it hard to get pretty wild.'

'Somehow I don't doubt that.' The smile that came back at me was carnal and knowing. 'When it comes to your own song, you could go for blatantly raunchy, sensual and atmospheric or even subtle and symbolic.'

I thought for a moment.

'I think it would have to be a combination of sensual with raunchy because that's how it feels to me. It's like my senses run riot. The more we do, the more I want it because it makes me feel so alive, and the more alive I feel, the sexier I feel. It fills me with a kind of confidence I don't normally have and that's like a drug; it's so addictive.'

'I know exactly what you mean. After my first time, I was like a kid with a new favourite toy for Christmas. I wanted to play all the time.'

'How old were you?'

'About the same as you: sixteen, going on seventeen.' He looked thoughtful for a moment. 'Okay, so we've got a start-point. What sort of musical style are you thinking, or are there any lyrics in your mind already?'

'No words yet, but style-wise I think it needs to have a groove, something you can really grind to. It's got to be dirty but still sensual.' Our eyes locked across the sofa. 'You know . . . like when we both lose all sense of time and space; when we build up to a really intense, sensuous fuck. Just . . . plain . . . hot.' I enunciated every word carefully, lips slightly parted at the end of each one.

By the look in his eyes, I could tell that he understood me perfectly. The bulge in his jeans left me in no doubt either.

'I love your way with words, Rebecca. Look what it does to me.' He pointed down at his crotch.

'Good. Hold onto that feeling. We need to channel that and turn it into a song that's just off the scale sexy.'

'It'll be interesting running that one past Jeff.'

'Never mind Jeff; we'll cross that bridge when we come to it.'

We reached for our guitars and were busy trying out ideas when the door opened. Mum came in with a tray of tea and biscuits. I wondered if it had been her at the door earlier, but apart from looking from me to Steve and back again, she showed no sign of concern or suspicion. She said nothing about it, and I certainly wasn't going to bring the subject up. I wasn't sure if Steve still had a hard-on but at least his guitar covered it.

Mum put the tray down on the coffee table.

'Everything going alright?' she asked brightly.

'Fine!' we answered together.

'Oh good: Jammy Dodgers! Bagsy first pick!' I exclaimed, diving for my favourite biscuits. 'Thanks, Mum.'

'The two of you look like you're onto something. I've seen that inspired look in an artist's eyes many times. Give me half an hour and I'll bring some sandwiches in so you don't have to break the creative flow of what you're doing.'

Steve chipped in.

'Thanks, Avril. That would be great. We are kind of on a roll.'

She left us to it, glancing briefly over her shoulder in our direction and smiling to herself, closed the studio door behind her. Positioning my left hand on the neck of my guitar, I began once again to pick out the chords for the verse.

-0-

By the end of the day, we had all the basics of the song. We'd even fired up the sequencer and laid down the beginnings of rhythm tracks we could work over. The pattern of the verses and choruses and quite a few of the lyrics were already in place. An infectious groove leapt out of the monitor speakers, building from seductively simple beginnings to a crescendo of raw sexual energy. By the time it reached the final notes, it punched the air in the room with savage, rhythmic abandon. As songs go, it wasn't exactly shy.

We were both glowing with pride and excitement and still more than a little turned on when I kissed him goodbye on our way out of the studio. I watched him drive away and went in for dinner, humming the vocal melody and popping my shoulders up and down to the imaginary beat with the bass line playing in my head.

CHAPTER NINE

I leant back against the wall with one knee up and my foot flat to the surface, waiting for Linda to emerge from her last lesson. A tide of grey and green uniforms swept along the corridor as the classrooms emptied and Linda appeared, slinging her bag over her shoulder. Scott and one of his friends were making their way past when they spotted us and threaded their way through the river of bodies.

'Hey, Linda!' They gave each other a brief kiss. 'Hi, Rebecca!' he said, turning towards me.

'Hello, Scott.' Our eyes met for a moment and he smiled softly, brushing a fringe of wavy, dark hair away from his eyes. His friend regarded me with what I could only describe as warm curiosity.

'So!' Linda interjected, clearing her throat. 'Are you still on for later?'

'Sure. I'll be over about eight after I've got my homework out of the way.' They smiled knowingly at each other.

Linda took hold of his school tie and pulled it towards her, lifting one foot up onto the point of her toes.

'Make sure you eat first. I don't want you fainting on

me.'

His friend looked the other way, not knowing quite where to put himself.

'Then I'd better go and make sure I'm prepared.' His eyes glinted with the prospect of whatever they had planned. I recognised that look. 'See you later. Bye, Rebecca!'

I raised one eyebrow at him and smirked.

'Bye!'

The two boys headed off down the corridor, picking up their conversation again. Scott's friend said something to him and they both looked over their shoulders towards us before rounding the corner and disappearing.

'He fancies you,' Linda announced.

'Who? Scott's friend?'

'Mark? No. Well, both of them actually, but I was talking about Scott.'

'But he's going out with you!' I protested.

'What's that got to do with it? He still fancies you. Don't worry; I'm not going to be jealous or anything. After all, open relationships are a two-way street. I learned that from my parents, remember?'

I blushed.

'I've got all the man I need right now, to be honest.'

'Well if you change your mind, I can always loan him out to you.'

'Linda, you're terrible!' Smiling, I shook my head in disbelief.

We began to walk up the corridor, heading the same way the boys had gone, and rounded the corner.

'Cupcakes at one o'clock,' Linda muttered under her breath when two girls from our year flounced past us in the corridor, noses in the air. Jenna and Brianne (or Barbie and Sindy as we sometimes called them) were both wearing too much makeup as usual, and their bleach-blonde hair took up an unwarranted amount of space.

'Cupcakes?' I asked once we were past them.

'Yes, cupcakes! You know . . . a thick layer of brightly coloured decoration and nothing of any real substance or interest underneath: pretty on the surface but ultimately disappointing.'

'That's so bitchy!' I sniggered. 'True, but bitchy.'

'The thing is they're probably overcompensating for poor self-image. They probably think painting themselves up like canal barges is what's going to attract the opposite sex. What they don't seem to get is that to attract anyone who isn't equally shallow for more than five minutes, it has to come from inside. You've got it in spades, especially since you started seeing Steve. All the boys have noticed it. That's why Scott and Mark couldn't take their eyes off you. I'll bet you don't even realise the effect you're having.'

'I didn't think I was doing anything.'

We exited the double doors and stepped outside. It was still cold despite the sunshine and we pulled our coats tighter around us.

'That's the point,' Linda continued. 'It's not something you 'do' at all. It's like a switch inside and at the moment yours is permanently in the on position. People pick up on it. Where do you think the expression 'turned on' comes from?'

'I don't know. I never really thought about it.'

Linda had a head of steam up now. When she was like this I could almost hear the machinery in her head clanking.

'There's a story I once heard about Marilyn Monroe. She was one of the great sexual icons of the twentieth century because she knew how to make love to the camera like nobody else; you couldn't take your eyes off her. One day she was walking down the street with a friend and nobody was taking any notice of them. They were dressed ordinarily, just minding their own business. She turned to her friend and said: 'watch this!' All of a sudden the sexy screen persona kicked in. Norma Jeane Mortenson transformed into Marilyn Monroe and within seconds people began to recognise her. They were surrounded by people clamouring for her autograph and the crowd of people barely even noticed the friend who was also a famous movie star in her own right. The point is, it's that magic, that spark that comes from within that makes for real sex appeal and you've got it. It strikes me that what you need to learn to do is to harness it, to use it to your advantage when you perform, considering the line of work you're going into.'

By now I was nodding in agreement.

'The funny thing is I know exactly what you mean, although I was coming at it more from the songwriting angle rather than performing. Steve and I have been working on something together. The only problem is I can't go to Jeff with the song because it's a bit, um . . . spicy.'

'You mean you're still actually working on music together?' Linda sounded surprised. 'I thought you were otherwise occupied.'

Now I was laughing.

'Not all the time: just most of it. I'm not completely sex

146

mad.'

'Not completely. You do rather enjoy it, though, and you certainly seem intent on making up for lost time.'

'And what's wrong with that?'

'Nothing! Nothing at all! It really has been like letting the cork out of a champagne bottle with you, though, hasn't it? All that pent-up sexual frustration to get rid of!' She shuddered. 'Mind you, you're obviously having a ball.'

'Or even two!' I couldn't resist.

'And there I was, thinking terrible puns were just my department.'

'Oh, I can give as good as I get.'

'I'm quite sure you can,' added Linda, her words weighty and smooth.

Somehow, everything always came back to sex with her.

'Honestly Linda, you're such a pervert!'

She couldn't have looked more shocked if I'd physically slapped her round the face. What had I said that was so bad? After a moment or two, her expression softened but there was an edge of steel in her voice.

'I'd rather not use that word.' She was making a conscious effort to relax. 'Kinky! I can accept 'kinky'. I'm happy to call myself that. I can own that word happily, but 'pervert'? No.'

'So what's the difference?' I asked, more than a little confused.

'There's a big difference. Someone once defined kinky as bringing feathers into the bedroom but perverted as bringing the whole damned chicken. There's nothing wrong with kinky; it's the healthy expression of people's natural sexuality without hang-ups or boundaries. Everybody comes out of it with something positive, whatever that might be to them. And anyway, one man's kinky is another man's normal. But perverted? Perversion is what happens when healthy sexuality gets turned into something damaging or repressed, something selfish or manipulative or hurtful. Perhaps the greatest perversion of all is chastity; there's nothing more unnatural than that!'

She was practically frothing at the mouth.

'Look at what happens when priests take a vow of chastity. Their sexual side often finds a way through in the end; it's only human nature. So many of them end up having a whole other life they keep hidden, or worse molesting altar boys, and for what? It's not about devoting themselves to God; it's about devoting themselves to the Church and its power over them and others. As for being anti-contraception, don't get me started. It's just another ploy to make sure the world is populated with compliant devotees, justified by dogma.'

Now she was completely absorbed, thinking out loud. There would be no stopping her.

'I guess the real difference comes down to whether it's mutual or not. I mean, no matter how extreme some people's behaviour might seem: if it's shared and consenting it's just kinky, but if it's one sided, one person simply taking pleasure in another person's long-term suffering, then that's perverted. I know there can be a fine line between pleasure and pain, but there's also a big fucking difference between role play and meaning someone serious harm. I mean, it doesn't even have to be sexual, although it often is. Take rape for example. It's not really about sex, that's just a means to an end; it's about power and the abuse of it.'

Give her a soapbox to stand on and Linda could proselytise for hours sometimes. If it wasn't for her dislike of organised religion, Catholicism in particular, she would have reminded me of a preacher in a pulpit. She may have been a filthy-minded philosopher but I usually found myself agreeing with her in the end, no matter how individualistic her ideas might be at times.

By the time we reached Linda's house, she had vented a lot of her frustration and was in a better mood again. I took the opportunity to ask her about something that had been playing on my mind.

'What did you mean earlier about Scott not fainting? What on earth are you planning to do to him?'

'Oh, that!' She shrugged her shoulders. 'I just meant for him to keep his strength up. I have needs you know.'

I couldn't help feeling that I still wasn't getting the whole picture but there was no point in pushing her.

'Well, enjoy your evening then. By the way, I can't believe your parents are okay with you doing all this at home.'

She shrugged her shoulders.

'Given their lifestyle choices, do you think they would have a leg to stand on if they didn't take a fairly liberal approach with me? It turned out fine with Ryan so they're hardly going to be difficult about things are they?'

I still couldn't help being just a little bit jealous of her freedom.

'Have fun anyway. Don't do anything I wouldn't do.'

'That leaves plenty of options open, then, doesn't it?' she drawled.

I stuck my tongue out at her and walked away, smiling.

CHAPTER TEN

Saturday morning dawned bright and cold. The days were lengthening again now, and it was already light when I came down to breakfast, dressed and ready except for brushing my teeth. It wouldn't have made the best impression if I went to the meeting with bits of muesli still clinging to my smile.

Jeff was pouring himself a coffee. Strangely, he usually had coffee rather than tea when he went into London. It was a habit with him.

'Do you want one?' he asked, holding up the pot. 'It's the proper stuff, not instant.'

Although I didn't normally drink coffee, I didn't mind it. Since today was going to be unusual, I felt like a change.

'Please.'

I sat down on a stool at the breakfast bar while Jeff placed a steaming mug in front of me and slid the milk and sugar closer. I never bothered with sugar in tea but to me, coffee was too bitter without it.

Jeff had dressed pretty much as normal: clean and smart but not overly casual, and I was glad I had done the same. A loose, white, open-necked blouse tucked neatly into my navy blue skirt which was pleated and gathered in at the waist, modestly making the most of my shape. He looked at me, pursing his lips and nodding slightly.

'That's probably about as dressed up for the occasion as you'll need to go with Mitchell. He's used to dealing with artists, so he doesn't expect people to stand on ceremony. Mentally he's as sharp as a pin but he's not really a suit and tie kind of person. After all, this isn't going to be a board room meeting.'

I nodded, listening while Jeff continued talking.

'It's all about building up a working relationship and setting out the stall as to where things go from here. You're not a passenger on this train, though; you're a co-driver from now on so don't be afraid to speak up and say your piece, okay?'

'Okay.'

He smiled gently.

'You'll be fine.'

I fought my way through a bowl of cereal, even though I didn't really feel like it, then downed a glass of orange juice and finished my coffee.

'I'll see you out front in ten minutes,' said Jeff, his tone light but matter-of-fact.

Upstairs I brushed my teeth in front of the mirror, looking at the young woman in front of me who was about to embark on another great adventure. My mind wandered back to the night before and the phone conversation I had with Steve while I sat up in bed.

'Jeff's dealt with Mitchell a lot over the last few years,' he said. 'I haven't met him personally but Jeff has done production work with several of his artists.'

I sighed.

'This is it then. This is where it starts getting real.'

'Yes, but it is what you've always wanted. It's what you've spent most of your life working towards.'

'I know; it's just scary.'

'Don't forget I know how fearless you really are underneath that soft exterior. I've seen how totally you throw yourself into everything. There'll be no stopping you from achieving your dreams.'

I fiddled with the hem of my tee-shirt.

'I'll miss you tomorrow. I miss your touch. It's really frustrating.'

'Hopefully there's next weekend,' he consoled.

'I know, but I wish there was a way we could see each other during the week. It is the Easter holidays after all.'

'Well, I'll be recording with Jeff in the daytime but I'm free in the evenings. The problem is whether you can get away or not.'

'I could say I'm going over to Linda's for the evening. She won't mind covering for us. We could go to your place. Monday's going to be complicated so how about Tuesday?'

He went quiet for a moment, thinking.

'That sounds great. We could stop off somewhere on the way for something to eat. I know this lovely little old country pub that does great food.'

'Are you sure you want to be seen out with a teenager?'

'What, in the company of such a beautiful young woman? I'd be proud to. Some people might frown at the age difference but we're not doing anything wrong. It would just be a nice thing to do together and besides, what good am I to you on an empty stomach?' I could almost hear him grinning down the phone at me.

'Have you been talking to Linda? She said something very similar the other day,' I snorted.

'No collusion, I promise.'

'It sounds like a plan then. I'll ring Linda in a minute. We should be fine, though. I'll text you to confirm what's happening.'

'I'll await further news. Until then, sleep well and good luck for tomorrow.'

'Thank you. Good night, Steve.'

'Good night.'

I didn't want to be the first one to end the call and neither did he.

'You're still there.'

'So are you!' Steve protested.

'Good night,' I said softly and hit the 'end call' button on the screen, holding the phone against my rapidly beating heart while I collected my thoughts on what to say to Linda.

A few minutes later, I texted Steve with the latest update.

> **Me**
> Linda's cool with it. In fact she even suggested I tell Mum I'm staying over at her house. That way we could spend the whole night together. What do you think?
> 10:04 pm

It wasn't long before he texted me back.

Steve
Brilliant idea. It would be so nice to have the time together without rushing to get you back.
10:07 pm

Me
Just what I was thinking. Glad you agree. I like the idea of waking up in the morning next to you. I'll go over to Linda's in the afternoon. If you let me know when you're leaving the studio, I'll meet you outside the gates to the park. You can drop me off outside Linda's on your way to work in the morning.
10:11 pm

Steve
I'm in awe. As usual you think of everything. Can't wait.
10:13 pm

Me
Me neither. Good night.
10:14 pm

I was still staring at myself in the mirror when my mind returned to more immediately pressing matters.

Never mind Tuesday; I have to get through today first.

I kissed Mum goodbye on my way out then pulled my coat around me. She called from the doorstep to wish me luck. There was something in the right-hand pocket; I could feel it. When I slipped my hand in, to check, I realised what it was straight away: doggy treats and an empty poop bag. Too late now; they'd have to come with me. Jeff was already waiting in the Range Rover when I clambered into the front passenger seat and pulled the door to with a smooth, comforting clunk. The latest demos by Whispered Scream were playing on the sound system. They sounded good already. When I looked around, Mum was still watching and waving with Rob at her shoulder. I couldn't help noticing how tall he was now, compared to Mum.

We pulled away down the drive and turned right onto the main road, leaving Westerbridge and the life I knew behind us. Passing through the surrounding countryside I still felt a little apprehensive. Jeff must have sensed my unease because he turned the music down and left me to my thoughts, concentrating on the road in front of him while I looked out through the window in silence.

The rural landscape of farmland dotted with oasthouses gradually altered. The rounded towers with their jauntily sloping cowls that punctuated the scenery vanished from the picture and green gave way to grey as we neared the outskirts of the capital. The Garden of England relinquished its dominion to urban sprawl, the streets becoming dirtier and more crowded. All the tumult of humanity tried to shoehorn itself into an ever decreasing amount of space. The traffic increased too, becoming more sluggish as it packed in tighter and tighter.

We turned into a multi-storey car park through an electronic gate which opened automatically and headed for the private parking on the underground levels.

'This is where I keep a space reserved,' explained Jeff. 'It makes life a lot easier when I go into town. Parking in Central London is an expensive logistical nightmare.'

It always struck me as odd how so many people referred to London as 'town'. Town to me was the centre of Westerbridge, not the sprawling city it took the better part of an hour to travel into the heart of.

'We're practically next to the underground station. It's easy to get to anywhere in London from here.'

We took the East London Line, heading north, and changed tube trains at Canada Water. I'd been through its clean, modern concourses of steel, concrete and glass a few times before and every time I did, I couldn't help being struck by how in tune with the surrounding docklands financial district and yet how different from most of the underground it was. Although it was a marvel of architecture and engineering, it bore the unmistakable fingerprint of money and influence. I wasn't sure how to feel about the place. In fact, I wasn't sure how I felt about London in general; it managed at one and the same time to be vibrant, fluid and exciting, but also rushed, self-absorbed and inhospitable. Sometimes the loneliest place in the world is in a crowd.

We changed trains and headed west on the Jubilee Line until we reached Bond Street. Although it had been modernised, it still held onto some of its traditional character, its white tiled walls retaining an echo of its Victorian past. We made our way back up to the surface and out onto the street among the hustle and bustle of the Saturday morning shoppers.

'This way,' Jeff gestured. 'It's only a couple of streets from here.'

A few minutes from the station we turned down a side street and found ourselves outside an anonymous doorway in the side of a plain brick building with no ground floor windows. There was no big sign, no fancy facade, nothing to announce what it was until I looked at a small plaque by the bell which read: 'M. Sacker (Management) Ltd.'

Jeff checked his watch.

'Five to ten: perfect timing. Go on then, you announce us. They'll buzz us in.'

I pressed the button and waited. After a couple of seconds, a muffled voice appeared from the speaker beside the bell.

'Hello. Can I help you?'

'Rebecca Taylor to see Mitchell Sacker. I believe we're expected.'

'Yes, you are, Miss Taylor. Please come in.'

There was an electronic buzzing sound, and the door unlocked with a click. We stepped inside a plain, unassuming hallway and Jeff gestured towards the stairs. The door pulled itself shut behind us.

'Up we go, first floor.' He sounded upbeat despite the rather anonymous surroundings.

I was surprised by what met us at the top of the stairs. It opened out into a spacious, modern reception area. Behind the well-dressed receptionist was a large sign with raised, metallic lettering which read 'Mitchell Sacker Management'. This was more like what I had been expecting.

'Good morning Miss Taylor, Mr Taylor. Please take a seat and Mr Sacker will be out shortly.' She was a model of friendly efficiency with a roundish face and short, dyed-blonde hair which stood straight up on the top of her head. She must have gelled it to within an inch of its life.

A large window which stretched from floor to ceiling looked out over the busy street below but up here there was almost no sound. The quiet of the office seemed at odds with the busy West End scene happening only metres away.

I'd barely sat down on one of the comfortable, over-large sofas when the double doors opened and a lightly-built man in his mid-forties with round glasses and short, brown hair stepped through and held out his hand in greeting. He looked more like an off-duty accountant than the archetypal, oily manager, yet he exuded quiet confidence.

'Rebecca! It's nice to finally meet you. Good to see you, Jeff. Come on through.'

He led us through another door into his office. Despite its size, it felt smaller on account of the sheer number of items that hung from the walls. Signed photographs of artists, gold discs and a collection of African tribal masks covered almost every available inch of space. There was even a gleaming, customised Harley-Davidson motorbike on a stand in the corner of the room. It didn't look like it had ever been ridden. Behind the large desk was a backlit glass case filled with awards.

He noticed me looking around in wonder and obviously felt the need to explain.

'I spend a lot of time here. This isn't exactly a nine-to-five job, so I tend to surround myself with things that I like and keepsakes of previous achievements. Stuff like that reminds us we're still human and not just machines, no matter how hard we work.'

He gestured for us to sit, not at the seats in front of the desk, but in the armchairs surrounding the coffee table in the centre of the room.

'Please, take a seat.'

The receptionist came into the room with a tray of tea and coffee which she placed on the table in front of us.

'Thank you, Penny.' Mitchell looked at her when he spoke.

She appeared to be the only other person in today, though judging by the number of other rooms off the corridor, he must have had quite a team of people working for him. Penny smiled, nodded and left, then Mitchell turned back to face me.

'We currently represent about a dozen artists.' It was as if he could read my mind. 'Most of them are quite well known now, and a few, like yourself, are up-and-comers. Some of them will become successful and some won't, and out of those only a few will achieve lasting success, but I'm a firm believer in investing in the future and you, Rebecca, have potential.' Mitchell reached for the tray.

'What can I get you both?'

'I'll have a coffee please,' I replied.

'The same please, Mitchell,' answered Jeff.

Mitchell poured three coffees while I sat, already reeling a little from his opening salvo, however softly spoken it might have been.

'Help yourselves to cream and sugar.'

We prepared our coffees and settled into the chairs again. I took a sip. It was richer than when made with milk. I liked it.

'So, down to brass tacks,' he continued. 'I've been listening to a steady stream of your demo recordings, Rebecca. Jeff has been very persistent.'

The two of them exchanged respectful glances.

'He has worked very hard to help develop your abilities and to get you out there. You have tremendous range and scope and your own songs are getting better all the time. There's good initial interest from a number of record companies. In fact, when the time is right there are potentially three types of contract option on the table. Obviously, there is a lot of negotiating to do and a lot of work to do first but all other things being equal, it comes down to two main factors and inevitably they are a compromise. If you sign directly to a major label then you are a small cog in a very large machine. They have tremendous marketing power but you are almost always a low priority compared to established artists. On the other hand, if you sign to a small independent you are a much higher priority to them, but they may lack the resources to make the most of your potential.'

He leant forward a little.

'Option three, which is my current favourite in your

case, is the interest from Pristeen Records. They have a smaller company mindset but also backing from one of the major labels, which gives them the financial clout to invest in you properly. What are your first thoughts?'

He sat back in his chair awaiting my response. What did I know? How did he expect me to answer?

'It seems like a good compromise,' I said simply, 'but I suppose there are a lot of things to take into account.'

Jeff sat forwards and listened closely. Mitchell seemed satisfied with my response.

'Quite. It's not just about the size of the advance; it's about the depth of the commitment. You can't afford to be put on hold by a record company and be forced through contractual obligations to sit by and watch while your career stagnates. Time is money for all of us. The more successful you are, the more successful we are.' He waved his hands around him. 'So, what I intend to do is see where each of the options goes, pursue a few others if possible, pay close attention to the small print and keep you up to date at every stage. Promise me, no signing the first piece of paper that gets waved under our noses. It's a decision that has to be taken carefully and everybody needs to agree on it, you included. After all, it's your career. Your talent is the foundation on which we need to build everything else. Agreed?'

'Agreed!'

'Good. Now then, speaking of your talent . . .' He steepled his hands together and gathered his thoughts. 'There are areas in which we need to focus so we can build you up into an all round performer. In the studio you are dynamite. The fact that you have the looks to appeal to an audience is not in question. Where we need to develop you as an artist falls into two areas. Firstly, we need to get you up in front of audiences every opportunity we can. To have any longevity in this business you have to be a good live performer. You need presence. You need stagecraft. To begin with, it will involve a much greater investment of time, effort and money than it appears to bring in, but stick with it and enjoy the ride because in the long term it will reap dividends. You've got some hard work ahead of you, and if you're serious about this it's going to take up all your available time once your exams are out of the way. The next few years are going to feel a bit like being on a rollercoaster at times; you just have to ride it out to the end of the track to see where it goes.'

He paused. I wasn't sure if it was for my benefit or his.

'And the second thing?' I asked. He looked quietly pleased that I was still up to speed with him.

'The demos you've made are very diverse. If anything they are too diverse. What you need as an artist is focus, identity. It doesn't mean lack of variety in what you do but what it does need is cohesion, both in the music itself and how you come across to people. There needs to be a unique selling point to make you stand out from the crowd of other hopefuls out there, but your music still needs to be accessible, otherwise neither the music industry nor the public will know how to categorise you, and believe me; that's more important than you know. Everybody wants to put things in little boxes so they know how to deal with them. Never underestimate people's lack of imagination. It's a bit like walking a tightrope; if you stray too much one way or the other then sooner or later you fall off into the void of obscurity.

There are no guarantees of success, sustained or otherwise.'

I was trying to absorb his words by osmosis rather than letting them wash over me. He gathered himself for a moment before continuing his carefully-considered deluge.

'Then there's image. The identity that you project, your public persona, is not the whole you or a fake you but a version of you; it's that part of yourself that you show to the public, magnified, made larger than life.'

If it wasn't for the conversation I'd had with Linda only a few days ago, I don't think I would have grasped the full meaning of his words. As it was, I nodded sagely and took another sip of coffee.

'There's certainly a lot to take in,' I said thoughtfully.

'That's for sure.' He nodded. 'I don't mean to bamboozle you with it all, but I'd rather lay everything on the line so you know what to expect. The more wholeheartedly you embrace the whole thing, the more successful you'll be at it. The music business is unpredictable, insecure and not for everybody.'

It was dawning on me how Jeff's words of warning to a naive fifteen-year-old might have prepared me for what was to come.

'On the subject of public image, there's the matter of the name the public know you by. 'Rebecca Taylor' might not be snappy enough if you are aiming at certain markets. You could go the route of completely changing the name by which you're known, which is how Reginald Dwight became Elton John and Gordon Sumner became Sting, or you could go for a shortened or amended version of your own. In this case, I'd recommend the latter approach unless you're truly feeling inspired by a complete change. 'Rebecca T' has a good ring to it perhaps, although there is another artist who goes by something similar. Ultimately the choice is yours, though. You are the one who has to live with it.'

I hadn't even considered that my name might be an issue.

'Rebecca T? I'll have to sleep on that one. It might take some getting used to.'

'That's fine. Act in haste, repent at leisure but think about it nevertheless. You may well find that the separation between the public you and the private you is really useful. It prevents you from feeling like public property all the time. There will be aspects of your life that you want to keep to yourself, otherwise this business can eat you up if you're not careful.'

By the time we emerged from the meeting and stepped back onto the street, the afternoon was well underway. My head was spinning.

'So, what did you think of Mitchell?' Jeff asked.

'He's pretty full-on isn't he?'

'He's got a mind like a scalpel: the best I know and straight as a die too. He doesn't mince his words but if you're fair with him he'll be the most loyal ally you could have in this business. Trust me; you need someone like him onside to fight your corner. You held your own in there too. Mitchell was impressed. He's very good at sounding people out.'

'I didn't think I said all that much. Mitchell can talk for the Olympics.'

'True, but what you said counted.'

'Tell you what, though; I'm starving now we're out of

there.'

'Me too, come to think of it! Come on, let's go and get some lunch before we head home; that is unless you want to go shopping while we're here.'

I could think of a few things I'd like to go shopping for in the West End, but not with Jeff in tow. Besides which, they probably wouldn't sell them to someone my age even if I managed to get through the door of the shop.

'No, not really,' then I had a flash of inspiration, 'unless you fancy having a look in some of the guitar shops.'

'There wouldn't be an angle to this would there, what with a birthday coming up?'

'No . . . ! Well, maybe!'

Jeff rolled his eyes and allowed himself a little smile.

'Let's go and get something to eat and then we can take a wander.'

The light was beginning to fade by the time we arrived home. By then I was tired but excited; excited because it really looked like this thing was happening and tired because of the thousand and one things milling around in my head. Mitchell had certainly given me plenty to think about. On top of all that, I couldn't help thinking about Tuesday. I was missing Steve so much. It had been two weeks since 'fruit salad'. Last weekend had simply worked up an appetite. I missed his touch, the feel of his body next to mine and his lips against my skin, but most of all I just missed him. Other than Linda he was probably the only person I could be completely myself with. I could tell him almost anything without being judged. I just had to hold out another couple of days without the frustration getting the better of me before we could be together again.

Mum wanted a full debriefing on the day's events of course. Jeff and I practically had to relive the entire meeting word for word, including the bit about having a stage name.

'I can see what he's saying. Lots of artists use shortened or amended versions of their names: Adele, Jessie J., Madonna.'

'You don't feel offended at my name being messed around with?' I asked.

'You've already changed your name once, remember? And what if you got married one day? Your stage name would end up different from your legal name then too, or you could go the other way and confuse the hell out of people like Cheryl Whatever-her-surname-happens-to-be-this-month. Sweetheart, you'd still be my daughter if you changed your name to Albuquerque Bluejangles.'

I couldn't help laughing at the ridiculousness of it.

'It would just be a bit weird being called something different.'

'Not that different if you think about it,' Jeff chipped in. 'You'd still be Rebecca to everybody if you went with something like Rebecca T.'

'Well, if you put it that way then maybe 'Rebecca T' isn't so bad. The trouble is, it makes me sound like a rapper and I don't really make urban music. It's just not me, and the one thing that connects everything I do musically is how genuine it is; it comes from within.'

'Mitchell sounds like a very shrewd man,' said Mum. Jeff nodded quietly. 'Whatever you decide, you have to be comfortable with it.'

I tried to calm the jumble of thoughts going through

my head by taking a relaxing bath after dinner. Big mistake! It did nothing to calm my aching need for Steve; in fact, it only intensified it. Every time I closed my eyes I could feel his hands on my breasts and my back against his chest in the warm, fragrant water. It wasn't helping matters.

I dried myself down and put some pyjama bottoms and a baggy tee-shirt on, then went down to the snug with a towel around my wet hair to watch the telly. It was a Saturday night after all. There had to be something suitably mind-numbing I could switch my brain off to. Fluffy padded over and curled up beside me on the sofa, her tangerine eyes watching me curiously while I flicked through the channels. Nothing really caught my attention.

Eventually, I settled on a wildlife documentary about the forests of Bengal and their fragile ecosystem with its graceful, powerful tigers, still holding sway at the top of the food chain despite the human threat to their habitat and livelihood. Everything was alright, and I was enjoying the programme until it came to mating season.

Oh, great! Even the flipping monkeys are getting more than me!

I shook my head in exasperation and hit the off button on the remote. It was only ten o'clock but I had to admit defeat. I stroked Fluffy's sleek, grey fur while she lay purring on the sofa, turned off the light and trudged upstairs to bed. After texting Steve to wish him goodnight, my head hit the pillow and I fell into an exhausted but fitful sleep.

Leafy branches give way in front of me as I push through the tangled growth of mangroves, away from the coastal marshes and deeper into the forest, my paws creating a trail of impressions in the soft, salty earth. The monsoon rains have left behind a metallic dampness in the air which clings around me like a halo, a mist of tiny droplets that pepper my fur and make a ghost of me.

I raise my nose to catch a scent on the air, my breath sighing deep and low in my throat. It's somewhere close by now; I can sense the beating of its fragile heart. Something small rustles in the undergrowth, but that holds no interest for me; I am on the trail of bigger prey.

I creep forward to the edge of the clearing, half obscured, at one with the backdrop of foliage and crouch, waiting and watching. My yellow eyes blaze in the dusky light beneath the forest canopy.

It wanders out of the brush on the far side of the clearing, emerging from the time-worn track that generations of its kind have followed before it, wary but still oblivious to my presence, heading towards water as all creatures eventually must. But first it has to get past me. I am the gatekeeper, the guardian on the threshold, arbiter of life and death.

Ears twitching back and forth, it moves forward, momentarily vanishing then reappearing in the dappled light and shadow of the forest floor.

I tense, muscles taut beneath my skin, the tip of my tail flicking, and I shift my weight, preparing for the moment. It draws nearer but it isn't close enough: not yet.

I wait.

My quarry moves forward another two steps then sees me, but too late. Eyes wide with terror, there is only the time for one short, piteous shriek but not enough to run. I pounce, claws tearing into its hide, gripping tight, the weight of my body *bringing it to the ground and pinning it there. My jaws close around its throat, crushing its windpipe, teeth puncturing the skin and sinking into softer tissues. The iron taste of blood fills my mouth. It stops struggling, eyes rolling back in its head then becomes limp, head drooping, antlers scraping against the ground. I drag my kill to the edge of the clearing.*

The deer's life is over but I will live to hunt another day, perhaps to find a mate and raise cubs of my own. I have obeyed my nature and done what I was born to do, what I had to do to survive. I tear into warm flesh, crimson blood staining the fur around my mouth and soaking into the earth beneath.

My eyes opened and I sat up in bed with a start. My hands were shaking and my heart was pounding. Waiting for the trembling to subside I rested my head in my hands, and although I wanted to shed a tear for the loss of innocence, the childhood I had left behind me, I neither could nor would. My decisions were made and my path was set.

I was a tiger now whether I liked it or not.

CHAPTER ELEVEN

I didn't recognise the car outside Linda's house. Maybe her parents had company.

Perhaps going over this afternoon wasn't such a good idea. Then again, it was the middle of the day: hardly Brian and Loretta Maloney's usual style. They would normally have been working and besides, the car was a small hatchback and not exactly new. It wasn't what I would have expected their usually well-heeled 'friends' to be driving.

The front door was unlocked as usual so I called out as I entered the hall.

'Hello! It's Rebecca. Is anybody here?'

Ryan appeared in the kitchen doorway looking effortless as always and inwardly I breathed a sigh of relief that I wasn't interrupting anything embarrassing.

'Oh, hello Ryan! I was wondering whose car it was outside. What brings you back here?'

'Seeing as it's the holidays I thought I'd better show my face for a couple of days and prove to Mum and Dad I'm still alive.' He cocked his head to one side. 'You're looking well.' Taking my hands he kissed me on the cheek then stepped back to look at me with my fingers still resting on the top of his. 'How are things?'

Where the hell do I start?

'Life is certainly interesting right now. So much is happening with the music and the exams are coming up too. There's never a dull moment.'

'Boyfriend?'

I lifted my shoulders and turned down the corners of my mouth in a gesture of non-commitment.

'Sort of!'

'Meaning yes. You don't have to be so shy about it.'

He was right in a way. I did feel shy about it, partly because if we were discovered it could make things difficult for Steve, but also because these days I felt so overawed in golden boy Ryan's presence. I changed the subject before I embarrassed myself.

'How's life at university?'

'Good. One more term and I've finished my second year. I moved out of the halls of residence and I'm living in a shared house with a few of the other students.'

I wondered what else they shared apart from a house. From things Linda had said, he obviously possessed his family's liberal attitudes and why not? Apart from being very easy on the eye, he was charming, intelligent and in the prime of his life. My mind began painting scenes in my head which I did my best to shut out, but they wouldn't leave me alone. I could feel myself starting to redden.

'What about girlfriends?' I asked.

'There's no one in particular. I'm just working hard and enjoying the social life.'

I'll bet you are. My imagination was going into overdrive.

'I'm in several of the clubs and societies that do outdoor pursuits like hill walking, climbing and canoeing. I like the outdoor life. It's nice to break away from the city at weekends, very refreshing.'

'Oh!' That was a surprise. I wasn't sure why. 'You're obviously making the most of things.' There was clearly more to university life than dusty academia and the opposite sex.

'Work hard, play hard: I think that must be our family motto,' he mused.

I was trying to think when I'd seen him last. It must have been the Maloney's Christmas party. It hadn't been one of 'those' parties, just drinks and nibbles and small talk with the neighbours, most of whom were trying a little bit too hard to be sophisticated. Mum, Jeff and Rob had been invited too, so had most of the street it seemed, but there were also some faces I hadn't seen before, probably some of their 'special' friends as well as family. Linda had been shocked when I expressed surprise that they had a regular social life too.

'They may have an unconventional marriage but they're not at it like rabbits all the time, you know,' she'd said. 'Most of the other couples they see are also good friends too. Some of them are kind of like an extended family and I've known them for years.'

Linda appeared at the bottom of the stairs, beaming at us.

'Don't you go stealing this young lady away from me, Ryan Maloney! I've got plans for Rebecca this afternoon and she's got a big night out to prepare for.'

He raised his eyebrows at me.

'Sounds interesting! Tell me more.'

'Oh, it's nothing,' I replied meekly.

'You can bring your bag upstairs, Rebecca. We're going into town shopping for an outfit for you before you get ready.' Linda seemed as excited as I was, despite my attempts not to show it.

'London?'

'No, Westerbridge town centre! There isn't time to go into London.'

'I've got stuff to change into in my bag,' I protested.

Linda shook her head.

'You're coming with me. Girl time!'

I turned back to Ryan.

'It looks like I'm in demand. I'll see you later.'

He nodded.

'Count on it. Enjoy your afternoon. Linda could turn shopping into a competitive sport.'

She gave him a familiar look of affectionate disdain and led me upstairs.

'Right!' She was looking me up and down. 'We are going to get you a proper makeover for your big night with Steve.'

'I'm going over to his place for the night, not attending a movie premiere. I don't want to end up looking like a Barbie doll.'

'You are off to spend a whole night of passion with your man for the first time in your life and I would be failing you as a friend if I sent you out the door looking and feeling anything less than a million dollars. I'm not trying to tart you up or overdo it, just make the most of your natural assets. Trust me; you are going to blow his mind by the time I'm done with you.'

I sighed.

'I guess you're right. I do have a rather limited wardrobe. I don't really dress up for the occasion very much.'

Now Linda was looking extra determined.

'We are going to show him the classy, sexy vixen lurking inside you. He won't know what hit him. First things first; we'll head into town to buy you a dress and some shoes to go with it, maybe some underwear too. I'm paying.'

'You can't do that!'

'Yes I can. It's my money.'

'I don't spend much of my allowance. I've got some money saved up.' I couldn't let her pay for all that. It wouldn't have been right.

'Then we club it together and get something extra special. No more arguments, okay?'

'Okay!'

I gave in. There was no point arguing with Linda when she was on a mission.

We were so busy talking all the way into town, the fifteen-minute walk passed by in a blink. Starting at one end of the high street, the first couple of shops we tried just didn't have what we were looking for and Linda shook her head at everything we pulled off the rail.

'Naah!' She pulled a face. 'Too tarty!' The next one was 'Too frumpy!' There was clearly a look she had in mind. 'I know where we can go. You know that little boutique on the corner about fifty yards down? I bet we'll find something in there.'

'But that'll be way too . . .'

Linda gave me a look that brooked no argument.

'All right! We'll take a look.' I resigned myself to my

fate. In fact, I would have bet money on Linda having had that place in mind all the time.

Even the mannequins in the window of the shop eyed us haughtily on our way in. A perfectly manicured and coiffed shop assistant glided over.

'Can I help you?'

Linda piped up before I could say anything.

'Yes, we're looking for a dress for my friend Rebecca to wear out for the evening. Not overly formal, but classic, feminine and understatedly sexy. Oh yes, and shoes to go with the ensemble.'

The assistant looked momentarily taken aback then regained her polite composure.

'Certainly. What dress size?' She was looking me up and down.

'Ten to twelve, depending on which way the wind blows,' I answered, gaining a little in confidence.

'What colour and style do you have in mind?'

My mouth opened but nothing came out. I didn't know. It was Linda who spoke for me.

'I reckon short-sleeved, above the knee, something that flows but still clings enough to show off Rebecca's shape. We'll see about colour from there.'

The assistant looked back at me with one perfectly plucked eyebrow arched.

'What she says,' I chipped in, shrugging my shoulders.

'I think I know what you're after. We've got a few possibilities. If you go over to the changing room I'll bring some over and you can try them on.' At least her initially frosty exterior was beginning to melt.

The first one was a blue-green coloured dress, which came to just above the knee and was pleated and gathered at the waist. None of us looked too sure about that one.

'It's too . . . old for you,' Linda pursed her lips, 'and the skirt's too long. What do you think?'

'It's a bit Roman-looking,' I added.

The assistant was starting to enjoy herself.

'Okay, let's go the other way. How about this one?' she asked, holding up a little black number.

I disappeared back into the changing room and tried it on. I knew this variation on the little black dress wasn't quite right straight away.

'I like it, but it's not right for tonight,' Linda said when I came out again. 'The sleeves are too long and the skirt's too short. It's a bit cocktail-dressy.'

'Okay. Try this one. Ignore the fact that it's grey. Tell me what you think when it's on.' The assistant had a gleam in her eye.

When I re-emerged from behind the curtain, Linda and the assistant both looked at each other.

'Oh yes.' Linda had a quiet glow about her. 'Now that's more like it.'

'Take a look in the mirror,' purred the assistant.

It was a made of a pale grey jersey fabric, with a sweetheart neckline and gathered in slightly below the bust. The skirt flowed to a little way above the knee, ending in a soft, lacy material layered into the slanted hem.

'What size is this?' I asked the assistant.

'It's a twelve.'

'Can I try the ten? I think it might cling a little more. The twelve is a bit loose.'

Linda looked triumphant. The assistant fetched one

from the rail.

When I reappeared from the changing room for the fourth time, both their jaws dropped.

'Now that's the one.' Linda's eyes were shining. 'That's what I'm talking about.'

'You don't think it's too blatant?'

Linda shook her head.

'It's just right. It shows you off to perfection.'

'What about where the material clings to my hips? Won't my underwear show?'

'Not if you don't wear any, sweetie.'

The assistant and I both stared at Linda.

'Aw, come on!' she protested. 'It'll give Steve a treat he won't forget in a hurry.'

It was the assistant's turn to blush and look awkward.

'So you like that one?' she asked, her professional composure returning.

'I love it. What about the shoes?' I was into my stride now.

In for a penny; in for a pound.

When we left clutching two fancy bags with the shop logo on the side, I had acquired a pair of strappy, grey, high-heeled shoes to match the dress. The straps extended up and around my calves and were the devil's own job to put on and take off, but they looked so good with the dress it was worth it. Linda was bouncing around like Tigger on speed.

'I can't believe how much money we just spent,' I said, still reeling. 'I don't think the rest of my wardrobe cost that much combined.'

'Never mind that, just imagine the look on Steve's face when he sees you. I've got to be there for that one. Come on; let's get home. We've got work to do.'

Back at the house, we dropped our haul on Linda's bed.

'Right, you hop in the shower and wash your hair. We can do your hair and make-up and stuff when you get out.' Linda was definitely on a mission now.

'Thank you. I was going to shave my legs too. I've got the shaver in my bag somewhere.'

A wicked glint appeared in Linda's eyes and I pulled myself to a halt.

'What? I know that look.'

'Why don't you go the whole hog and shave everything?'

'Linda!' Not for the first time, I raised my voice in shock.

'Well, why not? Can you imagine the surprise on his face when he finds out? Guys are very visual; they like to see what they're getting.'

'Well, that's one bit you won't be there to watch.'

'More's the pity!' she said wryly.

'Linda Jane Maloney, you're so bloody kinky!'

'Don't you know it? So, are you going to do it?'

I looked at her for a moment while I imagined Steve's reaction.

'Fuck it! Why not?'

'Good girl!' Now Linda was glowing with satisfied pride.

'You might need a hand with that if you haven't done it before.'

'I think I can manage. I'll let you know if I need you. Have you got any skin moisturiser? I forgot to put some in the bag.'

'Yeah, there's some in the bathroom cabinet.'

By the time I emerged from the bathroom with one towel around my body and another one wrapping my hair, Linda had set her dressing table up like a beauty parlour. She was looking expectantly at me.

'Come on then, give us a flash.'

I opened the towel for a few seconds then wrapped it around me again.

She bit softly into her lower lip, eyes gleaming.

'Very nice! Did you manage to get everywhere?'

'Yes, all the nooks and crannies. The big mirror in there helps. I still can't believe I'm doing this.'

'What time's he picking you up?'

'He should be finished in the studio by about six. He'll text me when he's leaving.'

'Good. That gives us about two hours of pampering. Nails first, then make-up, then hair I think.'

By about half past five, Linda had done everything she set out to do and stood back to take stock.

'There! You're all ready. Let's go and take a look in the big mirror.'

Linda had worked her magic. My hair was half up, half down in a waterfall plait. The braid ran round the back of my head, and the rest of my hair which wove its way through it tumbled in waves around my shoulders. My make-up and nails were immaculate but subtle and classic. I'd never seen myself looking like that. I turned one way then the other in the mirror, hardly believing my eyes.

'Oh Linda, it looks fantastic.' I went to fling my arms around Linda but she put her finger out in front of her.

'Uh uh! No smudging! We don't want you making a

mess of things so soon, now do we? You can get as messy as you like later.' She looked at me knowingly. I'd forgotten she knew all about the fruit salad incident. 'Anyway, what do you mean 'it' looks fantastic? *You* look fantastic. Come on. Let's show Ryan.'

She took me by the hand and led me down the landing, teetering in my new heels. They weren't particularly high but I was so used to flat-soled shoes that it felt like I was on stilts. There was a muffled reply from inside Ryan's room when Linda knocked on the door. She swung the door open and walked me in. Ryan looked up from the book he was reading and froze. His jaw went slack.

'Wow!' He sprang up off the bed and stood there, open-mouthed. 'Rebecca, you look amazing. So who's the lucky fella?'

'No one you'd know.' I had to think for a moment whether that was true or not, but I came to the conclusion they probably hadn't ever met.

'Well, I hope he appreciates you and treats you right or he'll have me to answer to. Linda, did you do this? You could do it professionally.'

'I have other plans. Anyway, all an artist needs is the right canvas.' She did look very pleased with herself, though.

My phone beeped. I could hear it from the other end of the landing.

Ryan smiled at me warmly.

'I hope you enjoy your evening. I guarantee your date will.'

'Thank you. I will.' I couldn't help smiling back. 'I'd better go and check that. It could be him texting now.'

I headed back to Linda's room to check my phone, not quite so wobbly on my feet this time and leaving a delicately perfumed trail behind me. At least I was getting used to the heels. Sure enough, there was a new message.

> **Steve**
> Just finishing up. I'm aiming to be out at six.
> See you about five past.
> 5:43 pm

I texted straight back.

> **Me**
> Can't wait. I'll be ready and waiting by the entrance to the park.
> 5:46 pm

Linda was rummaging in her wardrobe when I turned towards her. She held out a little clutch bag and a smart, black, waist length jacket.

'Here, you can borrow these. You'll need something to carry your phone in and it's going to be cold out. This should match the dress better than your own coat does, and seeing as you're not wearing a bra either, you'll end up poking holes in the fabric if you're not careful.'

It was dawning on me that it might also get a bit cold down there since I had taken Linda's advice and gone commando.

'Now that I'm minus any insulation, it might get chilly

elsewhere too.'

'There's nothing we can do about that, but I'm sure Steve will be happy to warm it up for you later.'

'Ha, bloody ha! Seriously, though, thank you for everything.'

'What else are friends for? I shall expect a full status report in the morning. I'm tempted to call it a debriefing, but you're already debriefed aren't you?'

I gave her a look of mock exasperation.

'Let's go before you unleash any more atrocious puns.'

It wasn't far to the park gates from Linda's, but we hadn't been there long when Steve pulled up. He stepped out of the car and came around to greet us, staring at me with a look of astonished delight and kissing me on the cheek.

'Hi!' He was transfixed.

'She scrubs up well, doesn't she?' Linda chimed in.

Steve glanced at her as if he'd only just become aware of her presence.

'Rebecca, you look amazing! Did you have a hand in this, Linda?' He looked back and forth between us.

'I helped.' Linda seemed to be looking at Steve with a whole new level of respect in the light of everything I'd told her. I would almost have called it awe.

'I must say I'm stunned.' He turned back to look at me, not wanting to draw his eyes away for more than a few seconds.

'Good, then take good care of her. Enjoy yourselves.'

'We will,' we both replied together.

Steve opened the passenger door and held it for me while I slid myself carefully into the seat, making sure my dress didn't ride up too far. After all, I wouldn't want to ruin the grand unveiling by playing all my cards too soon. Linda placed my bag on the back seat and stood back to wave us off while Steve came round to the driver's side. She gave us a final thumbs-up as we pulled away.

'I feel quite underdressed now,' admitted Steve, still looking over at me periodically while he drove.

'You keep your eyes on the road, Mr Bowes. It's not like these are going to turn back into tattered rags at midnight. We don't have to leave the ball this time. You can look all you want later.'

'Is that a promise?'

'You know it is. Anyway, you're not underdressed. You look lovely.' He did too.

He was wearing a collarless, mid-blue shirt which only unbuttoned partly down the front. The top three buttons were undone, revealing a wisp of hair at the lowest point. It tapered in at the waist then flared out slightly over his hips, all worn over the regulation jeans which hugged his thighs just tightly enough. This pair had a pattern of permanent, radiating, pale creases sewn into the seams. He looked and smelled good enough to eat as always. I was trying to picture how to take the shirt off him later. It would have to come off over his head.

'So, where is it we're going to?' I asked.

'It's a lovely little country pub called 'The Old Black Swan'. It does really nice food and it's about half way between Westerbridge and Coreham where I'm renting.'

'So, fifteen minutes between food and bed then.'

'Are we feeling a little impatient?' Steve smiled broadly as he drove, keeping his eyes on the road this time.

'It's just going to be so nice having you all to myself for a while. We always seem to be living on stolen time, even when we have the day to ourselves. There's always that chance someone will come home unexpectedly, like the other week.'

'Never mind; tonight is just for us: no interruptions, no pressure!' he reassured.

I closed my eyes and took a deep breath, then let it out slowly with a deep sigh and settled into the seat as we drove. My whole body began to relax. I hadn't realised how much tension I'd been holding on to, probably ever since the meeting with Mitchell. After a few minutes, the car turned tightly towards the left, circled round and pulled to a stop. Steve was smiling at me when I opened my eyes.

How did I get so lucky?

'Here we are. Feeling hungry?'

'Is that a leading question?' I replied.

'Food first, Miss Taylor.' He smiled to himself.

Steve stepped around the car and opened the door to let me out. The light was beginning to fade, but even so, the old pub looked inviting. There was already an amber glow coming from its little, crooked windows. None of its timber framed, white-painted walls were quite vertical and its red-tiled roof appeared to have given up trying to remain straight years ago. The whole thing exuded an air of old world charm that belonged to a time when life moved more slowly.

He bent forward to kiss me but not as far forward as usual on account of my heels. I wrapped my arms around his neck and kissed him back with passionate promise before he took my hand and led me towards the door.

'I thought this would be the perfect place to wind down a bit over a meal.'

'It's beautiful.'

'Just wait till you see inside; it's like time stopped.'

Steve lifted the latch on the weathered oak door and we stepped through into the bar, ducking to avoid banging our heads on the frame. There wasn't much more headroom inside, although the beamed ceiling lent it a cosy, intimate feel. Despite its age, the whole place felt loved and cared for. The horse brasses that hung around the walls were polished and gleaming, and the smell coming from the kitchen was making my mouth water. The bar was still relatively empty. Thankfully we'd beaten the early evening rush.

Steve spoke briefly to the man behind the bar, who pointed to a table in a quiet alcove.

'What would you like to drink?' he asked, turning towards me again.

'Can I have a lime and soda please?'

'Pint?'

'Yes please.'

'Make that two pints of lime and soda, please,' he informed the barman.

'You don't have to have the same as me, Steve. You can have a beer if you like.'

'The beer in here is very good. In fact, this place is in the Good Pub Guide, but I don't tend to drink when I'm driving, especially since I'm responsible for your well-being tonight and not just my own.'

He put the drinks on the tab and we sat ourselves down at the table. I slid my jacket off and placed it over the back of the chair then picked up the menu.

Steve gave me a look of gentle concern.

'You look nervous.'

Am I? I suppose I am.

'I've never been on an actual date before,' I confessed.

He shrugged his shoulders.

'It's just you and me and some quality time. No one has to stand on ceremony. You didn't go to all that trouble dressing up for tonight because you felt like you had to, did you? Don't get me wrong, you look breathtaking and I'm really proud to be seen in such stunningly beautiful company, but I know it's not how you're usually comfortable dressing.'

'Linda kind of insisted, to be honest. She can be very persuasive. Although dressing up for the occasion has been a huge load of fun. So, do you like what you see?'

His voice dropped an octave, suddenly gaining in gravity.

'Hmm.' His lips parted slightly. 'I certainly do.'

'So are you hungry too, Mr Bowes?'

'Yes, I am! Which reminds me, we need to take a look at the menus and order or we'll be here all night. Lovely as this place is, I think we both have other things on our mind. What do you fancy?'

I looked down at my menu with a smirk.

'Besides the obvious, I think it's a toss-up between the homemade steak and ale pie and the wild boar medallions. What do you think?'

'I had my eye on the steak and ale pie too,' he said. 'Why don't we order one of each and we can both try a bit of the other?'

'That sounds good. I don't mind trying a bit of the other with you. It's worked out pretty well so far.'

Now Steve was grinning from ear to ear.

'Yes, it has, hasn't it?'

He caught the eye of the waitress who came over, pencil poised at the ready. She looked about my age or maybe a little bit older. Thankfully we were far enough away from home for her not to be a pupil at my school. The atmosphere between the two of us must have been palpable because the waitress had become quite rosy-cheeked by the time she finished taking our order.

Steve insisted I give him chapter and verse on the meeting with Mitchell, even though I'd told him some of it the other night. We were still deep in conversation when the waitress arrived with the food.

'Thank you. That smells delicious.' I looked up at her.

She smiled briefly.

'Enjoy your meal'.

As I tucked into my wild boar with creamy sweet potato mash and seasonal vegetables I wondered how many lovers had sat here down the centuries, looking into each other's eyes and thinking the same thoughts of wild longing that were going through my mind right now. Each mouthful was a little slice of heaven.

'Try some of mine,' Steve entreated. A rich, dark and fragrant gravy clung to the tasty morsel balanced on his fork, which was ready and waiting for me.

I leant forward and wrapped my lips slowly around the proffered mouthful, cupping my hand under my chin, just in case stray food should fall down my cleavage and ruin the moment.

Then again, maybe it won't. Thoughts of fruit salad wandered through my mind.

I slid my mouth off the fork, taking the food with me.

'Mm! Delicious!' I announced when I had swallowed it down. 'Would you like to try a taste of mine?'

'Yes please,' he purred.

I cut off a piece, rolled it in the sauce and pressed a little of the mash with it before offering it up to his waiting mouth, unconsciously pressing my tongue against my top lip while he savoured the mouthful I had given him. We continued like that, alternating between what was on our own plates and feeding each other until we had cleared every last bit.

'Satisfied?' he asked.

'Not yet.'

'Shall I ask for the dessert menu? Do you fancy something sweet?'

'Not here.' Just in case Steve was in any doubt about how I wanted to round off my meal, I crooked my finger at him and beckoned him towards me. 'By the way, there's something I think you ought to know.' I leant in even closer and whispered into his ear. 'I'm not wearing any panties.'

He looked wildly into my eyes for a moment then called the waitress over.

'Can we have the bill now please?'

She must have been watching us because her lips were parted and her hands trembled slightly while she totalled everything up.

'Cash or card?' she asked, struggling to get the words out.

'Cash.' He glanced at the slip of paper on the little silver tray and reached for his wallet.

I checked the clutch purse. I checked my jacket. My money was in my other bag and the bag was still in the car. *Damn!*

Steve saw what I was doing and shook his head.

'It's my treat. Don't you dare!'

I didn't protest too much. I felt sure I would find some way to repay his kindness.

Steve put several notes on the tray.

'Keep the change,' he told her.

'Thank you.' The strangled words barely made it out of her mouth. She cleared her throat. 'Have a good evening.' She couldn't look either of us in the eye but couldn't look away either.

'Thank you. We will,' I assured her.

Outside it was dark now except for the floodlights that lit the car park and getting colder too. We slid back into Steve's car as another vehicle pulled in through the entrance. I leant across to kiss Steve but as I did, I noticed who was getting out of the other car.

'Shit! It's Sandra and Craig, two of Mum's old friends.' I ducked down as low as I could across the front seats, with my head in Steve's lap, trying not to be seen.

Steve held me gently in place and I kept my head down until the coast was clear.

'It's okay, they've gone in. That was close but I'm pretty sure they didn't recognise you. I got some pretty dirty looks, though, seeing as I was parked up in a pub car park with a woman's head in my lap.'

I put my hand over my mouth to staunch a nervous giggle and we both broke out into peals of laughter.

'Come on,' he said. 'Let's get out of here before anyone else sees us.'

A few minutes later we pulled up outside a small, modern development of flats. Steve switched off the ignition and killed the lights.

'Here we are, home sweet home. Paradise awaits!'

Inside the first floor flat, everything was new and well appointed. Steve had all the basic furnishings and everything was clean and tidy, it just lacked homeliness; it needed a woman's touch. I stood in the open-plan kitchen and lounge, looking around me.

'It's just a stopgap until I sort things out permanently,' he said. 'A lot of my stuff is still at the old house.'

'With Valentina?'

'Yes. She's not going to trash it or anything; we're not at war. I just haven't got the space here.'

Although I was tempted to ask him about what had gone wrong between them, I thought better of it. I didn't want to ruin the mood. I sat on the sofa while Steve pulled two glasses out of a cupboard and went over to the fridge.

'Glass of wine? White or red?'

'Maybe just one: white, please. You don't have to get me drunk to get me into bed you know.'

'I wasn't planning to.'

'What, get me drunk or get me into bed?'

'Get you drunk. I'm definitely planning on getting you into bed.'

I smiled to myself.

'Good. I was hoping it was that way round.'

He handed me a glass of white wine. It felt cool against my lips, the crisp freshness of it running over my tongue.

'Mm, that's lovely.'

'It's a Chablis. Nice, isn't it? I'll be right back.'

Steve disappeared into the bedroom and reappeared a

minute or two later, blowing out a match and smiling to himself.

'What are you up to now?' I asked. My curiosity and my lack of patience were both getting the better of me.

He put the box of matches down on the table in front of the sofa and took me by the hand.

'Come and see.' Picking up his glass he led me over to the bedroom door.

Dotted around the room were candles of all shapes and sizes, casting a warm, flickering glow and permeating the air with scent. Crisp, new linen covered the neatly made double bed which was scattered with a variety of cushions.

I looked at him, eyes shining in the candlelight.

'It's beautiful. You didn't have to go to so much trouble.'

'I know. You didn't have to either, but we both did, didn't we?' He put his arms around my waist and pulled me close; kissing me with glorious, simple honesty.

I stroked his face with the back of my hand.

'Take me to bed, Steven Bowes.'

I could see a thought crossing his mind and the heated look in his eyes returned.

'Is it true what you said to me in the pub, just before we left?'

'Oh, that! You'll just have to take a look and find out for yourself, won't you?'

Steve kissed me again and with his hands on my hips, lowered himself down until he was kneeling in front of me. He ran his hands slowly down my thighs until they reached the hem of my skirt then looking back up at me and biting his lip, he gradually lifted the material up until it bunched at the apex of my thighs, just covering me. He was looking directly in front of him again now, his eye line level with the object of his desire. Taking one last brief look up at me he lifted the skirt up to my waist and inhaled sharply.

'Oh Rebecca, Rebecca!' His voice was hushed. I could feel the heat of his breath on my skin. His lips brushed the smooth mound just above the cleft of my pussy and he began feathering me with kisses. By now I was breathless with anticipation.

'What do you think?'

'It's beautiful. You're beautiful and you certainly are full of wonderful surprises.'

Delicate fingertips caressed the line of my outer lips and followed the curve that led between my thighs, brushing the soft folds that lay between. His lips continued to administer their worship and he slipped a finger into the wetness inside, giving out a deep moan, at once animal and reverent.

I ran my fingers through his hair and shifted my feet a little further apart, allowing him to slide a second finger inside me. By now I was melting. Right at that moment, all I could feel was an urgent need that only one thing could satisfy. We could take our time later.

'Oh Steve, I want you inside me. Now!' My voice sounded heated, demanding, like it belonged to someone else.

He stood up, producing a condom from the back pocket of his jeans while I fumbled with his belt, all fingers and thumbs in my rush to get to him, but somehow I managed to undo everything and slid his jeans down his thighs. He quickly rolled the condom on and moved closer, tipping me backwards onto the bed, giggling. I hitched the skirt around my waist, lifted my legs and hooked them over his arms, heels waving in mid-air, and without any hesitation, he drove into me in one swift movement.

I cried out, not caring in that moment whether anyone in the neighbouring flats could hear or not.

'Oh yes, Steve! Fuck me! Do it hard!'

He obliged, laying into me with deep, steady strokes that fanned my flames until the inferno had engulfed us both and we threw ourselves at each other with wild abandon. I clung to him tightly, wrapping my legs around him, the heels of my shoes digging into the small of his back. Our mouths sought and found each other, pressed tight, breathless.

Hardly breaking his stride, he moved his body upright and lifted one of my legs, resting my ankle over his shoulder and kissing my lower calf as he drove himself into me, his hips rocking in a relentless rhythm, keeping time with my gasping breath.

I could sense the change in him as his orgasm approached.

'Yes, baby! Come for me,' I implored.

Steve shook his head and gritted his teeth, holding back the inevitable.

'No . . . Not yet . . . I'm taking you with me.'

He was right; I could feel it rising like a tide within. The conflagration was about to become a flood. He leant in towards me again and I held his face in my hands, looking beyond his eyes and deep into his soul. His gaze didn't falter.

My breathing stuttered.

'I'm . . . I'm coming.'

'Oh yes.'

'I'm . . .'

'Yes.'

Both rivers burst their banks together, releasing a deluge that swept away everything in its path. We clung to each other in the swirling waters; each with our head nestled against the other's shoulder and held on for our lives until the floodwaters had passed. Eventually, they subsided, and he lifted his head to look at me. Tears were rolling down my cheeks.

'What's wrong?'

'Nothing's wrong. I'm . . . happy,' I sobbed.

His lips met mine with an urgency that took my breath away again. It was as if they never wanted to let go.

CHAPTER TWELVE

We lay meshed together in the warm, flickering glow of the candlelight, luxuriating in the closeness of each other's bodies. Even though Steve was inside me, we were hardly moving. I lay on my front with Steve on top of me, his legs outside of mine, pressing them tightly together around his stiffness. It wasn't deep like that but the feeling was delectable. Every now and again I playfully tightened the muscles inside me and he would groan softly into my ear.

Steve's arms encircled me, his hands gently squeezing my breasts while he nuzzled softly at the back of my neck. Any last clothing had been dispensed with about half an hour before, shortly after we'd finished ravaging each other like wild things. Now the storm had abated and everything was calm.

'Steve?' I twisted my body and looked round at him over my shoulder.

'Mm-hmm?'

'You know you said I should tell you if there's something I wanted to try?'

'Yes.'

I wasn't quite sure how to put this delicately.

'There's something they often do in porn films.'

He looked amused. That wasn't the reaction I was expecting.

'And what have you been doing watching porn films?'

'If I'm old enough to do it, surely I'm old enough to watch it.' I felt quite indignant. 'Anyway, Linda and I found some. I think they must be Jeff's.'

'I've no idea if they're his; it's not something we've ever discussed. Besides, they do lots of things in porn films; you're going to have to be a bit more specific.'

'I want . . . I want you to . . .'

I heaved a sigh of resignation.

'You're bloody well going to make me say it, aren't you?'

'Of course. How do I know what you want unless you're prepared to tell me? I'm not going to make any assumptions, remember?'

Trying to overcome my awkwardness, I gathered myself. It just felt so taboo, so intimate. I cleared my throat, took a deep breath and looked him in the eyes.

'Steve, I want you to fuck me in the arse.'

There! I said it!

I had thought he might be shocked, but instead he looked at me with the same gentle kindness I'd seen on that first day together.

'Are you sure? It's not everybody's thing.'

'How will I know unless I try it?'

He conceded the point.

'If we do that, I'm going to take it slowly, okay? You can stop me at any time.'

'You make it sound like losing my virginity all over again.'

'In a way, it is. There's also the question of lubrication. I mean, that's hardly been an issue so far has it?' He glanced downwards with a look of appreciation. 'But that generally needs a little, um, assistance. I haven't got any lube; I wasn't expecting to need it, so we'll have to make do with what nature gave us, if you know what I mean.'

I did know. I had seen the movies after all.

Steve released his grip on my legs and as I parted them slightly, he slid himself gently away from me and sat up. Pulling myself up onto all fours, I wiggled my behind provocatively.

'Come on, Mr Bowes. You know you want to!'

For a moment he sat back on his heels, admiring the view.

'How did I ever get so lucky? You're so beautiful, so sexy and so adventurous. You take my breath away.'

He dotted kisses down my spine, following the line south towards the Promised Land; his hands firmly kneading the cheeks of my behind. Steve's fingernails raked the smooth, soft skin of my buttocks, sending tingling chills to every part of me, then brushing his lips against my skin he slid a finger into my vagina and worked it around, scooping up the moisture. Withdrawing it, he circled my anus gently with his fingertip before locating the opening and slipping it inside me. I gave a soft moan.

'How does that feel?' he asked.

'Different. Don't stop.'

He allowed a trail of saliva to run down his finger and slowly inserted it further. I gasped at the sensation. I felt so deliciously invaded.

'And that?'

'Fuck yes!'

With the aid of more saliva, he began to work his finger in and out of me and I reached down to touch my pussy at the same time. My hips seemed to have acquired a life of their own.

Then without warning the finger was gone and his tongue took its place, swirling and probing with delectable urgency. I pressed my fists into the soft pillow, gasping and moaning at his tongue's intimate ministration. Then the finger was back, slipping in and out. It was followed by another, filling me, testing me. It felt so forbidden yet so right.

'Oh my God, Steve! Do it! Please!'

He positioned himself behind me and I could feel him poised, pressing against my delicate opening. With great care, he eased forwards. I could feel myself yielding to him until he was just inside me. I clutched the bedclothes tightly in my fists.

'Relax Rebecca, please. I don't want to hurt you.'

I released my grip and lay my hands flat on the bed, willing myself to release the tension in my body despite the strange, alien sensation, and he inched himself all the way into me.

'Oh fuck!' I found myself sobbing softly into the pillow.

He halted, not daring to move.

'Are you alright? Do you want me to stop?'

I wasn't sure if my reply was going to be a request or an order but without any warning, the tigress, who up until then had been prowling in the shadows waiting for her moment, took command and answered for me. She bared her teeth and snarled at him.

'Fuck me! Just fuck me!'

He obeyed, although moving slowly at first, gently easing himself in and out.

'Oh yes, Steve . . . yes.' I abandoned myself to the feeling, somewhere between discomfort and pleasure. Fuck it felt tight, but good, oh so good.

Gradually he picked up the pace and we both gained in confidence, losing ourselves in the moment. With waves of intense sensation washing over me, I surrendered myself totally; unable to imagine a way I could have given myself to him any more completely than this.

We quickened, locked together in an intimate rhythm, undulating as one. I reached down, finding the wetness between my thighs once again and slipped my fingers knuckle-deep inside myself. The palm of my hand pressed against my clitoris as the tempo of our passion intensified. I ground myself against him with a fervent need each time he plunged himself into me, willing it to become ever deeper, harder, more forceful, melting us into one writhing, pulsing whole.

Although I could feel the orgasm building, I was unable to speak, my breath coming in short stabs as I fought for air. And then it hit me like a silent detonation that shook my whole body. I buried my face in the pillow, every muscle tensing simultaneously before disintegrating in a shower of sparks. The firework exploded, igniting Steve who followed seconds later. We collapsed together in a sweating, panting heap of arms and legs and skin and spent passion.

'Oh my God, Rebecca! I don't think I've ever . . .' His voice trailed away, lost for the means to express whatever it was he was thinking and feeling.

I eased myself off his fading erection and turned towards him, touching his face. There were no words. In that moment, none were necessary. I had willingly given Steve the last vestige of my innocence. We lay there for what must have been a long time, hands caressing each other's skin. The tigress stretched out, licking her paws and purring softly from somewhere deep down.

'Guys like that, don't they?' I asked eventually.

'Quite a few of them, yes.'

'Do you?'

He raised both eyebrows and blew air slowly through his lips, lifting himself up onto his elbows.

'What do you think? Anyway, more importantly, did you?'

'I don't know.'

He looked crestfallen, disappointed like he'd somehow let me down.

Maybe I should quit teasing and put him out of his agony.

I looked up at him, shiny-eyed and moist-lipped in the candle light, resting my hands on his arms.

'It looks like we're just going to have to do it again to make sure, aren't we?'

He grinned and descended on me.

-0-

It was the small hours of the morning before we finally reached a standstill. We lay there, exhausted and sated, arms resting on each other's bodies, our breathing falling into a steady cadence. Neither of us could move another muscle.

The tigress curled up and closed her eyes, her tail twitching from time to time as she drifted into unconsciousness. She was content.

CHAPTER THIRTEEN

I could hear Steve breathing slowly and steadily next to me. Although I had rolled over in my sleep, his arm still draped protectively over me, or was he just holding me close? I wasn't sure. I opened my eyes and looked around me in the light that shone through the bedroom curtains.

Our neatly arranged little love nest didn't look quite so neat anymore. The scatter cushions which had been so perfectly placed on the bed when we first came in, now lived up to their name and had been flung to all corners of the room, along with our clothes. Most of the candles had burned themselves out. Only a few of the larger ones still guttered and flickered in the draught that blew in between the curtains.

The window must have been slightly open all night. Heaven alone knew what Steve's neighbours thought of all the noisy lovemaking that went on until the early hours of the morning. I was almost surprised we hadn't crashed through into the flat below at times. Jesus, I ached. All the details of our night together were coming back to me and I smiled to myself, even though part of me still didn't quite believe some of the things we'd been doing. I might suffer today but I wouldn't have missed a second of it.

The wine bottle and the two glasses beside the bed were empty. My mouth felt dry but my head was surprisingly clear despite the fact that I didn't usually drink much wine. Sometimes we would have a glass with Sunday lunch at home, so it wasn't as if I'd never drunk it before, but still . . . although if I felt a bit dehydrated it was probably more down to exertion than alcohol.

I carefully lifted Steve's hand and slid myself off the bed, not wishing to disturb his sleep. He looked so peaceful, but I needed the bathroom. I slipped Steve's shirt over my head, padded my way to the room next door and looked in the mirror. Linda's immaculate make-up and hair-do were looking a little the worse for wear although they'd held up well, considering everything they'd been through.

By the time I came out, I had removed the make-up and let my hair down. The plait had started to come undone anyway, but still, it took ages to remove all the hair-grips. Linda had obviously anticipated some vigorous treatment because, given the number of them that were in there, she hadn't intended everything to come apart in a hurry. As always, I could rely on her to consider all eventualities. I slipped the hair-grips into the front pocket of my bag, put the kettle on and poured myself a glass of water.

I was busy popping tea bags into two mugs and humming a little tune to myself when I felt two hands on my hips and heard Steve's voice, close to my ear, soft and seductive.

'Good morning, Miss Taylor. You're up bright and early considering you had such a busy night.'

I turned to face him and put my arms around his neck.

'Hmm . . . Well, Mr Bowes, it seems I have you to thank for that. As for getting up early; I needed the loo and I didn't want to disturb you, although I was about to bring you in a cup of tea. It is nearly seven and I'd hate to think I made you late for work. I wouldn't want to get you into trouble, now would I?'

Whatever salacious thought had started behind his eyes was now trying to burn its way through.

'I think we're already way beyond getting into a little bit of trouble, don't you? The cup of tea sounds good, though.'

I turned back towards the kettle and poured the hot water over the tea bags. While I finished making the teas, his hands snaked their way up my thighs and underneath the hem of the shirt.

'Mm, still no panties! What am I going to do with you?'

'Steven Bowes, you're unstoppable.'

'I can't help what you do to me. I told you that.'

I held out the mug to him.

'Tea first, then maybe a slice of toast and some boiled eggs too. In the meantime, I'll try and work out if my nether regions haven't packed up and buggered off on holiday without me or gone on strike due to overwork.'

When we left the flat at half past eight, we'd had our tea with boiled eggs and toast then finished up with a bit of 'sausage and muffin' for good measure. Steve stopped the car outside Linda's house and pulled up the handbrake with a rapid series of clicks.

'Here we are. All back, safe and sound.'

'Even if we are a little bit knackered!' There was a little

hint of smugness in my voice.

'True! I've got to try and keep my eyes open in front of a screen in the studio all day.'

'And I think I'll sleep for a week. Thank you for a lovely evening and a wonderful night. Now I need to find a quiet corner to collapse in.'

Steve looked like the cat that got the cream.

'I don't think either of us will forget any of it in a hurry. I'll speak to you later, okay?'

What started as a quick kiss goodbye rapidly became something hotter, more passionate. Despite not wanting to let go, I tore myself away.

'You'll be late for work if we're not careful. We don't want Jeff getting annoyed. I'll call you later on when the coast is clear.'

I watched him drive off with a little wave in the rear view mirror and made my way up the drive to Linda's house. I felt surprisingly light of step, despite everything.

Linda was reclining on her bed, reading as usual when I went up to her room. She looked up from her book as I put my bag on the floor and sat down rather carefully on the edge of the bed. I tried not to, but I couldn't help wincing slightly.

Linda gave me a strange look and then realisation dawned across her face. Her jaw dropped.

'He didn't?'

'Didn't what?' I pretended not to know what she meant.

'You know exactly what, you brazen hussy.' She was hooked.

Unable to hold my excitement back any longer, I confessed everything.

Linda's eyes grew wider and wider. It was her turn to pretend to be shocked.

'And there's you, not even seventeen till the end of next week and already you're doing things that would make a seasoned whore blush.' There was a glint of humour in her eyes. 'Honestly, you're such a slut!'

'It takes one to know one, you kinky bitch!' I replied. Having exchanged compliments we fell back on the bed, laughing. 'You know what, though? It's almost like it's not me doing those things. Something animal takes over. I've been getting these dreams where I'm a tiger and . . . well, it's like it's her, not me sometimes, particularly last night.'

Linda propped herself up on her elbows.

'You know what it sounds like to me? You identify that aspect of yourself as a tiger and why not? I mean, it's a very good analogy, isn't it? You're certainly a bit of a wildcat in the sack! What you need to do is to accept her as a part of yourself and make friends with her.'

Sometimes I forgot she was studying psychology. She'd probably read all of the A-level material and more already, and she wasn't even half way through the course.

'Perhaps you should give her a name. That'll make it easier. You need to own it, baby!' She was sitting bolt upright now. 'What do you want to call her? How about, Gertrude?'

I rocked with laughter.

'Or Matilda?'

'Now you're being ridiculous!'

'Or Sadie? Yes. Sadie!'

I stopped laughing.

'Sadie?' I rolled the name around in my head. 'You know what? It suits her. Sadie: it's got the sensuality and the power and the independence. I like it.'

Somewhere in the back of my mind, a distantly remembered Beatles song was playing.

'It's like she is what she is, and she doesn't care what anyone thinks of her,' continued Linda. 'She follows her instincts and her desires without ever apologising for it. She could be a really powerful emblem for your sexual side, your feminine power.'

I was amazed.

'You know what? I think you're onto something there. You've hit the nail on the head.'

Linda sat back again with a self-satisfied look on her face.

'I love being right.'

'Oh, don't I know it!'

Now Linda appeared to be turning something over in her mind.

'Are you still using condoms?'

'Of course! What else?'

'I just thought you'd have sorted something a bit more long-term out by now seeing as the two of you have a bit of a regular thing going on.'

'There'd be too many awkward questions. I didn't want to risk getting Steve into hot water. Besides, I just felt a bit embarrassed about it.'

Linda looked surprised at my naivety.

'Oh, sweetie!'

There were only two people in the world who called me things like that, Linda and my mother.

'As long as you're over thirteen they don't have to

involve your parents anyway. Who you're doing it with is of no relevance. If you understand the information and they don't think you're being abused, there's no problem. This is the twenty-first century, honey. You think we're the first girls in our year to start having a sex life? Far from it! Some of them started ages ago, well before they were sixteen. The boys, on the other hand, are a different story; most of them were later starters. Us girls mature quicker. Boys in their mid teens make a lot of noise about things and some of them are full of bravado, but give them a real member of the opposite sex to handle and most of them wouldn't know where to start.'

'So who were the girls doing it with, then?'

'Older guys of course, by which I mean sixth-formers or the few boys who were a bit more together,' she appeared to be weighing her words, 'or each other, perhaps?' She looked at me with one eyebrow raised. 'Not many of them are screwing blokes ten years older, though.' If she'd been wearing her glasses instead of her contacts, she'd have been looking trenchantly over the top of them at me. 'Anyway, the point is, go and get it sorted, then the two of you can relax about it a bit more.'

'I didn't realise they'd be as understanding about it as that. It would be nice not to have to bother with condoms. We were talking about it a little while back.' It could only have been a week or two ago, but it felt like a lifetime.

'Think about it,' she said. 'The age of consent exists mainly to protect the vulnerable but if somebody is going to do it anyway, and let's face it, many do, then it's better to dish out contraception than deal with the fallout of teenage pregnancies, and you're well beyond the legal age of consent now anyway, so it's not an issue, is it?' She looked at me kindly. 'It's the holidays. You've got the time on your hands, so make an appointment. Why not give Steve a nice surprise? If you start on the pill you'll be fully covered inside a week, depending on when in your cycle you start taking it. It worked for me. Plus, even if you're still using condoms, it's extra insurance. You don't want any accidents right now, do you?'

'Oh, God no! I'm not ready for that yet. I've got a career to focus on and a lot of living to do first.'

'Well then, that's that settled!'

A thought crossed my mind.

'They don't have to examine you, do they?'

'Maybe, but probably not. Why?'

'It's just that I'm a bit . . . tender down there at the moment. I'd better leave it a couple of days. The doctor might think I'm being abused.'

'That's not abuse it's just vigorous, no-holds-barred sex.'

'No holes barred?' I wasn't sure if I'd heard her right.

Linda chuckled.

'Well, maybe that too by the sound of it. I think you've spent too much time reading the blurb on the covers of Jeff's porno movies. I see your point, though. Considering all the stuff you got up to last night you must be glowing like a beacon. Why don't you make an appointment for the end of the week sometime?'

'I will. On the subject of porn films: they've disappeared. I think Jeff must have realised they've been disturbed and moved them. Nobody's said anything, though.'

'Well, they wouldn't, would they? Can you imagine that conversation over the breakfast table?'

Her voice dropped an octave in imitation of Jeff.

'Hey Avril, you haven't seen my copies of 'Diving Miss Daisy', 'Nympho Sluts 2: The Second Cumming' or 'Whipped and Fucked', have you? I fancied a wank this morning.'

Shock turned to amusement as I pictured the scene. Linda's voice went up, this time mimicking Mum.

'No, darling. Maybe the kids have borrowed them.'

'Stop it! Stop it!' I crumbled into laughter.

Linda lowered her voice again.

'Oh well, that's alright then. You haven't got them have you, Beccs? Let me have them back when you're finished, will you? Just make sure you wipe the covers down first.'

There were tears were rolling down my face but Linda was relentless. My sides ached and I was finding it hard to breathe. Linda's impression of Jeff was surprisingly good.

'Oh Linda, you're impossible!'

'On the contrary sweetie; I'm highly probable.' She winked. 'In fact, I'm almost certain.'

CHAPTER FOURTEEN

'Happy Birthday, darling!' Mum held out the obligatory morning cup of tea. 'When you're ready, come down to the lounge.'

I threw a pair of jeans and a tee-shirt on and made my way down to find Mum, Rob and Jeff waiting with conspiratorial smiles. Rob was the first to hand me a card and a little gift bag, inside which was a bottle of perfume.

'I thought you might want some more. I noticed yours was getting a bit low,' he said.

I kissed him on the cheek.

'Thank you. It's one of my favourites.'

'I thought it was.' He looked quietly pleased with himself.

Jeff reached around behind the sofa and pulled out a long, brown leather case with 'Gibson' stamped along it in gold lettering. I knew what it was straight away. He placed it gently on the coffee table and stood back, putting his arm around Mum. My eyes welled up as I knelt down, unlatched the lid and lifted it. I glanced up at them. They were smiling.

'This is your main present, sweetheart.' said Mum. 'We thought you'd be ready for one of these, seeing as you're about to turn professional.'

I looked at the electric guitar and ran my fingers across its rounded, feminine curves. The gleaming, chromed hardware and pickups perfectly accented the halo of red around the edge of the body, topped with exquisitely figured maple. Beneath the lacquer the striped, golden grain of the wood spread like fingers, reaching out either side of the centre line to caress the cream-coloured binding which wrapped around the body and hugged the edges of the neck.

I looked back up at them, eyes still shining.

'It's a Les Paul Standard, a vintage reissue just like the ones we were looking at in London.'

Jeff nodded.

'It's shorter scale length than a Strat, so it'll suit your hands better. The richer sound will suit what you do better too.'

I picked it up and turned it over in my fingers. The backs of the mahogany body and neck were stained a translucent, cherry red. It felt reassuringly weighty, solid but hopefully not so heavy as to be uncomfortable when played for long periods. I couldn't wait to show Steve, although maybe he'd seen it already. We had lots of electric guitars in the studio and I'd played most of them at one time or another, but good instruments though they were, they were workhorses. This one was different; it was truly a thing of beauty. It felt alive to the touch; a living, breathing, sensual work of art.

'Of course,' said Jeff as I placed the guitar reverently back into its case, 'on its own, it's no good without something to play it through.'

He pulled back the curtains that covered the bay

window at the front of the lounge, revealing a guitar amplifier with 'Marshall' written in familiar white lettering across the front. Half the bands that came through the studio used them. It sat on top of a matching cabinet with four speakers lurking menacingly behind the grille like caged animals.

'It's top of the range, all valve,' Jeff explained.

'And it's going to live in the studio,' Mum insisted. 'It nearly rattled my fillings loose when Steve put it through its paces.'

So he is in on it. We shall have to have words when I see him tomorrow.

'Oh my God, thank you!' I bounced over and hugged all three of them.

'Make sure you keep tonight free,' said Mum. 'We're all going out to a restaurant.'

'Linda's still coming over this afternoon, isn't she?'

'Yes! In fact, she's coming with us this evening.'

This was news; Linda hadn't said anything about it. There must have been all kinds of plotting and scheming going on behind my back.

'Oh, and I'm staying over at Linda's again tomorrow.'

'Again?' Mum's voice was gentle, but I still felt uncomfortable. 'You've been staying over at hers quite a lot lately.'

I took a slightly deeper breath than usual.

'We're going to be busy with exams soon. After that, I'm expecting to be working on music for much of the time, and I don't even know if I'll be staying on in the sixth form, do I? We're just making the most of things while we can.'

Good recovery. Chalk one up to team Rebecca. Mum

214

pursed her lips and nodded.

I spent the morning playing my new guitar. Mum let me off using my amplifier in the house just this once because Jeff and Steve were still working in the studio before relocating Whispered Scream's album project to London the next week.

Linda arrived looking quietly excited while Mum, Rob and I were just finishing our lunch. I put my plate in the dishwasher and we headed up to my room.

'For a boy of his age your brother's getting quite a physique these days, isn't he?' she said on our way up the stairs. 'Not bad for fifteen.'

'Yes, I suppose he is developing; it must be all the sports. They start building the gym soon, next week I think. There'll be no stopping him then. I think he'll live in there.'

She sat down on the bed and held out the gift bag she had been carrying.

'Happy Birthday! Come on, open up!'

Inside, there were two neatly wrapped little parcels. I picked up the more rounded of the two and began peeling back the brightly coloured paper. The amusement must have registered on my face when I realised what it was.

'I figured you'd find a use for some lube given your sense of adventure. It's one you can use with or without condoms.'

'Thank you. I'll keep it handy. Steve did go and get some after last week but it won't last forever at this rate.'

I reached for the second package. This one was more rectangular and fitted into my open palm. Linda's eyes were shining with some secret delight as I began feeling for the edge of the tape. Inside the box was a smooth, purple object not much bigger than a thumb. Its tactile, soft plastic contours led down to a small button at the blunt end.

'It's a vibrator,' she said. Her voice was matter-of-fact, but seeing the bemused expression I must have had on my face, she clearly felt the need to qualify herself. 'I know it's not very big, especially since you seem to have been a bit spoiled in that department, you lucky girl, but it's not the size that matters, it's what you do with it, and this little beauty . . . well, let's just say it's got a myriad of uses and you can take it anywhere with you.' She gave a snort of wry amusement. 'If you use it around the back, though, for fuck's sake don't let go. They can disappear if you're not careful. That could be an embarrassing trip to A and E asking them to retrieve it.'

We both chuckled, although a part of me recoiled in horror at the thought of having to explain that little hospital visit to my family.

'Try it on the end of your nose if you're not convinced. Go on, I dare you.'

When I pressed the button, it buzzed to life. I rested it against the tip of my nose.

'Holy shit!' I blurted out with a nervous laugh.

'See what I mean? Surprisingly powerful, isn't it? Size isn't everything.'

Linda proceeded to illuminate me over the possibilities this innocuous little object opened up. I couldn't wait to try some of them out, with or without Steve. After all, I did get a little frustrated when we couldn't see each other. Once I was back in school and he was working in London with Jeff, we weren't going to have the freedom we'd enjoyed lately. Perhaps Linda had already thought about that.

'I'm sorry it isn't much,' she said.

'What makes you think I'd be disappointed? I'm going to thoroughly enjoy both presents. Besides, it was you who footed most of the bill for the dress and the shoes.'

'Aye, that's true enough I suppose.'

I put my arms around her in a big hug.

'Thank you, for everything. I got you a little surprise too.' Reaching into my bedside drawer I pulled out a rectangular box, wrapped up in shiny, gold paper. 'I saw this and thought of you. I couldn't resist.'

She tore off the paper and looked inside the box.

'It's a mug?'

'It is. Look at the design.'

Linda took it out of the box and realisation dawned. She grinned. There was a cartoon on the side of two women who even looked a bit like us, leaning towards each other and clinking their glasses together. Written above them were the words 'You'll always be my friend. You know too much'.

'That makes two of us,' Linda said.

If I hadn't known her better, I would have said she was welling up, although if there actually were tears, she choked them back before they could make their presence too obvious.

'You realise I'm going to have to get one of these for you too, so we have a matching pair! So what else did you get for your birthday?'

'Come downstairs and I'll show you.'

I led her to the coffee table in the lounge and slowly opened the lid of the guitar case.

'Wow! I mean, I don't know much about guitars but that is gorgeous. It's so you.'

'How do you mean?'

'Just look at it: it's one sexy beast; it's got curves in all the right places and look at the grain in the wood; it even looks a bit like tiger stripes.'

'It does too. I hadn't thought of it like that. And plug it into this thing,' I pointed to the Marshall, 'and it sounds frickin' awesome!'

'How many controls on the front? What do they all do?'

I patiently explained them all but Linda was still scratching her head.

'I think I understand the tone controls, but I'm afraid you lost me at the difference between gain and volume.'

'It's straightforward really. Gain determines how hard the preamp circuitry is pushed, drive controls the amount of harmonic distortion that the preamp valves produce and volume controls the output level to the power amp. Master volume controls the output from the power amp. Once you've got it sounding right, you can store the settings in the memory. This is basically four preamps in one box, each with three different drive profiles. Although the possibilities are endless, it's not rocket science when you get used to using it.'

'And you reckon I'm the clever one? Have you listened to yourself lately? Basically, when you turn them up it all gets louder, right?'

I sighed and gave up trying to explain the difference.

'Basically, yes.'

'And why do they insist on using something as outdated as valves alongside all the modern stuff built in?'

'Because they sound good, that's why! Nothing beats valves for guitar, particularly when you want to give it some hell. For rockier stuff, there's nothing else like it: so warm and musical sounding. Anyway, why are you so interested in that all of a sudden?'

'I'm not really, but you are. You're so passionate and so knowledgeable.'

'I'm lucky I guess. I've been fortunate to have learned from some of the best.'

Linda gave me her quizzical look.

'I think the apprentice may yet become the master.'

'Hardly!' I protested. 'I don't think you ever stop learning when it comes to music, though. I mean, I sing and write songs and play the guitar reasonably well, but I'll never play like someone who has devoted their whole life to that one thing. That's where a good lead player comes in; they're specialists.'

'So you're going to need the right band behind you then.'

I nodded.

'That's exactly what Mitchell's saying. Once my exams are out of the way we'll be in a position to recruit a band for playing live and in the studio, rather than just using session players who come and go. He thinks it's one of the things that will help to give it more . . . 'stylistic integrity' I think he called it. And you know what? I think he's right. You get a different vibe from musicians who are used to playing alongside each other all the time.'

'Come on then, give us a tune.'

I played her some of the song Steve and I had been working on, although Linda seemed more focussed on the words than the music.

'Oh, that's filthy hot! I like it.'

'It's not quite all there yet. There are some ideas I want to go through with Steve so we can finish putting the demo together. It's a bit of a joint project.'

'It takes two to tango, eh?'

'Exactly!'

CHAPTER FIFTEEN

Linda had styled my hair, this time in a more straightforward plait which hung loosely at the back of my neck, and I decided to wear my grey dress again. I'd managed to sneak it through the wash without Mum noticing. It had needed it. Thankfully the fabric shrugged off stains well and it looked like new again.

Mum stopped in her tracks when I came downstairs.

'You look amazing, honey. Where did the dress come from? I haven't seen that one before.'

I could feel Linda glowing with pride behind me.

'It was a present from Linda, the shoes too.'

Jeff appeared in the doorway, keys in hand.

'Wowee! Look at you all grown up!' He glanced towards Mum. 'Is everyone ready to go?'

On the way, Rob, Linda and I sat in the back of the Range Rover with Mum and Jeff upfront. Rob looked awkward sitting next to Linda during the twenty-minute journey, glancing across at her legs from time to time but trying not to be noticed. She seemed oblivious, but I had a feeling she wasn't. Despite wearing quite a short dress she kept crossing and uncrossing her long limbs, offering him the occasional, tantalising glimpse higher up her thighs. I don't think the poor boy had ever seen anything quite like it. His eyes were popping out on stalks.

When we pulled up outside our destination, the 'La Bella Ragazza' looked both inviting and intimidating at the same time. I wasn't used to going anywhere so swish. Pleated, burgundy blinds surrounded each window of the restaurant, through which I could just make out figures within, sitting at tables. The empty ones closer to the window were laid with pristine white tablecloths and napkins neatly folded into fans at each place. Rows of gleaming cutlery framed the settings and a row of wine glasses of different sizes and shapes stood guard behind them like a line of soldiers on parade.

We stepped out onto the pavement and stood at the front of the restaurant while Jeff parked the car around the side. When we all went in together with Mum and Jeff leading the way, I could barely see past them. Everything seemed unusually quiet. As I stepped through the door, they parted in front of me. The room erupted into cheers and the lights came up. I clapped my hand over my mouth.

The first faces I spotted were those of my grandparents who were sitting closest to me.

'Nanna! Pappy!' I squealed.

They stood up as I ran forward, and I flung my arms around them. Then I noticed the rest of the smiling faces in the room. Amongst the sea of family and friends were Linda's parents, Jeff's parents, Mum's friend Sandra and her husband Craig, Jayne and Sophie our friends from school, and Steve. For a moment I was completely thrown.

Steve. There was so much I wanted to ask him but I

couldn't, not right now.

I spent the next fifteen minutes greeting everybody and being wished a happy birthday more times than I could count. We were ushered to our tables by the head waiter just before the antipasti arrived. I knew which chair was mine; there was a heart-shaped, helium-filled balloon with '17' on it, tied to the back.

In the middle of each table lay colourful platters of cured ham, salami and other cold meats, olives and peppers, artichoke hearts, cheeses, flatbreads, and what looked like chopped tomatoes with herbs. That was just the first course.

A team of smartly dressed waiters came round and began filling glasses with wine. I was surprised when they filled mine. Mum leant across the table towards me.

'Happy birthday, sweetheart! It's a restaurant so you're allowed it.'

People were already beginning to spark up conversations while they filled their starter plates from the bewildering selection. I was grateful that Mum and Jeff weren't sitting next to Brian and Loretta Maloney. I shuddered to think about what would happen if they got talking about my overnight stays or lack of them.

Steve caught my eye and smiled. I wanted to talk to him, but there was no option but to bide my time. I could see that he felt the same. Pappy was sitting next to him and already had him well and truly monopolised.

'I hear you've had a big hand in teaching Rebecca to play the guitar amongst other things.'

'I helped out, yes. I can't take all the credit.'

'I think you're being modest. Avril says you've devoted a great deal of time and effort towards helping her develop her skills.'

I nearly choked on a stuffed olive.

'Are you alright, sweetheart?' Mum asked.

I cleared my throat.

'Yes, I'm fine. It just went down the wrong way.'

Every now and then, Steve was looking at me out of the corner of his eye while he talked with my granddad.

'It's been a pleasure, really. Rebecca's such a quick learner. She's got an abundance of natural talent and she's always looking to try out something new. She's blessed with an insatiable desire to push back boundaries all the time.'

I'm going to fucking kill him!

He was getting into his stride now.

'To be honest, there are times when I think I've learned as much from her as she has from me.'

That's it, you're dead!

He must have been struggling to conceal his mirth by this stage. I was finding it hard not to turn a delicate shade of beetroot.

Pappy looked at Steve warmly.

'Well, we're all very grateful. Rebecca wouldn't be in the same position she's in today without you.'

How right you are, Pappy. We certainly had managed to get into some interesting positions.

I kept my composure by focussing on making a little edible construction out of flatbread, salami and salad leaves, before taking a big bite to hide my smirk. Steve turned his attention back to his Bruschetta. At least he couldn't say anything else incriminating if he had his mouth full.

I'd like to give you something else to do with that clever mouth, Steven Bowes.

Although Linda was sitting with Jayne and Sophie, she glanced across in my direction. She'd obviously overheard the conversation too. I kept a straight face and took a sip of my Pinot Grigio.

Rob had a sour look about him. He seemed envious that I was now allowed to drink alcohol with a meal in a restaurant while he still had to make do with a Coke. His time would come. I had the sneaking feeling he was going to be more of a beer man than a wine buff, though.

After the antipasti, I took the opportunity to visit the little girls' room before the main course came. I was coming out again when I met Steve heading the other way down the narrow corridor.

'Oh good, I'm glad I caught you,' he said cheerily.

'You might not be in a minute. What was that conversation with Pappy all about?' I asked him in an urgent whisper.

'Your granddad was just asking me about your guitar playing.'

'You know very well you were talking about more than that. Right now I could slap you. You must enjoy living dangerously because Pappy may look like a sweet old man, but if he knew half the things we've been up to he'd flipping well shoot you.'

'Perhaps it's just as well for me that he's blissfully unaware then, although I know what you're saying. Just like the rest of your family, there are no flies on him.'

The door from the restaurant opened and we looked round as my uncle Jim squeezed past us on his way to the gents. I waited for him to disappear before carrying on.

'Anyway, how come you're here? You didn't say

anything.'

'How could I not come? I wanted to be here and besides, having been invited I could hardly say no or it would have looked odd.' I opened my mouth to speak, but Steve continued. 'As for not saying anything about tonight, what kind of a shit would I be if I'd spoiled your birthday surprise?'

I softened.

'Are we still on for working in the studio tomorrow morning and going over to your place later?'

'Of course! I'll give you your birthday present then. I don't think we'll get any time tonight and I'd rather wait until I've got you to myself.'

The door opened again and Nanna came past. I smiled at her. She smiled sweetly back at me before disappearing into the ladies.

'Although I'm desperate to see what it is, I think you're right. We're not going to get any peace right now.'

'Nine o'clock tomorrow morning then. I won't be late. I can't wait to give it to you.'

I raised one eyebrow at him.

Steve realised what he'd said and backpedalled rapidly.

'The present, the present! Honestly, I don't know who's worse; you or me.'

Jim came out of the toilets and sidled past us again. Steve's eyes sparkled with their now familiar mischief.

'Till the morning then.'

We stole a quick kiss and headed back into the restaurant. He held the door open for me and gave me a brief smile on our way through. We were just in time; the main course was arriving at the tables.

I retook my seat facing Mum and a plate magically appeared in front of me. Nestled on a bed of pasta with a name I couldn't pronounce were sautéed chicken and asparagus pieces in a tomato, cream and parmesan sauce with what looked like mozzarella on top. It looked and smelled amazing.

It was wonderful to see all my friends and family, relaxed and enjoying themselves. The wine kept flowing, as did the conversation. There were at least a dozen exchanges in full swing all around the room. In the midst of it all, Mum's friend Sandra occasionally looked across the restaurant at Steve with a peculiar expression. I wondered if she recognised him from the pub. She didn't seem to be staring at me so hopefully, she hadn't made the connection. Nonetheless, I shifted a little uneasily on my seat.

When the dessert cart arrived, we were all spoiled for choice. The hard part was deciding what to have from the colourful, mouth-watering selection in front of us. By then even Rob was in a surprisingly talkative mood, chattering nineteen to the dozen with Linda, Jayne and two of our cousins. He looked so grown-up all of a sudden.

Then, when the coffee and liqueurs came round, the lights dimmed and a glow appeared in the kitchen doorway. Two waiters wheeled in a large, iced cake, sitting on a trolley covered with a white tablecloth. Everybody sang 'Happy Birthday' and the trolley stopped in front of me. I looked around at the sea of smiling faces and paused to make a wish, then taking a deep breath blew out all the candles in one sweep to a round of applause. I couldn't believe all this was for me, and my wish . . . my wish was for everyone, even though I kept it to myself. The cake disappeared back into the kitchen then reappeared as neat slices in front of each person a few minutes later.

By the time we all spilt out into the cool night air I couldn't have eaten another thing and I was feeling pleasantly fuzzy round the edges. Throughout the meal, every time I'd looked at my wine glass it was miraculously full again. Everybody said their goodbyes and we clambered, tired and happy, into the Range Rover, all except Linda who returned home with her parents.

Ryan! Ryan hadn't been there. He must have gone back to university to prepare for the up and coming term or maybe to see one of his lady friends. Somehow I felt slightly cheated. I had no idea when he would be back next. I was still staring blankly out of the window when we drove away.

Mum looked round at me from the front seat.

'So, have you had a nice birthday?'

I reined my thoughts back in.

'The best, thank you. It's been amazing. I'm so lucky.' I stretched and yawned, flexing my shoulders back. 'I'm tired, though. It's been a long day.'

CHAPTER SIXTEEN

Steve was his usual upbeat self when he poked his head around the door of the kitchen.

'Good morning!' He looked around and his voice became more conspiratorial. 'Are all the others out?'

'Yes. Mum's taken Rob to one of his matches. Jeff's off running some errand or other. It's just you, me and Rolo.' Rolo lifted his head up off his paws at the mention of his name and looked at me expectantly. 'Even Fluffy is out hunting somewhere in the fields and hasn't been seen since first thing this morning.'

'Good, then I've got something for you.' He produced a small parcel with a shiny silver bow on top from the pocket of his jacket. 'It's only a little thing so don't get too excited.'

I peeled back the paper to reveal a square, flat, dark blue box and lifted the lid slightly, taking a peek. There was a glint of gold coming from within.

'You didn't have to . . .'

'You don't know what it is yet. Take a proper look.'

Lifting the lid right off this time, I looked at the gold anklet strung with little stars, teasing it around with the tip of my finger before kissing him on the cheek, eyes shining.

'It's beautiful, thank you!'

'Here, let me help you put it on.'

I lifted one foot up onto a stool at the breakfast bar. Steve placed the fine, gold chain around my ankle and clipped it into place, his fingers lingering delightfully on my skin.

'There! That looks lovely. Oh, and I also got you this. Hopefully, it will all make sense.'

He held out the large envelope he'd been carrying. Inside was a colourful, printed card with 'Star Certificate' written across the top in large letters. Maybe he could see that I didn't quite understand.

'I had a star named after you,' he explained. 'Somewhere out there is a star which is now called Rebecca. The coordinates are on the certificate. I'll show you how to find it after dark if the sky is clear enough.'

'I didn't even know you could do that.'

I looked again. This time I noticed the message at the bottom of the certificate.

Someday soon you're going to be a star, but you're already a star to me.
I hope it always shines brightly for you.
Happy 17ᵗʰ Birthday, Steve

I tried to swallow but the lump in my throat prevented me.

'Even though I'm so lucky to have the opportunities I do and to be as loved as I am, that's still got to be one of the sweetest things ever. Thank you.'

I wrapped my arms around his neck, held him close and kissed him, then kissed him again. I wanted him. I wanted him now, but that would have to wait. We had work to do. I pulled back and cleared my throat, patting him on the chest.

'I'll thank you properly later. For the moment, though, we've got a song to finish.'

'I've had some thoughts about that.' Steve was clearly on a mission too. 'I've got more ideas to help develop the arrangement.'

'And I've expanded the lyrics,' I added.

We spent the morning in the studio. By lunchtime the backing tracks were near enough complete and vocal parts had been recorded. We had ourselves a song, at least to demo standard. The problem was we still didn't know what to do with it without involving Jeff. It sounded good, though; we both thought so.

Nobody else had come back so we grabbed a bite to eat, took Rolo for a walk, then left for Steve's place. I sent Linda a text on the way there.

> Me
> Going straight to Steve's. You still
> OK to cover me?
> 2:12 pm

I settled into the seat and looked across at Steve while he drove. Every so often he would glance my way and smile. My phone beeped.

> Linda
> Hiya Slut. No problem. Have fun. Don't do anything I wouldn't do. ;-)
> Kinky Bitch
> 2:16 pm

I had to reply. I couldn't resist it.

> Me
> I guess that leaves my options open then. XX
> Slut / Sadie
> 2:17 pm

I knew when we'd arrived at Steve's, even with my eyes closed. By now I could follow every bend in the road.

Steve hung his jacket up on the hook just inside the door and went to the fridge to fix us both a cold drink. I flopped down on the sofa. From where I was sitting I could see a stack of guitar cases I hadn't noticed before. Maybe he'd been moving things around. I couldn't think where else in the flat he had room for them.

He slipped his iPod into its docking station, tapped the screen and handed me the drink. Even though the sound was turned down quite low, there was something familiar about the sound of the electric organ that came out of the speakers. It was joined after a few bars by a man's voice: doleful yet hypnotic.

'I know this song,' I said, 'although this sounds more sixties than other versions I've heard.'

'This is the original by The Doors and still the best in my book. None of the other versions of 'Light My Fire' smoulder in quite the same way, if you'll pardon the pun. You wanted to listen to some more examples of erotic music so I put a little compilation together.'

'Steven Bowes, are you trying to seduce me?'

'Maybe!' A familiar flash of mischief appeared in his eyes. 'Is it working?'

'You'll find out soon enough, won't you?'

He smiled to himself and put down his glass.

'I'm just going to the bathroom. I'll be back in a minute.'

An idea struck me.

As soon as he disappeared through the door, I launched off the sofa and made straight for the bedroom. By the time he came out again to find me missing, I was ready for him. I don't think I had ever moved so quickly.

'Rebecca?' called his questioning voice from the lounge.

'In here!'

He came through the door to find me draped over the bed, lying on my back with one knee raised and my head towards the door. I wore nothing but my gold anklet and a smile.

Steve gave a low, appreciative whistle.

'Now there's a sight for sore eyes.'

'I told you I'd thank you later. I've got a little surprise for you.'

'Other than this? It must be good.'

'I think you'll like it.'

I reached up to hold out the little silver bubble pack I'd been keeping hidden in the palm of my hand. Eight tablets were already missing. Steve looked at it for a moment and the penny dropped.

'When did all this come about?'

'Just over a week ago. I didn't see the sense in waiting any longer.'

'So are we . . . ?'

'Good to go, yes, so you can throw those condoms away for all I care. No more wearing a raincoat to go for a swim.'

I tossed the packet towards my open bag. It missed.

'I'll deal with those later. In the meantime, get yourself over here, Mr Bowes. There are more important things requiring your attention.'

He stepped closer to the bed, pulling his shirt off over his head, and I reached up to undo the buckle of his belt. That was easy enough, but the buttons on the jeans were not quite so obliging from upside down. Nevertheless, I managed. Steve eased them down his thighs and slipped out of them. From where I was lying it was one hell of a view.

Wriggling up so that I could lean my head back over the edge of the bed, I reached behind me and wrapped one hand around his growing erection, gently cupping his balls in the other. Steve groaned and leant forwards, spreading his palms across my breasts, caressing gently then trapping my stiffening nipples between his fingers. He pulled firmly and I gave a short, sharp gasp of surprise at the sensation. It wasn't enough to hurt me, but enough to catch me unaware. Even now after everything we'd done together, little things he did could still take me by surprise. There was still so much more I wanted to experience with him.

'I take it you're up for a little 'love in the afternoon' then?' he asked, his hands returning to their caressing motion.

'What do you think?' I replied.

Tipping my head back, I drew him into my mouth, my fingers wrapped tightly around his cock. Steve growled and slid his hands down my body until he was leaning right over me and parting my legs he rained kisses up the inside of my thighs. His hot mouth closed in on me, his tongue teasing my labia apart and finding the moist grove between, plunging into me.

It was difficult to concentrate on what my own mouth was doing. The overwhelming sensations from further down were very distracting, but I wasn't giving in to it. I raked my nails against his buttocks, lavishing him with my tongue and drawing him deeper into my mouth.

Steve groaned loudly, then not to be outdone he attacked hard, intensifying his tongue's rhythm and sucking the lips of my pussy into his mouth. Neither of us would give in to the other, each trying not to be overcome by the waves of sensation that were taking over.

I pulled back momentarily.

'Fuck my mouth, Steve.'

I wrapped my lips around him again and his hips began a rocking motion, his movement in and out of my mouth becoming deeper. Now he was finding it impossible to concentrate, torn between the act of giving and receiving. I adored doing that; I loved what it did to him, the way it drove him wild until he couldn't hold himself back any longer. I'd become quite adept at it, even if I do say so myself. This time I had other plans, though. I'd been waiting for this and Steve knew it. I stopped before I pushed him past the point of no return.

'I want you in me, Steve. I want to feel it.'

I flipped myself around on the bed, hooking my legs over his hips and pulling him towards me. I was so ready for this.

'Steven Bowes, would you do me the honour?'

Steve gave me a gentle smile.

'Gladly.'

He rocked forwards and sank slowly, smoothly, into me. Finally, I could savour the feel of him, skin against skin inside me for the first time. I pressed my heels against him, pulling him deeper, watching the way his expression changed as I welcomed him in.

'Yes, Steve. I want you to come in me.'

I didn't think he'd last very long. I'd already taken him as close to the brink as I dared, but he took it slowly at first and held on for longer than I thought he would, teasing my nipples between his teeth while gradually picking up the pace.

How about throwing a little more spice into the mix?

I reached my hand underneath the pillow to retrieve the little vibrator I had stashed there earlier and held it between us for him to see.

'Look what I got from Linda for my birthday.'

Steve gave me a look of amused surprise.

'And what are you going to do with that?'

'Let me show you.'

I activated the button, slipped it down between our bodies and pressed it against the base of his erection, right where our bodies met. The effect on both of us was startling. Steve's eyes went almost as wide as mine.

'Holy fuck!' The words exploded from his lips.

It's not just me then!

He slammed into me, sandwiching the diminutive wonder between our bodies, pressing it in even harder, and began a rolling motion with his hips. A hot tingle spread outwards through that whole area of my body. It must have had a similar effect on him.

I kept it there until his breathing began to change. I knew he was close by the way his lips parted slightly over his teeth and the tightening of the muscles around his eyes. Putting the vibrator to one side I tilted my hips so he was as deep inside me as he could go and he switched back to long, slow strokes that built quickly to a crescendo.

'I'm . . .'

'Yes baby, yes.'

'I'm going to . . .'

'I want you to. I want you to come in me.'

I stroked his face as he let go, pouring himself deep inside me. Whether I'd expected to be able to or not, I could feel everything. I pulled him close and we kissed, deep and slow, until his climax had subsided, our bodies still undulating in time with each other. He slowly regained his composure while I ran my fingers through his hair.

'Thank you, Steve. You don't know how much I've been waiting for that.'

He shook his head.

'But you haven't come yet. That just won't do.'

'So what are you going to do about it, Steven Bowes?'

There was laughter in his eyes now.

'Ve haf vays of making you come, my little fraülein.'

'Bitte, Mein Herr!' It was about all the German I knew.

Steve gently slipped himself out of me. I felt momentarily sad that he was gone but was delighted when his fingers offered their service instead, his fingertips caressing the sensitive spot at the front wall of my vagina, circling slowly. He removed his fingers and I intercepted them on the way to his tongue, steering them towards my own mouth.

'I want first taste,' I insisted.

This was a whole new twist to the honey pot game. He tasted of the two of us combined. I liked it. Not wishing to let go, I kept his fingers in my mouth and reached down to dip two of my own inside me before feeding them to him.

'Nice?' I asked, releasing his fingers from my mouth.

'Yes, but why lick the spoon when you can dive into the jar?'

In a moment he had moved down my body and his fingers were inside me, pressing against` my G-spot once more, his tongue lashing hard. I arched my back and flung my arms out to the side, my hand making contact with the vibrator again.

Why not? Let's take it all the way with this thing.

Steve accepted the vibrator from my outstretched fingers and circled around my pussy with it while his fingertips worked their magic. Pausing for a moment, he found my anus with one free finger and slipped it inside me as well. I reached behind my head, pressing my palms flat against the bars of the bedstead. The intense tingling from the vibrator circled closer which, coupled with the array of sensations that accompanied his probing fingers, rapidly drove me into sensory overload.

Now his tongue joined in again too. My body fought

for oxygen, losing its battle against the tension in my muscles. At the moment when I could stand it no longer, he pressed the vibrator directly onto my clitoris and I disintegrated, crying out for him in my moment of sweet release, every muscle letting go as I melted into the bed.

We lay there together, another song drifting through from the lounge; a slow, swung, gospel-tinged blues with a tight, rhythmic punch. A woman's voice slithered over the bass line, smoky and seductive; as intimate as if she were whispering across a pillow then powerful and unchained by turns. The song lifted, moving on into the chorus; the singer's voice peeling off into harmony with itself.

I had no idea how much of Steve's compilation I'd missed; I hadn't really been listening for most of it. He'd probably put it on repeat anyway. Steve rested his head against my thigh and stroked the lips of my pussy lightly with his fingertips.

'Enjoying the view from down there?' I asked him.

'Amazing! I could stay here all day. I love making you come.'

'I'll be honest, I don't mind it either.' I threw my head back against the pillow, still regaining my breath. 'I'm sorry about your bedclothes. I think we made a bit of a wet patch.'

'I don't care. It's more than worth it. Getting messy can be fun, can't it? Besides, it's a small price to pay for the extra freedom of going without condoms.'

'Plus it's still early and I've got you all to myself until tomorrow morning,' I beamed.

'Yes you have, so what would you like to do? Do you fancy going out somewhere?'

'First, we can take a shower.'

'Mm-hmm.' He nodded.

'Then we can have dinner and make love some more.'

He puffed out his cheeks and exhaled.

'All I can say is it's a good job I'm reasonably fit and healthy or you'd be the death of me, Rebecca Taylor. I think you must be intent on wearing me out.'

'If that happens, can I still keep him?' I asked, glancing down his body. 'It would be such a shame not to.'

'What are you going to do, keep him stuffed and mounted?'

'Something like that: stuffing and mounting might well come into it somewhere.'

Steve shook his head, breaking into a chuckle.

'Come on then,' he said, taking my hand. 'Let's go have that shower.'

He led me into the bathroom, slid back the cubicle door and adjusted the dial on the wall. The steady thrum of the water drowned out the faint music from the lounge when we stepped in, and I nuzzled in close to him under the falling water, the cascading droplets pummelling our skin.

'I love your shower,' I said. 'It's like having a massage; it's so refreshing.'

'I can do you a massage too if you'd like one.'

'Now there's a thought. Do you do everywhere?' I looked up at him, making big eyes; that always seemed to have the desired effect.

'Oh, especially everywhere!' he said.

I just loved how I could turn him on over and over again; it gave me a rush like nothing else. If I was his star then Steve was my moon and my sun. Aside from the music, he had become my everything.

Steve took a bottle of body wash down off the rack and gently rubbed some of it onto my shoulders. It quickly turned to a rich lather which ran down my skin, following the rivulets of water that trickled over my breasts and belly then ran down my thighs. His hands lingered on my skin and he worked his way south, fingers caressing the contours of my body as he went. By the time he reached the smooth mound between my legs I was ready to jump on him, but I resisted the temptation. I was at least beginning to overcome my impatience and enjoy the journey as much as the destination. His fingers lingered there, brushing against me just long enough to ensure I was left in no doubt about his intentions. They were fine by me.

'Your turn, before I come over all unnecessary,' I insisted, reaching for the bottle.

Steve appeared to be mulling over the opportunity for another smart comment until I stopped it in its tracks.

'Turn around,' I instructed, 'so I can do your back.'

He obliged.

I ran my hands across the taught skin of his shoulders and around to his chest, soaping him down and feathering my lips against his wet skin. My fingers found his nipples, gripping them between thumb and forefinger and tugging at them in much the way he had done to me earlier. Steve gave a soft groan which became deeper and more intense the more I did it.

'If you're not careful, Rebecca, I'm going to end up fucking you into the middle of next week. I don't know how you do it, but you've got me unbelievably hard again.'

It was music to my ears. I moaned appreciatively at the thought. I couldn't resist giving his nipples one last teasing pull before my hands continued down his body. They were met with the raging heat of his erection, made all the more startling by the coolness of the rest of his skin.

'Jesus, Steve! You weren't kidding were you?'

'Told you!'

I turned him round to face me and dropped to my knees, closing my mouth around him. He pressed his hands against both sides of the shower cubicle, steadying himself, and I went at him slowly and lasciviously, revelling in the multitude of sensations: the clean, hot taste of him; his stiffness pressing against my throat; and the droplets of water pounding the back of my head. When I looked up through the water that streamed over my eyes, he was clearly as lost in the moment as I was.

Coming to his senses, Steve took me gently by the shoulders and stood me upright, then hoisting me up with his hands underneath me, pinned me against the tiles and entered me hard.

'Oh fuck, Steve! Yes!'

I clung to him with my arms around his neck and lifted my feet off the floor, pressing them against the glass while he filled me repeatedly, drawing back every now and again until he was just inside me and holding there for a moment until the anticipation was almost too much before plunging into me again. Our wet bodies met each other over and over with resounding force beneath the warm cascade.

He brushed the wet hair from my face with one free hand while the other supported me from underneath and kissed me hard, our tongues entwining in an erotic dance all of their own. By now my feet were level with my waist, allowing him full access to me.

I found myself standing beneath a waterfall that tumbled over rocks and plunged into the pool around me from high above my head. Lush greenery sprang from the crevices in the rocks and tropical birds made their echoing calls high in the canopy of the trees above. Brightly coloured exotic flowers spilt from the overhanging branches amid the spray. I pressed my body against the flow, resisting the force of the living waters which tried their best to sweep me off balance and cast me into the deep swirl at the centre of the pool. Sadie looked on, occasionally batting one paw at the iridescent blue butterflies that fluttered from flower to flower in search of nectar.

We clung together, breathless, lost in each other, the pace intensifying.

Now we were together in the roar of the waterfall: two naked souls cast out in the wilderness, finding and holding fast to each other in our tropical paradise, making wild, passionate love with the water spraying off our skin. We cried out our orgasm together amid the deluge. We were animal, primal, complete and perfect.

We sank to the floor of the shower, still wrapped around each other and cradling each other's faces, unable to speak or move at first. Steve reached up and turned off the water. The roaring stopped, replaced by a steady drip from the shower head as it emptied itself. He ran his finger around my lips and looked at me in wonderment.

'What is it with us? I just can't fathom it. Sometimes we're like a tornado that rips through everything in its path.' He looked around. 'I'm almost surprised my bathroom's still intact.'

'Well there's no complaint from me,' I sighed, 'but I've got nothing else to compare it to except for a handful of Jeff's movies, and you can hardly say many of them are like real life. I wouldn't know if it's normal or not. I like it, though. I like the things that we do. Nothing else has ever made me feel like this.'

Steve nodded.

'It's funny, though. You can nearly always tell with that sort of thing whether they're just putting it on for the cameras or if they're genuinely into each other. It's a much bigger turn on when they are. Faking it's just not the same, not even close.'

He slid back the shower door, reached over to the adjacent rack and taking a fresh bath towel, opened it out and draped it around my shoulders. Suddenly the room didn't feel as warm as before now the shower door was open. Helping me to my feet, he tipped my head back slightly and kissed me once on the mouth. Even now, my legs still felt wobbly. I pulled the towel tight around me.

Steve took another towel and dried himself off. I watched the muscles flex beneath his skin, tensing and relaxing. He towelled his hair and shook it back out again before brushing it back from his face with his fingers.

'If I get the worst of the water out of my hair, will you plait it for me?' I asked.

'Of course. Have you got a hair tie with you?'

'There are a couple in my bag, I think.'

He came back a minute or so later just as I finished drying myself, with his jeans on and a scrunchie in his hand. He gave an appreciative sigh.

'You are one mighty fine sight naked, Rebecca.'

'The funny thing is I was just thinking the same about you. Sometimes I could just watch you all day long, even with your clothes on.'

He stood behind me, his nimble fingers dividing my damp hair at the scalp and working it into a plait that hung down between my shoulder blades before wrapping the scrunchie around the end.

'There, how's that?'

I tested it with my fingers.

'That's perfect, thank you. It'll be much more comfortable.'

'Are you hungry yet?'

'Starving!' I was suddenly aware of how much we'd worked up an appetite.

'Good. Me too! Fancy a nice bit of steak?'

'Now you're talking! With all the trimmings?'

'Naturally! And some Diane sauce if you're interested.'

'You're on.'

Steve busied himself in the kitchen while I put on a pair of knickers and a tee-shirt from my bag. Another song was underway when I came out of the bedroom. I knew this one; it was more recent than some of the others. Rihanna's sultry voice beckoned seductively from the speakers.

I sat on the sofa and propped my feet up against the edge of the coffee table, half listening to the music and half watching Steve brush olive oil onto the steaks then grind a little salt and pepper over them before setting them to one side.

He set a frying pan on the hob and looked at me,

smiling.

'Enjoying the music selection? How would you like yours done, by the way?' He pointed the pair of kitchen tongs he was holding towards the steaks.

'Medium rare please, assuming we're talking about the steak, and even if we're not, well . . . probably the same.'

I think he got the AC/DC reference, judging by the way he smiled to himself. Maybe 'A Touch Too Much' had been somewhere on the playlist, worming its way into my consciousness; it certainly deserved to be. For now, though, it was Rihanna's song that held my attention.

'S and M is a really hot song when you listen to it properly, isn't it?' I said.

'There are a few by Rihanna on there. She does like to get a bit saucy, musically speaking. Glass of wine?'

'Actually, can I have a cold drink first? I feel a bit dehydrated for some unearthly reason. I'd like to try a glass of red with the steak though if that's alright.'

'Of course!' He took a bottle from the fridge and poured me some sparkling water.

I watched him flambéing the juices in the pan and whisking in cream, French mustard and a mystery ingredient from a small bottle, but I was lost in the music when Steve brought our food over to the little dining table next to the window. Two places were already neatly laid with a large glass of red wine by each one. I hadn't even noticed him put them there.

'Penny for them?' he enquired when I sat down opposite him.

'I was just relaxing and listening to the songs. There's

some good stuff on there. You couldn't let me have a copy of the playlist could you?'

'Sure. I put it together mostly for your benefit anyway.'

'This looks delicious by the way.'

It did. Alongside the fillet steaks generously topped with the Diane sauce, he'd prepared chunky chips, mushrooms, steamed broccoli, and mange tout. The steak oozed just slightly pink when I cut into it. It melted in my mouth.

'What's it like?' he asked, picking up his knife and fork.

I started to reply through a mouthful of food but the words didn't come out right. I put my hand over my mouth, swallowed then washed it down with a sip of wine.

'It's really good. Sorry, you must think I'm so unladylike.'

'I wouldn't have you any other way than exactly how you are. You're a breath of fresh air in my life, even if you do seem determined to kill me. You make me feel young all over again.'

'Well, they say you're only as old as the woman you feel.'

I thought for a moment.

'Steve?'

'Yes?'

'Have you ever done the whole S and M thing?'

His fork stopped halfway to his mouth and hovered there.

'Not really: a bit of light bondage, nothing too major. Why? You've got your 'I've got an idea' face on again.'

'I mean, I'm not interested in making our relationship all about all that dominance and submission stuff, but it could be fun to play around with.'

'What have you got in mind?'

'What would you say if I asked you to tie me up? You could do anything you wanted with me and there'd be nothing I could do about it.'

For a moment there was a glint of steel in his eyes. I had a good idea what was going through his head, not that I minded.

'Anything?' he asked.

'Anything you like, within reason. There isn't much you could do to me that we haven't already done anyway, and it would be a real turn-on to be completely helpless and at your mercy.'

His fork finally made it as far as his mouth. He took a bite and appreciatively chewed over both the steak and my words.

'You trust me that much?'

'Of course I do. You've never been anything other than kind and considerate with me. I know you'd never do anything to intentionally hurt me. I just think it could be fun.'

'It could.' He nodded, sucking one cheek in thoughtfully. 'In case things get out of hand, though, there's usually a safe word for that sort of thing. 'Stop' is no good because you can say that and not mean it. It needs to be something you wouldn't say by accident.'

'What about 'antidisestablishmentarianism'?' I asked.

He broke out into a broad grin.

'I think by the time you managed to get that out it would be way too late.'

'How about 'Rihanna', then?'

He pursed his lips and nodded.

'That could work. Are you sure about this?'

'Yes I am, now eat up before your food gets cold!'

'Yes, Miss Taylor, or should I say, 'Madam Whiplash'? So who's taking charge now?' he chuckled.

I stuck my tongue out at him before taking another mouthful. Steve could cook; I had to give him that. He lifted his wine glass.

'A toast then: to adventure!'

I brought my glass up to his and our eyes locked.

'I'll drink to that.'

When we had emptied our plates and drained our glasses, I took them over to the sink and reached for the tap. Steve realised what I was about to do.

'Leave that! For tonight at least, you are a woman of leisure to be pampered and looked after.'

'And flogged and fucked?'

'I'm not exactly equipped for the former, but I'm sure I can manage the latter.'

Oh goody!

'I'm going to have to improvise a bit, though,' he continued. 'This flat doesn't come fitted with hooks in the ceiling. Go into the bedroom and wait for me. Make yourself comfortable and I'll be right back.'

'Is that an order, Mr Bowes?'

He looked at me for a moment, his expression darkening with intent.

'Yes it is; now do as you're told!'

I padded demurely over to the bedroom, even though I felt like skipping.

While I sat and waited patiently on the edge of the

bed, I could hear Steve rummaging in the lounge and the kitchen drawers before briefly going into the bathroom. The light was fading outside so I switched on the bedside lamp. What felt like an eternity but must only have been a couple of minutes passed before he reappeared in the bedroom doorway with a look of satisfaction, carrying the towelling belt from his bathrobe, a handful of leather guitar straps and a roll of thick, grey duct tape. He laid them out carefully on the bed, looking from the objects to me and back again.

I wondered exactly what he was going to do with each of them and looked at him helplessly, doing my best to remain still and calm, but inside my chest, my heart was pounding. Sadie paced expectantly.

He leant down to kiss me on my softly opened lips then stood back again. There was a look of resolve about him now, and he was trying to suppress a smile that was creeping into one corner of his mouth, but not quite succeeding.

'Take off your top and then lie back in the middle of the bed.'

'Yes, Mr Bowes.' I did as I was told.

'Now put your hands together in front of you.'

He wrapped a guitar strap firmly around my wrists then taking the roll of tape, bound the space between my hands to hold it in place.

'Comfortable?'

I nodded.

'Now try and free your hands.'

I couldn't.

He tied one end the towelling belt around the tape between my wrists, lifted my bound hands behind my head and attached the other end to the central bar of the bedstead, just close enough to keep me in place but allowing a little latitude for movement. Hooking the tips of my fingers around the bar, I watched him over the rise and fall of my breasts, eager to see what Steve was going to do next.

He reached over and picked up my phone from beside the bed.

Okay, I wasn't expecting that.

'Get ready to say 'Hi' to the camera.'

'What? You want to start filming me now?'

'I've never seen you looking more beautiful than you do right this moment.'

I pulled at the restraint but was unable to move.

'Steve! I've got no make-up on, my hair's still damp and I'm practically naked, plus I'm tied to your bed and unbelievably turned on right now.'

'Exactly! You've never looked more beautiful to me and that's saying something. Besides, this will be on your phone so you can do what you like with it afterwards. Delete it if you want to.'

I sank back into the pillow. After all, I had told him he could do what he liked with me.

'Next time I get the chance, I'm going to tie you up instead and then we'll see whether you like what I do to you or not,' I said with more than a hint of umbrage.

'I'll look forward to it, but in the meantime . . .'

He held the phone out towards me and pressed the screen. It beeped.

Showtime!

I kept my eyes averted downwards and did my best to look meek and mild, even though what I really wanted to do was tear his jeans off and fuck him.

'Say hello, Rebecca.'

'Hello.'

'You can look at the camera, you know. It is allowed.'

I looked up at him with what I hoped was doe-eyed innocence. Whatever it was, it was working; his hard-on was doing its best to break free of his jeans. After the day's escapades, I was surprised there was still enough blood flow to other areas to keep the rest of him supplied with oxygen.

'Hello,' I said again, biting softly into my bottom lip.

'So what would you like me to do to you?' he asked.

I wasn't sure the phone had enough memory for that little list.

'Surprise me.'

'Oh, I think that can be arranged,' he said, smiling to himself.

He panned away from my face and down my body. The camera followed his fingers skimming lightly across my skin and stopped at my crotch. I kept my knees tightly together.

'Let's see if you're ready for surprises, shall we? Open your legs.'

I parted my knees a little and with one hand, Steve spread them further, exposing me to the unblinking gaze of the camera. His hand slid up my leg and reached between my thighs to caress the area where my underwear hugged the line of my cleft. Moisture already beginning to seep into the thin, white cotton. He gave a sharp intake of breath.

'Oh Rebecca, you're soaking wet.' My breath sighed at the touch of his fingertips stroking up and down the damp material. 'I think we need to get these off you and take a closer look, though.'

Keeping the phone's camera trained on me, he eased them down with his one free hand, first one side then the other, and I lifted my hips slightly off the bed to assist him.

'I'd lend a hand,' I informed him, 'but I'm a bit tied up at the moment.'

'That's okay, I'll let you off.' He was just about managing to keep a straight face.

I turned my mouth down at the corners in mock disappointment.

'Not too lightly, I hope. Your discipline can be quite . . . effective.'

He allowed himself a little smile and slid my briefs smoothly down my legs. At the last moment, they caught on the toe of my left foot but I flicked them deftly away with a little kick. Keeping the phone in one hand, Steve slipped the index finger of his other inside me. He seemed pleased with the result; his lips parting slightly as, inch by inch, he slowly took me in, surveying me from top to toe.

He put the phone down again and taking two more guitar straps, loosened the adjustable parts where they looped through and passed one over each foot. I pointed my toes to make it easier. Once they were around my ankles he pulled them just tight enough to grip me and steering my feet towards the corners of the bed, tied the ends of the straps around the metal legs, taping them in place for good measure. I could hardly move at all now, completely exposed and at the mercy of whatever whim took his fancy. My only option was complete surrender.

253

Sadie settled down, licking her lips, waiting.

'I'll be right back,' he said and disappeared out of the bedroom door.

Sadie sat up in surprise. I would have if I could. The leather creaked every time I tried to move. All I could do was wait for him to return, although it was probably less than a minute before he came back with a glass of ice cubes.

Never mind fruit salad; we could make this into a smoothie.

Steve looked over at the phone.

'As much as I'd like to film this for posterity, I think I'm going to need both my hands from here on in. Never mind, eh?'

He popped an ice cube into his mouth and moved up my body, slinking like a blonde panther until his mouth was over mine, and kissed me, the warmth of his lips in stark contrast to the sharp coldness of the ice which found its way between my teeth. His lips left mine open and wanting and he trailed them down over my chin to my throat before taking another piece of ice in his mouth, sliding it across the skin of my left breast and planting it firmly over the stiffening nipple.

Even though I knew it was coming, the shock of the cold still made me gasp. His tongue flicked at the hardened bud, rolling the ice cube around it before moving across to the other side. One hand strayed down my body and teased at the lips of my pussy while the ice melted between my skin and Steve's agile tongue.

He reached for the bottle of lube. It hardly seemed necessary.

But, then again, maybe . . .

Now there was a delicious glint in his eyes, hard yet

irresistible. The liquid dribbled between my legs, running down my labia and into the crack between my buttocks. He slid two fingers deep inside me then held them there, quivering, before a third joined them. They slipped in easily. He rocked his wrist and rotated it back and forth, massaging the inside of my vagina. Then his little finger joined in too.

My eyes went wide. I had an idea where this was going.

'Jesus, Steve!'

'Shh! Relax.'

I released the tension in my body and gave in to the startling sensations. Steve tucked his thumb into his palm and gently worked his whole hand deeper.

'Fuck!' I gasped, tipping my head back, whimpering.

'If you're good and keep the noise down I'll let you come, but only if you're good,' he teased.

'Yes . . . yes, I promise.' It was an assurance I wasn't sure I would be able to keep. Now he was in me right up to the widest part of his hand, still rocking and rotating his wrist. As hard as I tried, I was finding it impossible to remain quiet. Steve stopped and gently removed his fingers.

'Seriously, we're going to have the neighbours calling the police if we're not careful. We don't want them banging the door down, thinking someone's being murdered in here.' His voice became hushed. 'I've got an idea.'

He slipped off the bed and retrieved something from the floor. In an instant, he was back with me.

'Open your mouth!' he instructed.

I complied.

'Wider!'

There was something white in his hand.

My knickers!

He fed them slowly into my open mouth, gently tucking in the last stray crease of material before I closed it again.

'There. That's better. Now you'll be able to come as hard as you like and I know what'll do it.'

I'll bet you do. Although I tried to say the words, they just came out as a muffled noise.

He slid down the bed and undid the leather straps, slipping them off my ankles then removed his jeans and lifted my legs, propping my feet on his shoulders. Taking hold of one foot, Steve ran the tip of his tongue up the sole, pressing into the instep with his fingertips and making me squirm. He worked his way across the toes, inserting his tongue into the spaces between them then sucking each toe one by one into his mouth. It tickled like crazy whenever his probing tongue found the gaps.

Then, taking both my feet he pressed them together on either side of his erection, sandwiching his cock between them, rolling his hips and moving smoothly in and out while holding my gaze with his, teasing me, taunting me. His swollen glans protruded obscenely from the space between my insteps while he slowly, deliberately fucked the soles of my feet, satisfying himself while my own need rose to fever pitch. A little bead of fluid gathered at the tip of his cock then smeared onto my skin as he withdrew then pushed forward again, all the while watching me, never wavering.

God, how I wanted him! How I needed him! I pulled against my restraints with what little noise I could make stifled by the underwear in my mouth, breathing heavily through my nose. My wide eyes were begging him for mercy; my mouth could not, but nevertheless he understood and took pity on my need. Steve released my feet, lifted my hips and positioned himself, smoothing lubricant over his engorged cock.

'You want this?'

I nodded, making a little, muffled sound and surrendering to the moment I hoped was coming.

Yes, I'm yours. Take me, please! Just take me!

As if in understanding he sank himself into my arse in one slow, smooth movement and set about fucking me with long, steady strokes, his face a picture of ecstasy and concentration.

Oh, yes! That's it! Just like that!

It was a good job my underwear was in my mouth because otherwise, I would have made enough noise to wake the dead. I strained against the ties on my hands, arching my body as he settled into his stride.

Yes, harder! Come on you beautiful bastard; fuck me!

He slipped his fingers into my pussy at the same time, their movement keeping time with the rest of him. I began to tense and convulse, my long awaited orgasm rising from the deep, a leviathan that was preparing to drag me back down with it into sweet oblivion.

'Oh yes, Rebecca. I know how much you love it when I fuck you like this. You're so sweet and so naughty; it just makes me want to do the sexiest, filthiest things to you.' His words carried the perfect combination of tenderness and menace which only served to turn me on even more, pushing me still closer to that delicious edge.

The creature reached out its tentacles and wrapped

them around me. With a sudden tug, it pulled me beneath the crashing waves and into the enveloping blackness, which swallowed me whole. My body was shaking as I plummeted downwards. Eventually, it released its grip and I swam back up to the surface, following the light and the rising bubbles, reaching for air.

Steve gently slipped the damp material out of my mouth and I filled my lungs with precious oxygen. The room and Steve slowly came back into focus.

He was smiling at me.

'How was that?' he asked.

'Oh my God!' I swooned, still unsure which day of the week it was, or even which direction was up. In the midst of it all, a thought crossed my mind, lending me a whole new resolve. 'I'm not finished with you yet, though, Steven Bowes. It's your turn now. Can you help me turn over?'

With my hands still bound to the bedstead, it took some coordination to get me onto my front, but once there I pulled my behind into the air.

'Come on, Steve. This time I want to feel you come inside my arse.'

He chuckled.

'What happened to the demure, submissive Rebecca of half an hour ago?'

'You didn't think I'd keep that up for long did you?'

He shook his head.

'No. Not really.'

Sadie sat back on her haunches. For now, at least, her work was done, the transformation complete. The shy little caterpillar had finally metamorphosed into a resplendent butterfly and taken flight. She was free, and she was beautiful.

Without warning Steve sank full length into me again, keeping me quiet by reaching out to put the fingers of one hand in my mouth. The other one periodically spanked the cheeks of my behind while he fucked me. I bit down on his fingers, deliberately trapping them between my teeth, lightly at first, then harder.

'Ow!' He withdrew his hand. 'It's like that, is it? You want to play rough?'

Steve took hold of my plait and pulled my head back, arching my spine as he thrust into me.

'Yes, pull my hair!' I ordered, trying and failing to look over my shoulder. 'Harder! Fuck me . . . FUCK ME!' I was almost screaming.

Sadie roared.

We no longer cared who heard us. The blood pounded in my head while he gripped my hair tightly and laid into me, making my whole body quiver every time he slammed himself forwards. I could sense the change in him as his orgasm approached.

'Oh Rebecca, you wanted it and you're going to get it.'

'Yes . . . come in me . . . I'm . . . I'm coming too,' I stuttered between thrusts.

'What, again?'

'Yes.'

Oh God, yes!

We both hit the peak as one, crying out and collapsing together, splayed out on the bed as he emptied himself inside me. With my outstretched arms still held tight to the bars, I could hardly move.

Steve recovered himself for a moment then reached up

to quickly untie the bonds and massage my wrists until the colour began returning to my hands. I'd been pulling so hard on my restraints that they'd gone white.

'I'm sorry if I hurt you.' He seemed suddenly penitent.

'No more than I wanted. No more than I could take,' I reassured him, reaching round with one hand to stroke his face. 'It's alright. I wanted this.'

Steve gently nuzzled my ear and I drifted, suddenly feeling tired. His lips grazed my shoulder and I closed my eyes for a moment, happy but exhausted.

-0-

'Hey you, wake up.' Steve's voice was gentle and melodious in my ear. His fingers stroked my hair while I drifted back to consciousness.

'Hmm?'

'I need you to get dressed and come with me. I've got something to show you.'

I was underneath the covers. I didn't remember putting them over me.

'How long have I been asleep?' My voice was still slurred and groggy.

'Oh, about two hours. It's a beautiful, clear night and I want you to see your birthday present properly.'

'Okay. Give me a few minutes to get ready, though.' I rubbed my eyes.

Steve smiled gently.

'It's alright, there's no rush.'

It was just as well. I needed the bathroom first, for a number of reasons. I looked round at him. He was already dressed.

'How long have you been up?'

'Not long. I think we've both kind of worn each other out today.'

'You think? Tell you what, though; I could murder a cup of tea.'

'So could I, come to think of it. I'll stick the kettle on while you get sorted.' He kissed me on the forehead and went off to make the teas with a little backwards glance and a smile as he left the room.

I made my way awkwardly through to the bathroom. My ankles weren't too bad, but my wrists were still a little sore and . . . Eugh! I had a bit of tidying up to do, but it was worth it.

When I came back from the bathroom, I dressed again. I had a pair of jeans with me and a slightly warmer top I could put over the tee-shirt. Thankfully there was another pair of knickers in my bag. The last ones were still a little soggy; no wonder my mouth felt dry.

Steve was ready and waiting with two mugs of tea.

'Here you go.'

'Thank you. So where are you taking me?'

'Just out of the village, away from the street lights so we can get a better look at the night sky.'

'Has anybody ever told you you're such a romantic?'

Steve shrugged his shoulders and took a mouthful of tea.

It was only a short drive out of Coreham to the lay-by where we stopped. The lights of the surrounding towns and villages formed distant patches of amber on the horizon; otherwise, the night was dark and moonless. There was a fresh bite to the midnight air when we stepped out of the car and turned our eyes towards the wheeling, infinite blanket that stretched over our heads. I stood on the verge, shivering slightly.

'Here, take my jacket,' he said.

'Won't you be cold then?'

'No! No sense, no feeling!'

He retrieved his phone from the pocket and draped his jacket over my shoulders. It was way too big for me, but it was warm and welcoming and it had the scent of Steve on it. I pulled it tight around me.

'How do you find the right one?' I asked.

'There's an app. on my phone. I wrote down the numbers off the certificate. We've just got to line it up with the night sky and move it around till the co-ordinates match and that's your star.'

He held it up in front of us and moved it slowly around for a few seconds.

'There!' He pointed and I followed the line of sight along his arm. 'You see that bright one just to the right of the cluster. That's it. That's Rebecca. Now you know where it is, as long as you remember that pattern you'll be able to find yourself.'

All of a sudden it seemed so much more real than before. I could see it. I felt like I could reach out and touch it. I wrapped my arms around him and laid my head against his shoulder.

'Thank you; it's wonderful. You're wonderful.'

We lay side by side on the bonnet of his car, holding hands, looking up and marvelling at the stars in the clear night sky until eventually tiredness caught up with me again and I began to yawn.

'Tired?' Steve asked.

'Yes. I need the rest of my sleep now.'

'Come on. Let's go back to bed.'

I raised one eyebrow.

'To sleep!' he qualified. 'I don't think I've got the energy left for anything else.'

'Nor me,' I assured him, 'not after the day we've had!'

I was on the edge of sleep again when we arrived back at the flat. Steve ushered me upstairs and helped me undress. I felt so exhausted I could hardly move. He lay down facing me and pulled the duvet over us, holding my hands between his and kissing me on the forehead, our breathing falling into step. The warmth of his naked body next to mine was especially welcome after the chill night air.

As I drifted into slumber I could feel Steve's hand stroking my hair and hear his whispered voice, soft and mellow on the edge of my consciousness.

'Goodnight my sweet, beautiful, amazing Rebecca . . . I . . .'

CHAPTER SEVENTEEN

Looking at the girl in the mirror, I barely recognised her. Dressed neatly in her uniform ready for what might probably be her final term of school, she was a far cry from the young woman I knew; a woman on the cusp of her dreams, confident, secure and sensual. The girl who looked back at me was another creature altogether, an empty shell I no longer inhabited.

School was the same as always, and yet it felt different too; it was somehow alien. Not that I'd ever truly felt like I belonged, but now I was going through the motions, marking time until the exams finished in just over two months. Then I could begin my life in earnest.

Steve and Jeff would be in London during the week for quite some time while they recorded Whispered Scream's new album, so Saturday would have to be my only Steve day once again. I just needed to keep my head down, revise for my exams and persist with the songwriting while I waited for the weekend to come around.

The songs! Always the songs! Mitchell had a point, though. The last time I spoke to him on the phone he'd been going on about the writing.

'Sometimes you'll write great songs that don't fit with what you would record yourself as an artist. That doesn't matter. Don't second guess yourself; just create, because what isn't right for you might be right for someone else. A good song is a good song.'

He wasn't done.

'A significant proportion of the artists' royalties go to the songwriter, not the recording artist, no matter who actually performs it. If other people record your songs, it's a great calling card in this business. It's a foot in the door. It can also be a career option that goes on long after the solo career dries up because fame can be a fickle mistress.'

Sometimes the biggest challenge with Mitchell could be getting a word in edgeways, but his advice was always worthwhile. I couldn't argue with the sense behind the things he said; it was just a bit like attending a lecture at times.

A couple of times during the week, Scott came back with us to Linda's after school. He had a youthful charm that was quite sweet really when I got to know him a bit better. I never saw much of Dean, though, and Linda didn't discuss him very often. She kept him under wraps like some kind of guilty secret. He didn't even strike me as being her type; in fact, I'd have called him a little effeminate if pushed, although he obviously wasn't gay. I could imagine Linda together with Scott (and sometimes, in private moments, I did), but not somehow with Dean. Something about him always seemed out of place: a puzzle with one piece the wrong way round, only I couldn't make out which piece.

Linda could still be quite a challenge to fathom at

times. I promised myself that one day I'd actually get to the bottom of what went on in that clever, impenetrable head of hers but it was never easy. When pressed about herself she would simply shrug her shoulders and say something like: 'I'm complex not complicated, multi-faceted but never two-faced,' and leave it at that. She never laid all her cards on the table, at least not all at once, and her comments left me none the wiser, but I cared about her deeply and I knew she cared about me.

Linda would move Heaven and Earth for me if I asked her to, and sometimes if I didn't. Having had my back more times than I could mention, she was always there to listen to me and always had good advice when I needed it, but only ever opened up about herself when she was ready to. We trusted each other despite her rather secretive side and that was what mattered. I could tell her things I told no one else and I knew they would go no further. She was my priestess of perspicacity, my kinky confessor.

I was so relieved when Saturday came around. It didn't matter if the rest of the family was home or not during the day; Linda would cover for us later. Steve and I spent the morning in the studio as usual, still tweaking and perfecting our song and laying down basic demos of other ideas I had been working on, but he seemed a little more subdued than normal; maybe the long recording sessions in London had tired him out. Jeff hadn't made it back until well into the evening all week.

'Time is money when you're paying for a top studio,' Jeff explained when I asked about the late working. 'When you're paying for them by the day, bringing the project in on time and on budget is crucial. Record companies don't like having their funding messed with by over-ambitious production values and wasted time.'

He'd looked so tired when he finally made it home each night, only to get up in the morning and do it all again. Every day had to be approached with the same vigour and energy like it was something constantly fresh and new, no matter how exhausting the schedule was.

'There's no let-up if you want to be up there with the best,' he'd say sometimes. If that was what showbiz required, then sooner or later, and probably sooner the way things were going, I would have to get used to doing the same.

For all his thick skin, though, Jeff did everything out of love: love for music and love for family, even though we were never his by blood. He'd devoted so much of his time and energy to my future, so had Steve, and so had Mum. Each had given me more than I could measure in their own different ways. I wasn't going to let them, or myself, down. The tiger in me dared not flinch from her purpose. Her goal was not just to survive, but to thrive.

It was mid-afternoon when we arrived at Steve's flat. When we got out of the car, a middle-aged woman was staring at us from a first-floor window with an expression like a bulldog chewing a wasp. I smiled and waved. The face disappeared with a twitch of the curtains and they fell back into place.

'What's so funny?' asked Steve.

'Oh, nothing!' I smiled to myself and sashayed through the outer door of the vestibule, swaying my hips to a rhythm that only my ears could hear. The jungle drums were calling.

Inside the flat, Steve pottered around the kitchen

straightening up when we got in. Normally everything was already tidy. He was as sweet as always but his usual sense of mischief was missing. It was obvious there was something on his mind, but I'd learned to be patient with Linda so I showed the same restraint with him, despite my concern.

We made love anyway, clinging to each other with such beautiful, sweet, tender simplicity that when he came inside me, in that moment of total honesty when there was nowhere left to hide he laid his head on my shoulder, sobbing softly into my hair and trembling like a leaf. With my legs still wrapped around his hips, I held him close to me like a small child, cradling his head against my breast and running my fingers through his hair. Almost instinctively I was afraid to let him go. I wanted to keep him inside me like something precious.

'Steve, what's up?'

He shook his head and slowly sat up, drinking in my face like a man dying of thirst.

'Just some stuff I need to deal with. It'll probably come to nothing: baggage, you know? I don't want to darken your day with it.' He brightened. 'Come on! Let's go out to dinner: my treat.'

How could I refuse? Suddenly he was back to something like his usual self. I knew there was more to tell but he had to be ready to share it so I bided my time. What else could I do?

'Where would you like to go? The Old Black Swan?' I asked. 'I think the waitress would run for cover if she saw us coming through the door again.'

The laughter returned to his eyes.

'Can you imagine if it was the same girl? I think she

died with embarrassment last time.' His expression became more lascivious again.

That's more like it.

'Or maybe she was just turned on,' I added. 'We were all over each other. It's a wonder we didn't get thrown out.'

'I know. I was about ready to take you over the table right then and there.'

'And I don't think I would have stopped you. That would have been good, wouldn't it: getting barred from a pub before I'm even old enough to drink in it?'

We both laughed at the scene in our heads. He was definitely in a better frame of mind now.

We decided it might be wise to try somewhere else a little further afield; after all, we didn't want any more close calls with Mum's friends either. The countryside was dotted with villages, each with gorgeous little pubs.

'Most of the pubs have to do food in order to survive as a business these days, so we'll be spoiled for choice. After all, man cannot live on beer alone, although he's probably willing to give it a damned good try,' Steve joked while we dressed.

'How come you know so much about it?' I asked him, pulling on my shoes.

'I grew up around it. My parents ran a pub but they saw the changes coming and got out of the trade while they could. Running a pub isn't what it used to be; the pub and the church used to be the twin hubs of village life, now neither is. Sign of the times I guess: not all change is progress.'

We drove out of Coreham, heading east until we hit on a suitable candidate. It didn't take long.

Dinner was lovely and the weather so unseasonably warm that we were almost tempted to sit outside to eat. As darkness fell the air became chillier, so in the end, we were glad we'd stayed inside and settled down at a quiet table with our drinks. At least he allowed himself one beer this time and he seemed more relaxed again as we chatted. We even managed to act with a little more decorum this time. From time to time, though, Steve would become quiet for a moment and stare at his drink before brightening again.

We had to make the most of our time together since I would not be seeing him again until the following Saturday. I still wished he would tell me what was playing on his mind, but failing that I came to the conclusion that the next best option would be to kiss it better instead. Steve didn't complain when on our return to the flat, I kicked off my shoes, undid his shirt buttons and with a smouldering look, led him back to bed.

I had just the medicine he needed.

CHAPTER EIGHTEEN

Steve was late. Steve was never late.

The others were all out and I'd been sitting in the kitchen, waiting for him for over three-quarters of an hour now. Through the window, I could see how dark the sky had become, and it was just starting to rain. I was already on my third mug of tea and I'd been to the loo twice. Why did I feel so nervous? It was just another Saturday.

He sent me a text on the Friday to confirm he would be coming over, and there had been no message this morning. I checked my phone again.

Nothing. I decided to text him.

> **Me**
> Is everything alright?
> 9:53 am

My phone remained silent.

Finally, I heard his car pull up in the driveway and my heart began to sing. Saturdays with Steve were the highlight of my week, my light in the darkness. I went to the side door to meet him with open arms but as soon as I saw him I knew something was wrong, badly wrong. I could feel it. The cloud hanging over him was as black as the skies above. Gone altogether was the carefree jauntiness, the irresistible spark of mischievous energy that I had come to expect from him. His shoulders had dropped. He looked like he hadn't slept.

'What's wrong Steve? You look awful.'

His face was a mask of grim determination.

'There's something I need to talk to you about,' he said flatly.

Had somebody found out about us? Mum? Jeff? What if Mum's friend Sandra had confided her suspicions? Nobody else had said anything about it, though. Now I was being overtaken by a cold dread that prickled right up my spine. I felt sick. My stomach had gone into freefall.

'Come in and sit down,' I said, my voice filled with concern. I ushered him into the kitchen and placed the mug of tea I'd already prepared for him on the breakfast bar, while he sagged disconsolately onto a stool. 'It's probably getting a bit cold. I made it a few minutes ago. I thought you'd be here sooner.'

'Thank you. It's fine.' He tried to smile at me but instead of being his usual easy-going grin it was thin and tight. It never reached his eyes, which were trying not to look down at the floor.

The waiting was agony.

'Rebecca, I . . .' He took a deep breath and closed his eyes before exhaling slowly and opening them again. 'I've been talking to Valentina and we've decided to give our marriage another try.'

In an instant, my world collapsed. I wanted to smash everything within reach. I wanted to scream and throw things at him. I wanted to beat him with my fists and call him every name under the sun. Instead, I slumped on the stool opposite him with my head in my hands while my brain tried to process what he'd just said. My skin had gone numb all over: cold, anaesthetised. I slapped my palms against my forehead in a vain attempt to make sense of the jumble of thoughts and feelings that were now taking over then sat in silence, staring at the counter top. My fingers rocked the mug of tea in front of me while circular ripples played on the surface of the liquid inside.

Steve looked at me forlornly, waiting for my response, fiddling absently with his fingers. Some part of me knew he was just trying to do the right thing because I could see how he was tearing himself apart, and even though I felt like giving in to hysteria, what good would that do? Eventually, I pulled myself together enough to reply. I needed to know what was behind all this.

'Okay. Talk to me,' I said simply.

He relaxed slightly, looking strangely relieved. Perhaps he'd been expecting World War III. Maybe he didn't have a clue how I'd react.

'The reason we split up in the first place was that we were trying for a baby, and it just wasn't happening. There was no medical cause for it. There's nothing wrong with either of us but we just couldn't conceive. We both had a whole bunch of tests and they all came back fine. We'd even married quite young so we could start trying for a family but she was so desperate for it to happen it put a huge strain on our relationship. We started arguing about the stupidest stuff and it all went downhill from there until the stress and the bickering got so bad that neither of us could stand it any longer and I moved out.'

'So what's changed?'

'I suppose that spending time apart made her think again about what she wanted. I'd have been happy with her, children or no children, but for her it was different, especially being from Spain. The Spanish are all about family. It's a huge thing to her, not having kids. Now she wants us to try again and take the future as it comes.'

'What do you want?' I asked him.

He paused for a moment then looked straight at me. His eyes were still reddened and glistening, the skin around them blotchy.

'I never completely gave up loving her, Rebecca. I've been feeling so guilty, so conflicted lately after she started talking about getting back together again. I'd never mean to hurt you.' His voice trembled. 'That's the last thing I want.'

My heart was breaking. I wasn't sure if it was for him or for me. Second by second he was slipping away from me, the distance between us becoming a yawning chasm that grew ever wider. I was losing my Steve and there was nothing I could do about it. I took a deep breath.

'Listen.' My voice was as matter-of-fact as I could make it, but the hollowness within threatened to engulf me. 'We both knew what this was when we got into it. If I remember rightly it was me who asked you and you said no to start with, or tried to.' At least I was making an attempt at humour. 'I've been having the time of my life and I can't begin to tell you what you've given me and how much it means.' My mood lifted a little. 'You've been so good to me and so kind.'

'And so horny?' he chipped in, trying to lighten the atmosphere further.

'And so horny.' I smiled thinly. 'You've made me feel like a woman in ways I couldn't have imagined only a couple of months ago, but we wouldn't have had a future together. Given everything that's happening with the music, we both knew that, didn't we? I guess I'd hoped we could have more time together but, in fact, it's kicking off already. Mitchell's already starting to speak with record companies and he's talking about putting a band together and getting out there gigging. I have no idea how crazy this is going to get or what the future holds. Now you have a chance to save your marriage and I care about you too much to stand in the way of that; it wouldn't be right.'

Then a thought struck me.

'Does she know about us?' I asked.

His mouth set in a grim line and he nodded weakly.

'She does now. How could I not tell her? If we're going to have any sort of future there has to be honesty between us, no matter how much the truth hurts. I didn't tell her who I was seeing at first but she worked it out quickly enough. Strangely enough, being jealous of us was one of the things that made her realise she still wants us to be together.'

He gave a short spluttering laugh, more one of relief than good humour. The colour was starting to return to his face; up until then, he'd been deathly pale.

'She's not going to tell anybody, is she?' I asked. 'About us I mean.'

He shook his head.

'No. She's not the vengeful type. I explained

everything. I spared her the um . . . details, of course.'

I wondered if he did all the same things with her; if it made her feel how it made me feel. Of course he did. Why wouldn't he? I tried to picture her in my head. She would be tall and slender with long, black hair, flawless olive skin and eyes like deep, dark pools of Latin passion and desire. How could I possibly compete with that? My mind was trying to paint her into a long, red, ruffled dress with castanets in her hands and a red flower in her hair.

Stop it! You're being ridiculous. I pulled myself back into the here and now.

'Have you . . . ?'

'No.' Steve shook his head. 'We've just been talking.' He seemed lost in thought for a moment or two. 'You know, it's strange, the parallels between my situation and Jeff's. It's one of the things apart from our working relationship that makes us as close as we are. We're on the same wavelength.'

'How do you mean?' I asked him, confused now.

He looked at me in amazement for a moment.

'You mean you don't know about what happened with Jeff's first marriage?'

'I know he was married before but I don't know the details. He doesn't really talk about it.'

'That's understandable I guess. His marriage broke down because he can't have children. Ginette was fine but Jeff discovered he's infertile. They both wanted children but couldn't have them. She started sleeping around. Eventually, she found herself someone who got her pregnant and left Jeff to have babies. I don't even think she's together with the other guy anymore. She basically used him as a sperm donor.'

'The bitch!' I spat the words out with even more venom than I expected. What Jeff said during our conversation about the music industry came flooding back to me.

You're my daughter now, the daughter I would never be able to have if I hadn't met your mum.

All of a sudden it made sense: why he had embraced us as a family so wholeheartedly and why he had devoted himself to helping build our futures. I loved him now more than ever. Sniffing and wiping a tear away from my cheek with the heel of my hand, I could feel myself starting to well up but I kept it under control.

Now Steve was being the strong one.

'Jeff just fell apart, and I was there to pick up the pieces when all of this was going on. That's why Jeff and I are so much closer than just employer and employee. I'm so sorry to have hit you with all of this, but I couldn't carry on seeing you and try to save my marriage at the same time; it wouldn't be fair on either of you.'

'Still friends?'

'Of course we're still friends! I'll always be here for you. You've got an amazing future ahead of you and there is still so much work to do. It makes me very proud to be a part of that. You know, I really do . . .'

'No!' I interrupted him, putting my hand over my mouth and desperately holding back the tears. 'No, don't say that. Please don't say those words, not now. It was what it was, but we both knew it couldn't last forever.' I steeled myself. 'Go to her. Go and save your marriage. I want you to be happy; you deserve it, and you can tell Valentina from me that she's a very lucky lady to have you.'

We both stood up. Steve's tea, now stone cold, still sat untouched on the counter. We made our separate ways around the breakfast bar and went through to the vestibule, turning to face each other at the bottom of the stairs. I put the flats of my hands against his chest and kissed him meekly on the cheek.

'I'll never forget what we've had together. It means more to me than you will ever know. Thank you for everything.'

'You will be alright won't you?'

'Of course I will. Now go to her. Go and be happy.'

He leant forward to kiss me but I put my finger to his lips. I shook my head gently.

'You save that for Valentina now. You hear me?' I was choking on the words.

By now the heavens had opened and the rain was coming down in sheets. It drummed on the roof of the studio and erupted from the drainpipes, spilling out onto the courtyard. Steve nodded, turned and disappeared through the door. He didn't even try to shield himself from the onslaught; in fact, I think he barely noticed it. He hunched his shoulders and made towards the car, not even daring to let himself look back.

Steve was gone. My beautiful, sweet, exciting Steve was gone.

Feeling numb, I made my way upstairs. I needed the solace, the quiet sanctuary of my room. I closed the bedroom door behind me and leant against it. It felt cold and hard on my back.

My light in the darkness had been extinguished and there was a growing tightness around the hole where my heart had been ripped from my chest. I couldn't breathe. The stinging behind my eyes became an intense burning, the first trickle growing to become a deluge once the floodgates opened.

I threw myself onto the bed and sobbed into the pillow until there were no tears left.

ABOUT THE AUTHOR

D.V. Williams was born and grew up (sort of) in the southeast of England. After eminently sensible careers in industry and teaching while spending any free time writing songs and poetry and performing in bands, he finally carried out a lifelong threat to do something life-affirmingly un-sensible and write a book. The creative urge had finally taken over. There was a story to be told that refused to go away.

Two years on, and the first three books about Rebecca's life and loves had been completed. All that was needed now was to get them published, and that, as anybody who's ever tried it knows, is another journey altogether.

The author is married with two teenage sons and lives in southwest Wales. They share their home with two cats, a neurotic collie, and an ever-growing collection of musical instruments.

www.dominic-williams.co.uk

www.facebook.com/DVWilliamsAuthor

www.twitter.com/DomVWilliams

COMING NEXT . . .

EMBRACING THE WILD

D.V. WILLIAMS

Fame is a strange thing. Some people crave it. For others it's the price of following their dreams, but one thing is for certain . . . it changes everything.

After her first love affair comes to a sudden end, Rebecca Taylor is devastated. Thankfully there's the inimitable Linda to help her pick up the pieces of her life and move on. With Rebecca's sexuality fully awakened, the tigress inside her is hungry for more, and Linda is always ready to lead her astray.

While Rebecca devotes herself to carving out a career in the music business with her new band and trying to put the past behind her, Linda has plans of her own . . . and secrets too. Her unusual lifestyle draws Rebecca into a hidden world where the pursuit of pleasure is the greatest currency of all.

However, nothing could have prepared Rebecca for what lies ahead. It seems fame and money also have a dark side, especially when you're not always sure who you can trust.

Tigers Book Two

Lightning Source UK Ltd.
Milton Keynes UK
UKHW04f0004160718
325758UK00001B/8/P